VIRTUOSO

Yelena Moskovich

Two Dollar Radio
Books too loud to Ignore

Two Dollar Radio
Books too loud to Ignore

WHO WE ARE TWO DOLLAR RADIO is a family-run outfit dedicated to reaffirming the cultural and artistic spirit of the publishing industry. We aim to do this by presenting bold works of literary merit, each book, individually and collectively, providing a sonic progression that we believe to be too loud to ignore.

TwoDollarRadio.com

Proudly based in

Columbus
OHIO

@TwoDollarRadio

@TwoDollarRadio

/TwoDollarRadio

Love the
PLANET?
So do we.

Printed on Rolland Enviro.
This paper contains 100% post-consumer fiber, is manufactured using renewable energy - Biogas and processed chlorine free.

Printed in Canada

100%   PCF   BIO GAS ENERGY   PERMANENT

SOME RECOMMENDED LOCATIONS FOR READING *VIRTUOSO*: Under a table at a New Year's Party, at bar called The Blue Angel, at a gas station, in the window seat of a plane, before and after a date, while looking at photos of long-lost friends, in a slightly worn-in velvet theatre seat, in the throes of jealousy, despair, or nostalgia, and when horny or while dreaming. Or, pretty much anywhere because books are portable and the perfect technology!

AUTHOR PHOTO→ Inès Manai

COVER PHOTO→ Nikita Nikiforov

When I dream it's of you
My love, my friend
When I sing it's for you
My love, my friend
    (Marie Laforêt, "Mon amour, mon ami")

. . . and huge stars,
above the feverish head, and hands,
reaching out to the one,
who hasn't for ages existed—and won't exist—
who cannot exist—and must exist.
    (Marina Tsvetaeva, "Nights without the beloved . . .")

PART ONE

Soliloquy

Face down on the hotel linen, the body. Just one hand drooping off the side of the bed, resting on the bristles of the rose-colored carpet, fingers spread, glossy nails, raw cuticles, wedding ring in white gold like an eye frozen mid-wink.

The rest of her is emptied flesh, breasts smothered into the bedsheet, pillows crushed against the headboard. Her contorted shoulders a grimace, the back of the knee a gasp, skin already dimming. This woman is alone.

*

Her wife has set the bag of lemons down on the coffee table of the hotel suite. She is approaching the closed bedroom door. Hand on the knob, turning. The metal spring jumps and the door is sliding over the flush carpet fibers.

*

When her wife sees the body—how alone it is—she pounces on top of it.

Outside, the whirling sound of the ambulance. Closer and closer to the hotel. In the bedroom, on the nightstand, the phone hangs off its tight-curl cord, beeping hysterics. The wife is scavenging the body for breath, hair in her mouth, she's pulling it out. She's dragging the body down, *thump*. Millions of rose-colored bristles. Her hands clam at the sternum. The phone is beeping and she's thumping the ribcage and rubber-soled footsteps are nearing. The hotel clerk is young and lean, he steps forward then back, then forward then back, he wants to look, he doesn't want to look. A heavier pacing behind him, the manager is here now, he says, "*Volte agora para baixo*," to the kid, Go downstairs now. As the kid is fumbling away, a man and a woman in forest green medical uniforms brush past him. "Go!" the manager repeats. The kid is going but he keeps looking back. The wife is screaming now: "*Por favor!* She's going to die!"

The defibrillator is unpacked. The man in uniform has a patch on his breast pocket, a medical emblem with a thin red snake. The woman in uniform, same patch, nudges the thumping wife, pulls her aside, pulls her aside again. "I don't speak Portuguese! We're on holiday!" The woman in uniform is touching her shoulder and making eye contact. The wife is yelling in French like chewing, and the woman in uniform is holding her back and nodding. The wife is sloshing her blond hair away from her eyes, trying to gawk back toward the body. Her tongue is fidgeting with words, she's thinking, *I just want to touch her*, as if touching the body were all it would take. The woman in uniform is pulling her into the adjacent room. "I understand," the woman in uniform is repeating in her nasally English, "I understand, madame . . ."

"Clear," the man in uniform pronounces in Portuguese and sends the body a shock, its chest curves up, the wife jumps toward the woman in uniform, the woman in uniform catches the wife, something like a hug, the body falls back down to the carpet. The wife's tears split like hairs. "Clear," the man pronounces again, the woman in uniform is squeezing the wife's forearms. The wife shuts herself up with her own gasp and peers. The current races through the flesh to the heart and pulls the body up, chest bowing, ribs splintering beneath her skin, and for a moment, the wife thinks she's getting up this time. But the body cinches in and collapses, *thump*, back down into the millions of rose-colored bristles. Her shoulder blades hit the floor and spread, and the head winces then stops. The mouth inert. From her slack, parted lips, a viscous blue foam is seeping out.

*

Later, the sun has set. The wife fills out the forms, empty stare, stiff wrist, runny nose. The body's name and age and social security number. Her own name she writes haltingly, having to look away and then back down at the paper several times. When her pen finishes the last letter, she picks up the paper and stares at her full name: *Aimée de Saint-Pé.*

It is then that she feels an extra presence in the room. Something like a color where there was no color. She looks around her: the doctor's a brunette in starched white, sitting in her chair; behind her, light gray window panes; below, a floor of pale freckled tiles. And yet, there is an extra weight within the room, like a movement finishing itself.

The nurse puts a hand on Aimée's shoulder. "Are you all right, madame? Do you need another glass of water, maybe?" Aimée looks up at the nurse. Her lips are oily in the crevices, her skin is darker after sunset, and her eyes—Aimée's stare is gliding past the nurse, behind her head, toward the wall of the office. Something is there.

The nurse is waiting. "Do you need . . . ?" she starts again, but then lets the phrase go. It is behind her, yes. The weight, the movement, the color.

The doctor looks up and then back down at the paperwork. The nurse is speaking to Aimée again. But it—it is untucking itself from the air, groping its way along, moving toward her like flesh.

A click pinches metal and Aimée's chair fills with a wet heat. The doctor has stapled the forms, and urine drips onto the floor.

A little to the left, mon amour

It was an ambling humidity, as August exhaled and the ocean knocked itself against the coasts, beating out the fever. In Paris, the cars shuffled back with their passengers after the holidays, and the mugginess hovered at the tops of cars and the chests of pedestrians and the ground-floor windows.

*

I knew your friend, the Malá Narcis, was how Mr Doubek's email began.

*

Jana's armpits were once again damp, despite the deodorant she had reapplied in the train-station toilets. She was just coming back to Paris from her solo holiday to the South.

She had had the idea to go to Marseille in the first place when she was translating a brochure for import/export petroleum, which mentioned the city was France's major center of oil refining, having extensive access to the French waterways up into the Rhône through the canal. She looked at the train prices and found them reasonable.

In Marseille, she took the ferry to the island of If and visited the dungeon from Dumas' *The Count of Monte Cristo*; she ate swordfish with ratatouille and saffron rice; she looked at the Opéra de Marseille from the outside and saw that nothing was on; she sniffed the various local soaps; she eyed the flopped fish on the blue tarp with crushed ice at the fish market on the Quai des Belges at the end of the harbor; and then she went to the beach, took a seat in the shade, and tried to imagine how someone like Antonin Artaud, the misfit avant-garde theatre artist and Marseille native, could have grown up here. She pictured him with far-flung eyes, pacing around his home city, philosophically infuriated. As she watched the blot of his silhouette jerk along the sand, she realized it wasn't him at all that she was envisioning, but a girl she used to know back in Prague, who everyone called the Malá Narcis, the Little Narcissus.

That evening, Jana meandered toward the city center and the so-called lesbian bars she had spotted, went into one, sipped on a gin and tonic at the bar, and then walked back to the hotel. Five nights of it was enough, she didn't need seven, so she went to the train station and changed her ticket.

Back in Paris, in her studio apartment on the dead-end street stemming from Place Monge, just above the shop that only sells toolboxes in various assortments, on the sixth floor, she plugged in her phone and opened up her laptop and saw the strange email from a "Mr Roman Doubek." He explained that he had requested her services from her agency for his upcoming trip to the Paris Medical Trade Show, where he would be representing Linet, the famous Czech hospital-bed supplier, but her agency had told him that she was unavailable during his requested dates. They must have hired their other Czech interpreter in her absence, Jana thought, the young, orb-eyed Alicia, who started as a discreet and thankful foreigner with visible panty lines, but had recently spurted into a self-assured, cat-eyed, thong-wearing young woman in part because of her new French boyfriend and how well things were going with him, and how far away the Czech Republic now felt, and how naïve she had been, and how glad she was to no longer be naïve like that.

Jana read the email and thought of Alicia, her taut breasts in her cheap, ecstatically patterned blouses, her stare somewhere between expectant, shy, and vengeful. The way she began to ask Jana if she was seeing anyone and footnoted their exchanges with anecdotes about her boyfriend and his funny French buddies. Once she wouldn't let it go, insisting on confiding to Jana that she found her to be isolated, and it might do her good to open up a bit because she was actually an attractive woman at the end of the day, and she could, if she wanted to, go out with her and her boyfriend and his funny French buddies, and who knows. Jana folded the feelings into one straight line, which drew itself on her lips.

*

I knew your friend, the Malá Narcis, the first line read.

*

The next day, Jana got a pressing call from her agency coordinator who was thrilled to find her back in Paris early. They needed an urgent substitute for Alicia, who was supposed to have come back a couple of days ago from her holiday in Biarritz, but, while climbing some rocks at the beach to take a sunset photo in her new bikini, as her French boyfriend coaxed, "A little to the left, *mon amour*," and his buddies and their girls drank beers, the

Czech girl felt the sun setting on her back, watched the waves rolling toward her, and felt that she had finally found her place in their world, when the rock tilted and she slipped and her ankle cracked.

Jana agreed with the agency coordinator that she would take over Mr Doubek the following morning.

*

Jana put on one of her professional suits—a knee-length skirt and matching blazer in midnight blue, with a simple cream-colored V-neck blouse and dark-blue heels.

She arrived early at the medical trade show at the Paris Expo in Porte de Versailles, held in the largest pavilion of the seven-halled convention center, an enormous metal-beamed structure with lofting skylights over its grid-work of stands. She walked along the alleyways between the stands, familiarizing herself with the layout. She passed the Bs and Cs, checking her map so as not to miss the right turn at J14 toward the International Meetings Lounge, where she was to greet Mr Doubek and his French clients at 10 am.

The booths were already filled with people chattering in many languages, setting up their boards and medical apparatus. She passed by D32, where a wheelchair was on display, the cushion a tan and beige ying-yang design, the back of the seat lined with soft-ridged paneling. Behind the wheelchair, a banner listed the product's assets: *bedsore prevention cushions, a remote-controlled electric rise to stand-up position* . . . Jana glanced at the right-hand armrest, a slide-out remote control with a rubber blue grip sticking out.

She walked on, then slowed at H40, gazing at a poster of a plump heart, veined with blue arrows in various directions. Two compact chest defibrillators were being taken out of their case and put on display on the foldout table.

"*Excusez-moi*"—the voice came from behind her. Then a hand touched her shoulder. Jana turned sharply, almost nicking the woman with her elbow.

"Oh, I'm sorry!" said the woman, stepping back as Jana pulled her hands to her gut.

The woman was also wearing a skirt suit, but hers looked completely different. The skirt a bit shorter and a little tighter, the color a little darker—a midnight between blue and black. The blazer cinched at her waist, with just a hint of an ivory blouse peering from between the crevice. She had a black silk scarf around her neck, but her collarbone was bare. Jana looked down at her feet: similar heels, but with a pointed toe.

"I didn't mean to startle—" the woman said nervously.

Her blond hair was parted neatly in the middle and sleeked back into a tight ponytail that hung between her shoulder blades. Her cheekbones opened up on her face, making her eyes look thin, drawn back, mooning with a private embarrassment.

"Do I know you?" Jana asked flatly.

"Oh . . . Oh!" the woman was putting her hand up to her mouth. "I'm sorry, I thought you worked here," she said through her fingers.

The woman's eyes floated down to Jana's badge on her lapel. She pronounced the letters in red out loud, "Liné . . . ?"

"Linet," Jana corrected her pronunciation. "Czech manufacturer. The top hospital-bed supplier worldwide. I do work here. I'm an interpreter."

"Oh . . ." the woman continued uneasily, "well, maybe you can't help me then, but I'm looking for the Dupont Medical Booth. Well actually, between them and a group with the oxygen generators. I've already made two circles through the pavilion, but . . . I can't find it."

"You're in the internationals section," Jana said.

"I am?" the woman replied.

Jana began unfolding her map. The woman quickly pulled out hers and showed it to Jana.

"I got one of those too, but I swear it's as if the spot I'm looking for doesn't exist!"

The two women put their maps side by side as if they could complete each other's scope and traced their eyes up and down the grid of numbered letters.

"The doctor that's speaking at the Global Plastics round table," the woman began speaking aimlessly as she searched, "that's my father. He's a prosthetics specialist."

"You work with your father?" Jana asked.

"I mean, I used to be his assistant, like a welcome-desk secretary, to be honest, but that was years back. No, now I work for a friend of his actually, a gynecologist. His clinic is right next to the Portuguese Embassy, above Parc Monceau, on the—"

"N39," Jana pointed to a small square in the south-east corner of the hall.

"That's funny," the woman said. "I walked around N36, N37 over and over again and didn't see it . . ."

The two women parted their maps and folded them into their respective blazer pockets.

"Do you think you could help me with one more thing?" the woman said shyly, reaching into her pocket and pulling out a badge with a safety pin glued onto the back. She extended the badge toward Jana.

Jana took the badge in her hand and turned it over. She undid the safety pin and looked up. "Where shall I pin it?"

The woman took out one finger, the nail painted in a creamy rose, and pointed to her lapel. "Here. Thank you."

Jana leaned in toward the woman's bare collarbone, pinched a bit of the coarse dark fabric and drew the needle point through, clipped it and then let go, careful not to touch the woman's chest.

She stepped back and looked at the badge fixed on the woman's lapel.

Aimée DE SAINT-PÉ, the badge spelled out.

"*Merci*," the woman said.

Just then, Jana had the idea to introduce herself, but the woman gave her a brisk smile, turned, and began walking toward N39.

Jana watched the woman walk away, her skirt shifting at the curve of her buttocks, then pulling over the slope toward her thighs.

Jana

For the first 19 years of my life, I was a simple Czech girl, a watercolor.

Those days were a clock run by the workers and the ŠtB, the Czechoslovakian State Security. Workers, dressed in stained beige, loading a truck with big square canvas bags. Workers, wearing buttoned-up shirts, walking to work. Workers, carrying their briefcases with stiff arms. The ŠtB, walking in their plainclothes, snapping hidden photos. Man on steps. Woman with buggy. Man and woman hand in hand. Famous artworks of our era. They tapped telephones, opened letters with their steam apparatus, crawled through the veins of the city and pulled people out, out of their own biographies. People disappeared, reappeared, confessed, reported others . . . Much fervent artwork was created, in the preferred medium of photography: *Man Subverting Republic* (Black and White), *Woman Distributing* (Tryptic), *Man and Woman Organizing* (Reprint).

These events closed over like wounds made of water. Life continued. Bubbles of breath rose to the surface and popped. The streets filled up with the absent minded, people walking heavy in their head, burying one worry with another. Anthills and craters. Warm steam from boiling potatoes seeped out of an open window. Pigeons pecked at the bland earth. The ration lines for sugar, coffee, salt, bread . . . Shadows pinched together in the alleyways, then quickly separated. There were kisses. There were pamphlets. There were foreign bills slipped from one pocket to another. At the corner, a woman crossed the street. On the walkway, a kid fell off his bike. Code or meaningless events? The cat in the window stretched her jaw wide open, as if she were a tiger.

*

I was just a particle, a frequency, a rainbow in the sky, a melody on the tip of someone's consciousness in January 1969, 13 years before my birth, when, in Prague's Wenceslas Square, Czech student Jan Palach set himself on fire to protest the continued Soviet domination of Czechoslovakia.

And I was still that immaterial soundless refrain when, a month later, another Czech student, Jan Zajíc, traveled to Prague to the same square for the 21st anniversary of the Communist takeover, on February 25, 1969. He was a nobody kid from Šumperk, where he was attending a technical college, specializing in railroads, and also writing poetry. An hour or so after noon, he walked into the passageway of No. 39 on that square, his white shirt completely soaked. He lit a match and drew it to his chest. His shirt burst into a fur of flames and the body within twitched against itself.

He had planned to run out of the door into the square, the square where Jan Palach burned like a torch. But fully aflame, his body of 18 years only made it into the hallway, where he collapsed.

"Why did they do it?" I remember asking my mother.

"Do what?"

*

Let's just say I know those boys set themselves on fire, not because someone told me, but because floating particles talk among themselves.

In fact, we were very chatty when, a couple of years after Palach's protest, the ŠtB tried to destroy any trace of his actions and existence. They exhumed his body after the burial and cremated it. His mother grieved erratically. It's terrible to mourn a son one never had.

*

Then, all of a sudden, I had to leave the chatty circle of particles and be born—and of all places, in Prague—and of all days, on the 1st of January—and of all names, Jana.

"Why did they do it? Didn't it hurt a lot? Especially on your face. On your cheeks and on your eyelashes . . ."

My mother looked up from the sink, over at me.

*

I thought often about this act, so unusual, so special. I kept trying to decide if it's something I would like to do, or would like to reserve for a very special occasion.

Once I was bored, I mean *so bored* I felt like the air inside of me was cracking, so I pleaded with my brother to play with me. He was older and uninterested in my games. Usually, I accepted his rebuff, trudged away and ran traces into the carpet with my fingernails. But this time, my boredom was so immense and unending, the boredom of rooms and rooms of bed-ridden children, eyeing springtime through the window. I told my brother that if he didn't play with me, I'd set myself on fire. I turned to leave. He grabbed my wrist and pulled me toward him into what I remember as my first hug.

*

I gave up on playtime and resigned myself to endless hours with my face pressed against the window, watching people in the streets below come and go. I felt like I could read their thoughts.

I followed a woman with my eyes, in her listless walk, carrying a bag, her mind twisting. *I should have said—no, just keep quiet, that's it, silence will show him—remember to save a garlic clove—but who does he think he is, professor's son—that chicken smelled bad this morning—it's about getting a little respect—I hope it didn't go bad—now that she's eating chicken—I'll take her to the park this Saturday—That son of a bitch and his goddamn face—Why does my leg itch?—If it comes, it comes. I refuse to be afraid to die.*

*

Paranoia was our specialty. Before that final autumn of 1989, I remember my uncle telling my father that he shouldn't sit on the toilet without looking first into the bowl.

*

The Communist regime in Czechoslovakia made everyone pragmatic and self-serving. To an alien eye, ironically, we might have looked like a capitalist mental asylum, obsessed to the bone of each day about getting more or less than someone else, and why, and why not, and how—tomorrow, next time—not to let him, not to let her, get more, get mine, get me.

The young mothers took to the park for information. They'd take a seat on a bench, send their little ones to fumble around together as the gossip began. The park bench was the only safe place to talk, one eye on your child, and the other on the mamkas. They spelled out the necessary information, encoded seamlessly in their chit-chat. *Her mother's dying* meant the apartment was up for grabs: A two-bedroom like that, and right on Janáčkovo nábřeží, third floor, windows facing the river, I'll pay her a visit, poor woman—Lenka, don't put your face on that, that's filthy! Your Lenka's gotta stop touching everything. You know what's-her-name's little girl just kept sucking on nails she picked up from the ground. Then she got tetanus and died. Her mouth just rotted away. I know, I know, I'm always telling Lenka if she puts her face and fingers in everything, she'll get tetanus and die . . . but you know kids, they're stubborn. *By the way, does Lýdie still come by* meant what kind of Western products does she have? *And Karel is cheating on her with the director of the mathematics department* meant your son better make friends with his. LENKA, I SAID GET YOUR FINGERS OUT OF YOUR MOUTH UNLESS YOU WANT IT TO ROT AWAY LIKE WHAT'S-HER-NAME! . . . Poor girl. She sure was pretty before her mouth fell off.

*

I was a clean-handed little girl. I was not curious about things that could leave a stain. I did not touch dirt. I did not touch puddles. I never secretly plunged a finger into a pot of jam. Although I followed, in my quiet vigor, the initiative of those children, the ones who got onto their stomachs at the curb and shoved their full hand into the gutter, then pulled it out and ran around, chasing the others, all of us shrieking out of the fear and delight we could not voice at home. At home, we had to keep quiet. Your grandma's sick, keep quiet. Your mother's got a migraine, keep quiet. The neighbors'll complain we've got a spoiled child, keep quiet.

Of course, we—the quiet children of the neighborhood—were bottled up with the desire to shriek. We would have welcomed any occasion. We would have chirped in ultimate joy at the sight of someone being stabbed in the street, wishing our hearts into knots that this stabber would pull out his meaty blade and run with it at us, so we could shriek even louder! We were so desperate for every giggle.

*

My brother, in his loose blue T-shirt, kneeled down by my side. He took the two shoelaces out of my hands and pulled them up like magic ropes and twisted them around each other. Then in one swift gesture, he released his hands and I marveled at the perfect bunny-eared bow on my shoe.

*

There were two rules to my childhood. Don't get stolen and don't get molested.

*

There was a girl I knew who had disappeared. She used to live in the building across from me. Milena. A year or so older than us. I would see her, walking through our courtyard, the one we shared, my building, her building and the other one in front. Our parents just sent us children out—"Go play"—so they could get a little quiet in their small shared living quarters. So each banished child would kick their feet around in that courtyard until someone else was sent to "Go play," then we'd join together in our exile and do something with a rock or the spaces between the trees or the cracks between the bricks or, if we were really in the pit of an insurmountable boredom, someone would resort to the hand-in-the-gutter trick.

But Milena, she only walked through, holding her daddy's hand, and looked at us with a still, floating presence like she was a czarina being led to her carriage. Even if we were in the heat of it, whatever game it was we had scraped together that day, we would stop and stare at her as she crossed the yard. She was never sent to "Go play." She never let go of her daddy's hand.

*

Milena was a doll. Or the closest thing any of us had seen to a doll—since there were no toys really, except for the rag-dolls our grannies would sew for us if we really pleaded. But there she was, blond pig-tails and candy eyes, in her neat clothes, the hem of her rose-and-yellow dress smooth, unlike our wrinkled cotton prints, always pinched into our underwear or twisted at the side, where you could see the stitched tears our mothers had scolded us for getting and our grannies had sewn up for us.

Milena's eyelashes fluttered in a quick gesture when she blinked, like those paper-thin hand fans. Her skin was always sun-kissed, even when it was gray for weeks, I'm telling you, and, although her body was small like ours, her arms and legs and neck all had something quite refined, unlike our kiddish, knotted limbs, blotted with bruises and scrapes and itched-off mosquito bites.

Every part of her was a doll. Even her knees were mesmerizing. Like wax molds. Mine were always grated from sitting on the carpet for so long, or crouching on the cement to count the weeds, or kneeling on the wooden stairway to look through the small window at my neighbors (especially Ms Květa on the second floor, who painted her lips red "as if she had nothing to be ashamed of," according to Mamka, and who was always fixing her breasts through the front opening of her dress).

*

I had veiny white skin, puddle-colored hair, and flat gray eyes. Milena's eyes always sparkled—always; even from the distance of her crossing the yard, they glimmered above her fresh round cheeks, which flushed and framed those lips, so pink and perfectly drawn.

*

I had assumed that molestation was inevitable for all little girls, like getting your period—it may include some mystical pains, but you get over it, and you learn bodily maintenance.

When my cousin, my father's bad-seed brother's son, came back from prison, my dad kept standing in front of me—he wouldn't let Jiří lay his eyes on me. I was fascinated by this buzz-cut, pug-featured kid with a tattoo on his neck. I kept trying to squirm around my father, to catch Jiří's eyes—just then, he looked over and I looked up and there it was, my eyes sparkled like Milena's perhaps, and I thought, *finally!*

*

I spent much of my childhood waiting to be molested, like waiting for womanhood. Try as I might to make myself molestable, it never came.

I heard Milena got molested.

Oh, Milena made me terribly jealous those days.

My cousin Jiří did have a predatory feel about him. But he was a kid. He was 17. And he couldn't keep himself out of prison. Also, someone once told me I looked a bit like his older sister, rest in peace. She was the one who had raised him, but then ran off in a young-love marriage, and Jiří joined a pack of boys who all had the same scar. So maybe seeing me was a case of being haunted, as happens when people die, but the anger stays. I think Jiří's squinty eyes were on me in that way, twisting oddly like damaged fingers, trying to peel the layers of the package before him to get to what he truly saw in front of him: his late sister Frida. He must have been staring at me, the frame of a child holding the shadow of that young woman, with his eyelids quivering—*why didn't you stick around for me . . . I was so scared.*

Or maybe he did want to touch my young formless body, just because he was bigger and stronger than me. Or maybe he wasn't even into the struggle. Maybe he wanted to use some of his drugs on me, until I was passed out, just so he could hold a warm limp body, like a rabbit freshly passed away, long and flimsy, so he could say the words that would inexplicably come to his mind: "Now you're safe."

Poor Jiří. But everyone back then was a bit damaged or violated or hungry or bored. Marcel Proust was banned for our parents, and our national anthem is still *"Kde Domov Můj?"*—"Where Is My Home?"

*

They eventually found Milena's body. It was laid out on the dirt beneath the square shrubs at the side gate of Saint George's Basilica. She had been dug up and dropped off there, half-decomposed. After all those years, she was still seven. It all remained a mystery. Since we are telling the truth, the first feeling I had was, well, at least Milena will never get her period. Now we are even, I suppose. I forgive you, Milena, for being beautiful, for being molested, for being my first love.

The new girl

Milena's family moved out, and in came a new one. A bird-eyed mamka in a heavy fox-fur coat, a stubble-faced papka with a hernia-type stride, and a little raven-girl.

*

It was almost December. I was six and the new girl was six too. I saw her in the courtyard from my window, holding her winter hat in a small mittened fist, the top of her head sleek with dark hair. She turned to look at the buildings and I saw her left eye was slightly puffed up, and below it a streak of violet-blue. Then she looked up, straight at my window. Her pupils pointed into mine.

New Year and my birthday came around and a couple of the families in the building celebrated together as usual, except that year, the new one was invited too. All of us children knew each other except for the little raven-girl, so we all just stood around and stared at her, and she crouched against the wall and leaned her spine into the light socket, glaring back at us. Slavek's mamka said, "What's the matter with you all standing like stones? Go play." She meant inside, it was a holiday, she wasn't kicking us out into the courtyard. Plus it was snowing. Anyway, the adults quickly forgot about us and got drunk and opened and closed the window to smoke or coat the tops of their glasses of liquor with snowflakes. Since the Communist takeover in 1948, the Czechoslovak people had grown less and less interested in politics or having opinions about anything bigger than their neighborhood or family. They planned their countryside summer holidays, they drank, they bickered, they recited poetry, they went to bed.

Some of the kids snuck in sips. Slavek was already getting drunk, and his little cheeks flushed as he ran around his father's legs, saying, "Papka, Papka, show us the knife!" It was the famed knife, with a thin snake coiled on the metal handle, that Slavek's father's father had apparently killed a Nazi soldier with—slicing him right across the throat below the Adam's apple—but Slavek's father just used it to shear a chicken's skin in the kitchen sink or sharpen the ends of electrical wires. "Not now," Slavek's papka said and he pushed the boy out of the way. Slavek twirled a bit, then played swords with my brother, then vomited by the couch. After the women cleaned it up, his father put a hand on his son's shoulder, knelt down and said, "Now, Slavek, if you drink the booze, you gotta keep it down."

Slavek pouted, then murmured, "I'm sorry I yacked, Papka . . ."

*

The raven-girl and I stayed still like stones and stared at each other until the countdown began. Ten . . . Nine . . . Eight . . . All the adults were hurriedly refilling their glasses. Three . . . Two . . . But suddenly the raven-girl sprung away from the wall and ran and threw her limbs out greedily and sang a loveable song in a nasty voice. Her mamka tried to pull her down by her wrists, but the girl kept springing back up until her mamka gave her a sharp smack to the back of the head and her sleek black hair whisked up. The girl stopped, touched her skull with her palms, then grew very quiet.

Her mamka excused her right away and told everyone not to mind it too much—her little girl was prone to these fits of stagecraft and this was precisely why they called her the Malá Narcis, because she's a Little Narcissus who can't get enough of herself from time to time. The other kids started laughing with their mouths closed, the sound bursting out like spit. The adults turned the music up and began to dance, now that it was a new year, and the raven-girl looked around, then crawled under a chair. She sat there, watching everyone's calves. It was a couple of minutes past midnight and I was officially seven years old. I went over to her, crouching down in such a way as to try not to mess up my dress in case my mamka was watching, and crawled under the table to sit near her. She looked over at me. I sucked my lips in, then let them go. "Hey," I said. Then we both looked at everyone's calves. I saw my mamka's knee slide past her daddy's trouser leg. I saw his sock showing as he took a step back to the beat, the hem of his gray suit trousers lowered because of his long legs. I saw her mamka's white heel cross over and her tanish-colored stocking crease behind the knee. "I'm Zorka," I heard next to me. When I looked over at her, she was picking her nose.

*

Zorka. She had eyebrows like her name.

*

Aeque pars ligni curvi ac recti valet igni. Crooked logs make straight fires.

Like I said, I knew your friend

Jana held her purse to her pelvis as she waited outside the International Meetings Lounge.

*

"You must be Ms K——," the man in the gray suit said.

Jana extended her hand. He wrapped his around hers and shook it while opening up a mindful smile.

"Mr Doubek," he said, then cleared his throat. "Roman Doubek."

*

Roman Doubek looked too small for his suit somehow—his shoulders were inordinately narrow, or else his head, balding and shiny on top, was too wide at his jaw, or else his potbelly was too apologetic, like a stolen grocery store item tucked into a coat. On top of his bulbous nose was a pair of light silver-rimmed glasses.

*

"Here I was on my way to Paris and here you were living in Paris. Here I was seeking an interpreter, and here you are working as one," Mr Doubek said. "Like I said, I knew your friend—the Little Narcissus."

"How so?" Jana enquired, maintaining her disinterest.

"I had considered it a nightmare, and then—I went online, Ms K——. I'm delighted you were available, in the end, for this meeting," he replied. His face formulated back into a smile and he said no more.

*

Jana was burning to say her name, Zorka, you knew Zorka, is that it? But to say her name now, out loud, after so many years of it remaining purposefully unsaid, would be as freakish as this man's nightmare claim.

Besides, Jana had no patience for riddling when it came to men. There was always a condition to the suspense, and the anticipation was as finely nauseating as a string of saliva being drawn out slowly from the mouth, and the reveal usually revealed nothing more than men's inherent privilege to withhold information. Even if he did know Zorka, it no longer concerned her—this knowledge, her existence, the man's betting chips clattering in the palm of his wording. Did he think he'd make a little girl out of her by mentioning the Malá Narcis? She wanted to tell him that she had never been a little girl in her life, and she wasn't about to start now.

Jana cleared her throat and informed Mr Doubek that she would be using the toilet before the meeting.

In her cubicle, Jana closed the door and pulled up her skirt. She wasn't sure if she actually had to urinate. She pulled down her underwear and ran her palm over her pubic hair, incrementally against the grain. *Zorka*, she whispered out loud, and the stream came all on its own.

*

"As I'm sure you've observed." Mr Doubek sat beside Jana, across from the two French clients. "Linet has been dynamically developing. Since our beginning in 1990 in Želevčice u Slaného, we have expanded our production to reach hospitals, retirement homes, and long-term care facilities worldwide, exporting to over 100 countries and growing."

He spoke assuredly and evenly, sliding rehearsed coins that Jana flipped routinely into French for the clients.

"Our main plant in Želevčice manufactures 40,000 beds a year."

The shorter client, with a mole on his cheek, asked, "Tell me more about the Eleganza 3 bed?"

"The Eleganza 3 bed is for intensive care units," Jana translated.

". . . sold greatly in the United Arab Emirates after being exhibited at the Dubai convention."

"Very innovative," the second client added, nodding his dark head full of brushed hair, his cleft chin pointing at the table.

"Anti-pressure ulcer mattresses . . ."

"Can we just go back to the CliniCare 20+ mattress?"

". . . made of cold polyurethane foam, which is also covered with a layer of thermoelastic foam . . . with transport handles on the side, of course, for easy transfer."

"Oh no, the EffectaCare 20+ has a greater foam density."

". . . in collaboration with top healthcare professionals and experts in the scientific fields!"

"Listen, we're not only on top of the newest equipment in the area of medical care, we set the trend. So, let's get to why we are really here, gentlemen."

"Yes, let's," the man with the mole agreed.

Mr Doubek pulled out a glossy brochure from his folder and slid it across the table to his clients.

The Virtuoso Mattress, the front page read, *when care is critical, each fiber counts.*

"There is no mattress system for high-risk patients like this in the world."

The clients opened the brochure to the second page and Mr Doubek reached over and pointed to the diagram of the multi-layered mattress with information bubbles around the design.

"The three-cell technology holds the body of the patient in 'zero pressure.' Allow me to further explain what this means, gentlemen. Zero pressure, let's just say these patients, on the verge of complete organ failure, for example, on the precipice of expiration, in addition to the stellar care that the best medical facility can provide, they require a sort of organic reunion with their own gravity, a homecoming to the distribution of their mass, a realignment comparable with the original state of symbiosis within their mother's womb—so to speak.

"But let's discuss more concretely. Here," Mr Doubek turned the page for the clients as Jana spoke, "the system of connected air cells between the two-layered mattresses creates the therapeutic effect that has been proven to accelerate wound healing.

"And as you can see," the page was turned again and Mr Doubek's finger pointed to a photo of a nozzle-like apparatus adjoined to the side of the beige bed frame, "the Virtuoso mattress system is also equipped with a one-hand-operated CPR system."

The French clients began nodding in sync, then flipped backward in the brochure.

"Very impressive," the cleft-chin client said, "but it is also quite an investment, you would agree."

"The investment is on a par with the service, gentlemen," Jana said calmly. "This is state-of-the-art medical care. This one-of-a-kind mattress, this complete bed system," Jana continued as Mr Doubek held down the brochure with the fleshy side of his fingertip, "this is the human sleep wherein science can reach its hand the farthest it has ever reached to intervene."

*

Mr Doubek gestured, letting the clients leave first. After they'd left the meeting room, Jana stood up, and Mr Doubek followed suit. She took a couple of steps toward the door, but Mr Doubek slid around her into the doorway and turned to face her.

"The meeting went very well," he said.

"I'm glad to hear it," Jana replied and waited for Mr Doubek to step out of her way. But he just stood there, looking at Jana.

"Can I get you a coffee . . . and a pastry . . . ?" Mr Doubek asked.

"No, thank you," Jana replied, looking beyond his shoulder.

Mr Doubek maintained his gaze on Jana, continuing to speak in a weighted tone.

"I know I am intruding, Ms K——. I was under the impression you might want to hear more about your friend . . ."

Mr Doubek reached his left hand inside his jacket pocket and pulled out an inky-colored business card and gave it to Jana. On the card, the letters were embossed.

She angled it toward the light and read:
THE BLUE ANGEL
Underneath, *Bar à vin.*

Then the address. A street named "Prague," in the 12th arrondissement.

"We could get a drink there," Mr Doubek said. "At 9 pm . . ."

Jana's eyes were going over the contours of the card, dropping into the grooves of each letter.

"I hope you like sad music, Ms K——. . ."

Zorka

The other kids were mush. Except her, she was solid, I knew that from the courtyard when I looked up.

Sure I get what the gossip was, even back then, Slavek's big brother with his big mouth was spreading it, saying me and my mamka and my papka had been kicked out of our last apartment for our "dynamics" and we were on our best behavior in the new building and that truth be told, I was the nutjob of the family.

*

Yeah, I had a pee trick when I first moved in, six going on seven, but for the record, I did behave most of the time 'cause Papka said we can't get kicked out any more, but then Mamka would scream, clang a dish, take a hard footstep, how she did, close the window abruptly, and I knew she was coming for me. So I stood in the middle of the carpet and pulled down my tights and my underwear and let it stream.

"Stop it stop it stop it," Mamka would run in, trying to pick me up, getting pee all down her stockings, cursing, kicking me with her pee-stained leg, screaming, "Malá Narcis!!" when I fell to the floor, then me standing back up, the stream starting again between my legs, Mamka slapping me across my face, me falling back down on the wet carpet, Mamka getting on top of me, Mamka whacking me on the shoulder, on the temple, the cheek, the wrists, the arms, the mouth, whatever, it was all the same to Mamka's hands. She'd slap herself tired, then get off me and stand up, take a moment of solitude like I knew her to take. She'd place her face into her still-hot palms and hold her head up like that, eyes closed. And I'd get up, careful, checking things out, my face stinging, my lip bleeding. I'd give her dress a little tug. I'd say, "Mamka?" in my not-so-nasty voice.

There were dashes on my cheek from Mamka's wedding ring.

I'd give the dress a tug and say, in my quiet, not-weird voice, "I'm all out of pee now, Mamka," to let her know.

Then she'd take her hands away from her face and look down at me and say, "When you call me your mother, it makes me want to die."

*

It was the anniversary of the Soviet invasion, and the adult talk was: "Twenty years now of this Warsaw Pact crap"; the Czechoslovaks were a slow-boiling people, they were a cautious people, but now, even they had had enough of this shit. I'd been collecting my saliva in a cup I hid under my bed. "Everything you don't say," I told Jana, "becomes liquid." I didn't want my words, said or not, to go to shit. Jana played it quiet, like she did. She was good at that. But then she whispered to me that she was already full of wasted words, so maybe she shouldn't speak at all. I snuffed at her then, "Yeah right, Janka, never! You gotta keep speaking, and if it don't sound right in one language, just learn another."

Jana knew what I meant, and everyone could see it. She was sharper than sharp. Her mamka was always bragging about her brain. She got her big books, dictionaries, Russian and French and German, and Jana started learning words that looked confident.

*

Maybe I'm not telling it right. Or when I hear myself describing Jana, I get sorta pissed off about it, like, that's not right. I don't know how to make it sound like how it was, for us.

She was solid, Janka. She was my best friend.

*

We were seven when the first cracks began to appear in the cemented communism we had grown up with. In November, the news came that the Berlin Wall was coming down and refugees were trying to sneak through Czechoslovakia; the Vltava shifted beneath its icy skin like life heckling a corpse. The adults were asking each other in private, "Well, what do you think, what about us?"

Janka and I, we sat under the kitchen table, daring each other to swallow the pebbles we had collected that autumn. Big pieces, little pieces, country by country, communism started crumbling everywhere.

*

"Janka . . ."
   "Huh?"
   "Guess what?"
   "Huh."
   "Guess though."
   "Um . . ."
   "You'll never guess."

"What?"

"Know how I'm supposed to be like . . . greater . . . than this."

"Yeah."

"Like . . . my eyes the size of the planets out there."

"Yeah."

"And like, my heart beating, splitting land masses into islands . . ."

"Yeah."

"And like, big tits. In everyone's face."

"Yeah."

"Well . . . I'm getting outta here."

"Outta here where?"

*

The first time I ran away from the new building, Mamka smoothed things over with the neighbors so we wouldn't look too weird as a family. Sure, her eight-year-old girl went missing for a couple days, she sang her tune, but she probably reminded everyone that I'm a Little Narcissus, and assured them one by one in the hallway that I'd been pulling these stunts since I could walk, and please, did they want to help themselves to a portion of her poppy-seed cake, freshly baked?

I came back a couple of days later, and Jana asked me where I'd gone and I told her I was hanging out in the forest and then we both looked at the curtains in the kitchen and I could feel her feeling it 'cause I was feeling it too, the nothingness of time, as thin and stretchy as your eyelid if you pull it up with her fingertips. If we had known how to cry about those feelings, we sure would have. But we were kids, we only knew how to cry about the stuff that didn't really hurt, we cried to show everyone we were still kids, in case they started worrying we were up to some adult shit. But I remember those curtains and how much I wanted to cry about my destiny and I'm sure Janka did too, and so I just reached out my hand and Janka took it, and that was enough, and actually, it was incredible, to hold on to something instead of wetting myself.

*

I don't know what to do with History, the big one that belongs to all of us and my small one, like a keychain.

*

Yeah, we were about 10, I think, and yeah, I just hit Janka on the sternum and yelled at her. Asked her where her revolution was, for fuck's sake. The sun was out. Jana was clogged up beneath her thin auburn bangs, the rest of her hair long and flat. She had that good-girl look down. Even when I brushed my hair, I still looked like I'd mess something up for somebody.

They were announcing the withdrawal of the Soviet forces, those last T-72 tanks and armored vehicles rolling through the streets with their artillery snouts and gouged-eye stares. Jana got real good at fingering her hair quickly into two straight plaits. I was testing out my middle finger at cloud formations, sunsets, horizons . . .

I told Janka, listen, we've been pooing and peeing on each other for too long in this country and it's about time someone built a modern toilet.

By that time, my mamka had sloped from her flirty mania back into a subdued and self-conscious stare, stirred up by that early case of electroshock therapy she had. Those days, she was too depressed to be political. And my papka was just getting really sick then, before we knew it was a terminal disease.

"Janka, you gotta be your own person!" I yelled at her. (That's why I was hitting her in the sternum. 'Cause she wouldn't say nothing in response, I mean . . .)

Then finally she said, "I want a nice modern toilet too, you know."

*

Politics got full of wonder, miraculous even, not knowing what would happen. Other things, we did know. Like my papka who was sick. We bought a grave ahead of time. Still the world kept on folding and unfolding, creasing itself this way or that, borders, agreements, yeah I was showing off the scars on my body to Janka, like guarded checkpoints I snuck myself past.

*

She told me she wanted to cut off her hair, I said good idea, it's weighing you down. She asked her mamka and her mamka said no, absolutely not, your hair looks nice the way it is, so I stole the big pair of sewing scissors from our neighbor Ms Květa and Janka pointed where, and I chopped it off straight at the chin. Her mamka freaked, what have you done, then of course, turned on me, got my mamka involved (bad idea). My mamka showed her how to freak out properly. She got my papka's belt and started lashing it in the air like a horsewhip, so of course I took a run for it, and she went after me, and got a couple of lashes in, but I also gave her the tongue twice and a solid two-finger salute, so we were even.

Jana asked to see my welts so I showed her, shoulder-blade, neck, forearm, but said it was definitely worth it. She looked out of this world with her new hair. I wore sweaters for a while, sweat it out in spring, till the welts healed.

Fuck, we were almost teens and it was tough. We'd go up and down Dvořákovo Street and stand outside of the Prague Conservatory, that yellow building like a huge plastic stick of butter. One July it got so hot, I thought it smelled salty and oily. I was wearing long trousers because I was trying to hide three fat bruises on my right thigh.

In school, people thought my papka was a military man and he was strict, so I just let them think that, and Jana added a comment or two to keep the rumors going on my behalf. Yeah, her mamka was mush, and her daddy was out of it, but the thing is, she didn't know about getting a beating, really. The thing is, it's kinda embarrassing when it's your mamka that does it. Janka said her mamka never slapped her or her brother Vilèm around. They only got spanked by their daddy's hand, and Vilèm got the belt a couple of times because he liked to have the last word, but he grew out of that, and Janka was attentive by nature.

I churned a bit of spit in my mouth and shot it as far as I could. "What if my spit was made of fire?" I asked Janka.

*

We'd go by the Vltava River, kicking pebbles with our shoes. We'd walk by that old Jewish cemetery, past the Staroměstská metro, to the astronomical clock tower, the biggie tourist trap, now that tourists were flocking in. Near the bottom of the clock tower was a series of layered astronomical dials—the sun, the moon, and the zodiac—just below two windows out of which would appear a rotating circle of apostles. Placed around the astronomical dials, there were small statues representing the evils of life: *Vanity*, a man admiring himself in a small mirror; *Greed*, a man holding a bag of gold—you get the picture—and lastly (my favorite) *Death*, a skeleton holding an hourglass in one hand and the clock's bell-ringing rope in the other.

On the hour, *Death* rung his bell, the apostles rotated in their windows like, "Ohhhnooo!" and the three evils shook their heads from side to side, saying, "Please, please, I don't wanna go" (too bad, suckers).

Afterward, we'd cross the bridge to Letenské Park, and just hang out at the *kolotoč*, the old carousel in the middle, a closed-up mustard hexagon with those grinning life-size horses, carved from wood and covered in real horse leather, stuck in mid-gallop on their metal stakes.

*

I got my period before Jana despite being as flat and skinny as a birch tree, so yeah, I bragged a little. Then Jana got hers soon enough, right on her birthday, and our country, the former Czechoslovakia, split. I told Jana her ovaries burst and cracked our nation in two, ha ha. That New Year, people danced a little harder as the snow dusted down the black sky. Janka and I were both sitting under the table, our heads touching the top when we sat up straight, so we hunched and chatted and snuffed at anyone who told us that we were too old to sit under the table on New Year's Eve. All the adults were so involved with their own bodies, they danced with closed eyes, then Slavek's papka plugged in the strobe light that Slavek had gotten him, and everyone swiveled around the thick rays of white and yellow and green and blue.

Then we saw it, between two flashing strobes of white, her mamka kissed my mamka on the lips in a quiet, lag way. They held each other, with their mouths pressing together, as around them hands and elbows jutted into the multi-colored flashes. It looked like forever, but before we could say anything out loud, it was done. Our mamkas parted and soon they were dancing with our daddies. I climbed out from the table and stood there, wanting to run around their legs like the Malá Narcis that I was. I could feel it swelling up in me, I could have even given my pee trick a go, but that stunt was old news. Janka climbed out and stood next to me. She pulled out her hand and I reached it and took it. We were anonymous pillars, standing the test of time.

*

I followed my mamka into the shared kitchen and stood behind her until she turned around. Then I asked, "Why did Mrs Táňa kiss you on the lips?"

Her eyes flashed.

"It's not what you think," she said and began to feign rubbing a stain out of her dress.

She stopped, looked up at me, and said, "If you must know, *your father* is going to die." She took a breath and I kept looking at her, so she said, "He is ill and he's going to die young and I will be left all alone." Her eyes began to heat up, then she grabbed her skirt again and began rubbing, like sparking the fabric against itself.

"It's awful, *awful*, the diseases that climb into your body and putrefy the organs. You think it can't happen, or someone else, or later, but it swells right up inside you, deep inside and makes room for itself until you're wheezing for mercy—" then she just stopped talking.

I knew what it was. My index finger was high and snug in my nostril, grabbing at something promising. She slapped my hand out from my face and screamed, "Don't pick your nose when I'm explaining death to you! *Bože na nebi*, Zorka, you're almost a woman!"

My nail scraped the inside of my nostril, and a ring of blood and some nose hairs pulled out.

My mamka looked at my finger, then at my face, then pulled me into her chest with a frantic grab, my forehead bumping into her collarbone.

Yeah, she was trying to hug me.

She began murmuring in her silky voice, "Please, please, please, my love . . . don't be weird."

She let go of me and walked back toward the party. At the doorway, she stopped, two men shouted her name at the same time. She bent her knees and shook her ass, holding the sides of the door, then propelled herself forward and was dancing inside the strobe-light colors that were tearing holes into the room. Everyone danced like bodies being resurrected in gunfire. I licked the blood off my finger and told Janka to come dance with me.

*

So our pubic hair had begun to grow in enough to shave it off. Jana did like I asked her and stole her dad's razor.

We took turns with it in the bathroom, sliding the razor in and out over our cunts and all the way back to our assholes, and all around, pulling the lips out one by one to get it good. We wiped away the flecks of blood and looked at the curled black and brownish strands floating in the toilet bowl, then flushed and faced each other, with our underwear and jeans still down at our ankles.

I ran my hand over my bald cunt and said, "Agnus Dei." Like the Lamb of God, like they were teaching us, in the Book of Revelations: "*Slain but standing.*" That was my cunt's name.

Jana did like me and ran her fingers over hers and thought about it. I thought about it too. But we couldn't think of a name for hers. I crouched down and looked at it head on to get some ideas, pulling apart her cunt's lips with my fingers and having a good look around and then I saw it!

"Woah!" I announced. "It's the Jan boys in there!"

"What?"

"Jan Palach and Jan Zajíc, you know! The divine heretics, hello, our shooting stars, our punk meteors, our—" I plucked the air like an electric guitar and sang out, "Great balls of fire!"

I reached out my hand and Jana helped me up.

"Agnus Dei and the Jans," I said. "That is, number one, a great title for the past and the future, and number two, an even greater band name, which is our cunts, Janka, jamming like—" I crunched my eyes and got the high notes of the air guitar, "like . . . hell no, hell nooo, Hell FUCKIN NOOOOOO . . ."

"Agnus Dei and the Jans," Jana repeated as she hit some air drums around her.

Then we straightened up and took each other by the shoulders and leaned in close. Our jeans and everything were still bunched at our feet, it was just us, all bare, all shaved, just in our sweaters, me in my bright-red turtleneck and Janka in her blue-and-tan striped. I told her to close her eyes and I closed mine.

"You see us?" I whispered. "We're floating above, you see it?"

"Yeah . . ." Jana whispered back. "Above . . . everything . . ."

"Below us . . . everything's in flames . . ."

"Yeah. I see it."

"See our ugly apartment building there . . . ?"

"Yeah . . . there's fire . . . in the windows . . ."

"And our ugly school . . ."

"The side just collapsed."

"And our ugly *kolotoč* in the park . . ."

"The horse leather is broiling and the wooden bodies are splintering off their poles . . ."

"And look!"

"What?"

"You see it?"

"Yeah . . . I think so . . ."

"The Vltava . . ."

"The river . . ."

"The water's even on fire!"

"And . . . the trees too!"

"And the birds."

"And the gravel roads . . ."

"And even *us*!"

"Us?" Jana asked.

"Yeah *us* . . . You see us?"

"Sure . . . where are we?"

"Look . . . There we are . . . I mean just our ugly bodies, that is . . ."

"Yeah . . . our ugly bodies."

"They're burning. You see that?"

"There's flames on my eyelashes—but it doesn't hurt."

"We're running across Wenceslas Square . . ."

"And all our ugly limbs, like hands like shoulders like knees, and our ugly clothes, all on fire . . ."

"There're the benches . . . and the row of yellow taxis . . . and the saint on his horse in front of the National Museum . . . And there're people all around us, stupid people, flocks, people and pigeons and cars honking. And the stupid police blowing their whistles . . ."

"And we're running across in flames . . ."

"And the more we burn the higher we get! Look now: There's our ugly city, and our ugly country, and our ugly world! . . . Even the stuff we thought was okay or even nice or really beautiful, it wasn't, it's not . . ."

"It's all the same. It's all on fire."

"And now we're just . . . finally . . . essential . . ."

"And it feels good . . ."

"It feels so good."

"Fuck off, *ošklivý svět* . . . ugly world, peace out. Agnus Dei and the Jans have risen, baby!"

*

When I opened my eyes, we were already kissing. Maybe we were doing that the whole time. Janka's tongue was strong, I remember. I thought, wow, so that's where she keeps all her strength then. I remember it, strong, in my mouth.

Girls only

0_hotgirlAmy_0 has joined the group <GIRLS ONLY>

Dominxxika_N39: Hey hotgirlAmy, A/S/L?

0_hotgirlAmy_0: 15/f/Milwaukee. U?

Dominxxika_N39: 35/f/Prague.

Dominxxika_N39: . . . too old?

BabyBoi_whatup8: For real.

0_hotgirlAmy_0: Whatev BB. It's hot.

Dominxxika_N39: *smile

Dominxxika_N39 has left the group <GIRLS ONLY>

Dominxxika_N39 has joined the group <GIRLS ONLY>

Dominxxika_N39: Sorry hotgirlAmy! I sign off quick cuz
I thought husband come home.

0_hotgirlAmy_0: Oh . . .

Dominxxika_N39: But its OK, is just bird outside who
make noises.

BabyBoi_whatup8: Ummmm Dominxxika, it's GIRLS ONLY—If u not a dyke—GOODBYE>>>

Sexy_Kimmie_: Not everyone here's a dyke, btw, gross.

69Beachgirl69: Seriously BabyBoi. Go back to the butch/ femme chatroom.

~GlitterCrush~: F U Kimmie & Beachgirl. BabyBoi stay.

BabyBoi_whatup8: Holla GlitterCrush.

~GlitterCrush~: *bites her glossy lip

BabyBoi_whatup8: Damn.

00ps-I-did-it-again00 has joined the group <GIRLS ONLY>

00ps-I-did-it-again00: *waves to everyone

00ps-I-did-it-again00: Anyone here from Nebraska?

~GlitterCrush~: Hey 00ps, u a heart-breaker?

00ps-I-did-it-again00: *dusts her shoulders off

~GlitterCrush~: *giggles

Mybigbootie56: Any other latinas here?

JLoJLoJLo: . . . Duh. *waves at bigbootie

Mybigbootie56: *shoots herself in the head

JLoJLoJLo: lol. 17/Houston

Mybigbootie56: All my exes live in Texas! JK. Me = 15/ HOTlanta, Georgia holla!

Sexy_Kimmie_: KatieCutie, Id totally just make out with her. Like even if she's all, I'm not like that, just kiss her.

69Beachgirl69: Yeah do it!!!

KatieCutie16: What if she tells our swim coach?

69Beachgirl69: Then we'll like come over there.

Sexy_Kimmie_: KatieCutie we got ur back girl.

KatieCutie16: Haha thanx guys. Itd b so funny if u just showed up in Toledo.

Sexy_Kimmie_: I could whatev. Ohio is like what a 12 hour drive from Vermont.

69Beachgirl69: Yo swing by Detroit and pick me up too! *rolling on floor laughing

Sexy_Kimmie_: For real!

0_hotgirlAmy_0: Dominxxika, wanna go private *wink

Dominxxika_N39: I follow u . . . *takes hotgirlAmy's hand

Dominxxika_N39 has left the group <GIRLS ONLY>

0_hotgirlAmy_0 has left the group <GIRLS ONLY>

00ps-I-did-it-again00: I played with ur heart. Got lost in the game . . .

~GlitterCrush~: *reapplies lip gloss

Global Plastics

Aimée shifted in her plastic seat in front of the stage across from N39. Four men were on stage, wiry mics hooked up to the table. Framing them, two banners spotted with logos, each bearing the title—in leaning blue lettering—*Global Plastics*.

*

". . . to most accurately mimic the strength, resilience and flexibility of a human hand . . ."

*

Aimée shifted again. There was an odd sensation, as if right behind her shoulder. She turned discreetly around and glanced at the seated public in the rows behind her, suits and blazers, attentive to the lecture. Everyone's eyes were on the speaker. She turned back to the stage and tried to listen.

"Yes, metal devices are durable, but they are frustrated by their limitations—"

The speaker had a small head with white hair and pinkish lips at the center of his graying beard. His bright-red tie spotted with white dots stood out against his pale-blue shirt and his dark-blue suit-jacket. The name-card in front of him read: *Docteur de Saint-Pé*.

*

". . . more supple, coated with polyurethane."

*

Next to the doctor, the man in the black suit nodded dutifully, his brown hair thick and neat. On the other side of the doctor, a long-faced man with deep indents leading to his mouth pursed his lips like a question mark, his thin blond hair catching the overhead lighting. The last man at the end of the table in the asphalt-colored suit flared his nostrils as if punctuating the doctor's speech.

*

"And, of course, injection molding technologies . . ."

Aimée tried to concentrate on her father's words, but she felt as if her seat was being budged. She glanced down at her hands holding her mobile phone on her lap, and gripped the device more firmly.

". . . this biofeedback is precisely what the amputee has to rely on in order to determine how much pressure to exert in any given movement . . . something metal devices don't and can't offer . . ."

The doctor gestured to the brown-haired man on his left and smiled.

"Like the V3 Remotion Knee in California . . ."

Both men smiled at each other. The asphalt suit itched his nose.

"These plastic sockets are based on vital primary anatomical principles."

*

She was clutching her mobile phone, trying to force her eyes forward, but her head was drifting over her right shoulder again, resting on the man sitting beside her, with long earlobes, who was jotting something down on his notepad. Behind him, there was a woman, dry skin coated with layers of make-up, dark eyebrows colored in, her eyes loyal to the speaker. Aimée twisted her torso farther round in her plastic seat, sweeping over the faces of the sitting people, looking for the source of her agitation. But not a single person's eyes were on her, everyone was looking straight ahead at the speaker.

". . . as with Touch Bionics," the doctor continued.

It was there though, the feeling. Behind the audience. A man had halted his step. Gray suit, eggish body, balding head with a thin pair of glasses on his nose. His head was facing the stage but his eye was directly on her. She met his stare and the two held each other's gaze. The man lifted his left hand and began moving it toward his chest. Aimée watched his hand disappear between the jacket lapel and his button-down shirt. She felt her own blouse shift and wrinkle at the ribcage. Then she saw his hand reappear, first wrist-bone, then knuckles, and she exhaled as if he were pulling something out from inside her. He held a square sky-blue silk handkerchief and put it to his mouth to cough. He coughed several times, then crumpled up the handkerchief and began sliding it back into his jacket pocket. Aimée's shoulders shriveled into her heart.

Then the man was walking away, into the rows of stands, toward the internationals section.

Aimée unwound herself to turn back toward the stage. She lowered her eyes to her lap, where her hands were still gripping the mobile phone, as if sensing it was about to ring between her two palms. She looked up again to the panel and saw a different stage altogether, an elevated theatre stage, deep in its black-painted floor, framed with a heavy curtain drawn open, lights crossed and fused over the body of a woman standing barefoot in a white satin nightie. In her shadow, a younger lookalike, white satin nightie, thighs, knees, spread toes.

FEMME (facing audience, looking at horizon)
I was young once.
FILLE (facing audience, looking at public)
I was old once.

*

Aimée was a miracle child, meaning her mother had had her when she was deemed past her prime, and it was the last mistake her parents had shared. Their other two children were already grown up and making their own lives when Aimée came into the emptied nest, and not two years in, her parents filed for divorce. Her mother moved to London in a sweeping gesture, underlining how many years her father had kept her from doing what she had wanted to do all along. Incidentally, she had a beau waiting for her there.

Her older sister, Sylvie, followed suit, calling Paris a dwarf-ish stone-hearted city, but looking directly at their father. Her brother, Benoît, had always had a thing for South-East Asia, and long before the women of the house proclaimed their British leanings, he turned his medical volunteering into a stable job at a hospital in Thailand, half a world away from the father who could not help but mention that he thought Benoît was too sharp to be a generalist for coughs and sneezes. Over time, the mother and sister and brother became less family and more painted figurines, shrunk and motionless, from a childhood Aimée had too abruptly outgrown. And so, she and her father grew closer together as if it had always been just the two of them in their family unit.

*

Her father tried his best to cultivate the girl, whom he promised himself would be different from Sylvie and by-God nothing like his wife.

*

He had gotten them front-row seats at the theatre for a show starring the French film actress Fanny Ardant, which was getting some buzz in the papers. Aimée was 13, her thin blond hair brushed and tucked behind her ears.

*

One woman came on stage wearing a white satin nightie, barefoot. It was Fanny Ardant. The public sat up in their seats. The famous actress took a breath and said, in her velvet voice, "I was young once."

From the other side of the stage a younger woman came out, also wearing a white satin nightie, also barefoot. Her dark hair was brushed out like Fanny Ardant's and her face held a resemblance to the actress's sagely luscious features. The younger woman came forth and stopped at Fanny Ardant's level. Looking out into the audience with an invigorated glare, the younger actress proclaimed, in a broad voice, "I was old once."

∗

The stage was so high, and the perspective so sharp, and both actresses' matching nighties so short, that young Aimée spent the whole play inadvertently glancing up the two sets of thighs above her, between them to the end point, then blinking hurriedly away.

After the show, young Aimée kept mispronouncing the leading actress's name. Her father corrected Aimée—Fanny *Ardant*, Arhdaen—but Aimée kept saying *Arendt* so her father had to explain that "Arendt" was someone else's last name, Hannah Arendt, the Jewish philosopher and theorist. Then he felt that he should explain Arendt's essay "On Violence," and why it was such an important gesture to question the relationship between violence and power, and the quintessence of defining terms like power, strength, force, authority, and violence. "Power is never the property of an individual; it belongs to a group and remains in existence only so long as the group keeps together," whereas strength is individual, force is contextual, and authority is vested and carried. "Out of the barrel of a gun grows the most effective command, resulting in the most instant and perfect obedience." Immediate and immediately unsustainable. So what is violence, her father asked 13-year-old Aimée. She glanced up blankly at her father, then back over to her right, where the stage had been and the actresses' matching pair of thighs became one.

∗

The following weeks her father got increasingly agitated because he was trying to educate Aimée further on Arendt's ideas, but kept accidently referring to her as Hannah *Ardant* and his mind snapping immediately to that film with Fanny Ardant alongside Gérard Depardieu, Truffaut's *La femme d'à côté, The Woman Next Door*. In the film, Bernard (Gérard) is living happily with his wife in Grenoble until a new couple moves in next door. His new neighbor's wife (played by Fanny) turns out to be a past lover of his.

Aimée, who had by this point been mispronouncing both the actress and the philosopher's names out of nervousness, began to stutter in addition. Her father switched to his role as the doctor; though he was not a speech therapist, he felt that cases of dyslexia and speech impediments were analogous to ghost pains of phantom limbs, and he just had to make his daughter understand her own body—that her tongue, her mouth, her throat operated in full function within each pronunciation. His diagnosis was that Aimée's oratory mechanics still somehow felt the attachment of previously pronounced sounds to those she was currently trying to voice.

*

Aimée was sent to her room to recite the name "Fanny Ardant" clearly and coherently 100 times before bed.

Night after night she said the actress's name 100 times like a bedtime prayer, and by her 14th birthday her stutter was gone.

*

When Aimée was 16, she heard about a new club that had just opened on Boulevard Poissonnière, near the Rex cinema. Like a struck match, the word spread quickly, girls, ladies, dykes, cunts . . . It wasn't shy or hidden like most places one crawled into to be gay between their walls. It was unapologetic, loud, messy, the place to be for girls who liked girls, and boys who liked boys if they came with a girl, and punks and actors and musicians and anyone who wanted to dance hard. Wednesdays was rock, Thursdays electro, Fridays more experimental, and Saturdays Girls Only.

Le Pulp.

A couple of Saturday evenings she passed by it, not daring to go in, veering into the metro station right in front and going home. But then her father prescribed himself some sleeping medication and Aimée began to sneak out.

*

The entry way had a large slab of black-painted wood hanging off two metal chains, with the cut-out letters in a dirty, scraped pink, yelling out *PULP*. There was no entry fee, part of the motto, anyone was welcome—well, any girl or any boy accompanied by a girl.

Inside, it was murky with people, wallpaper peeling off the walls, armchairs in cherry-red imitation leather with a couple of slashes across the cushion, and the dance floor with its scuffed floorboards.

A tall girl leaned into Aimée and asked if she wanted codeine and Aimée yelled over the music, "No thanks," but the girl shrugged and yelled back, "No, I asked if you *had* any . . ."

Aimée walked away and got onto the dance floor. She found a shadowy spot and began to dance, glancing around her at flashes of faces, rounded cheeks, sloped noses, dark eyelashes, frizzy hair, straight bangs, short crops, red lips, purple lips, plain lips, mouths slightly open or pinned shut or exhaling cigarette smoke.

She was scanning the room for a girl she'd like to kiss.

She went as many nights as she could. Kissing, groping, hoping for the next song, the next drink, the next cigarette, and the next touch.

*

It was electro night and the bodies were jumping with their heads hooked down and their hair swinging over their faces. Hips and elbows. Hands in the air, cutting through the lights.

At the bar, a guy in a dark-green T-shirt was arguing with the bar woman. Aimée stepped to the side, waiting to order. The bar woman leaned over the counter.

"Out there," she pointed to the door, "the world's yours. Dick around all you want. But these 100 meters squared in here, they're ours. So if you hear my cunt say No, it's NO. End of story. Enjoy your night." She stamped her palms on the counter and turned to Aimée. "What can I get you, darling?"

*

Aimée had been stuck on a girl name Céline with eyes the color of absinthe and mean-looking lips protruding into the flashing lights. She had kissed her and they had fondled each other on the dance floor but Céline seemed to be neither interested nor disinterested, which made 16-year-old Aimée desperate for her attention.

*

Aimée had reached the tautness of her longing. She lay in bed masturbating, thinking of Céline, when her hand froze and her breath cut off.

She had a vision of the Seine, pushing dully forward, the top skin wrinkling over itself, the skylight a pinkish white, the water like mud. Aimée exhaled and got out of bed. Without deciding, she pulled on her jeans, clipped on her one sexy black lace bra from H&M, pulled over a loose gray sweater, and snuck out. She thought she was going to the Seine to jump in. She went to *Le Pulp* instead.

Céline was on the dance floor, moving her body like a wrench, her wavy dark bob behind her ears, her eyes lined with black, and those glimmering green pupils, always as if she'd poisoned herself. Her lips, thickly coated with red, were staining the cigarette hanging from her mouth.

Aimée watched Céline dance. She stared. She went over every part of her with her glare. But Céline wouldn't even glance up. Her eyes were nowhere. They were diamonds being cut from smut. Aimée felt the chiseling in her chest. She felt the mud of the Seine. All the times she had glanced at a girl in school and clenched her gut. All the words she had stumbled over in her life. All the ways she hated herself and everything she couldn't bear to leave behind. Céline, her eyes of green venom glowing in the spotlight, smoke crawling out of her red mouth.

*

Don't we all ask for death before we know how to ask for what we really want? Usually it's night-time—out of its stem, a rose blooms open with a fragrant scream.

*

Aimée stood there and swallowed. Over and over again. Watching Céline. An oracle. A knife's blade. Petal by petal, to the moon. Then someone else spoke.

"Oh la la . . ."

Aimée turned around.

"Don't tell me . . ."

The girl was taller, her features velour in the darkness. By the way she stood, Aimée could tell that she was not only older, but already knew who she was and had some agreement from the world about it.

"*Pardon?*" Aimée said.

"That girl. The one you're watching. *Elle est chiante.* She's a waste of time."

Aimée glanced over at Céline, then back at the girl.

"But you like her, huh?" the girl continued.

Aimée nodded without meaning to.

"What else do you like?" the girl asked.

Aimée hesitated. ". . . Gin and tonics."

"Now that's interesting."

The girl knew the DJ and bought Aimée all her drinks. The girl was no girl either, but 26 to Aimée's 16.

"Hey, Dominique!" the girl's buddy, Olivier, called out to her. He opened up his cigarette box and pulled out a small baggy with two blue pills. Dominique took the baggy out and tucked it into her bra, then pulled out a cigarette and offered one to Aimée.

Olivier turned to Aimée and said, "You know you're smoking with a star, right?" and gave her a wink.

*

At that time, Dominique was a star and felt like one, though her main claim to fame was that theatre piece she'd co-starred in alongside Fanny Ardant, at Théâtre de la Madeleine, which Aimée's father had taken her to. Fanny Ardant, with her dark brows and dark hair and buttery eyes and her lips imbued with that voice, assured and coy . . . Fanny Ardant, the woman who was always wearing red, even when she was not. Dominique had assumed that she had the makings of a woman like that, who owned a color all to herself.

The director had cast Dominique to play Mme Ardant's younger ghost, somewhere between herself as a child and her daughter. It was a symbolic mise en scène, both women wore sleeveless gray tweed dresses, ending at mid-thigh, then in the last scene both women were in white satin nighties. Fanny Ardant was "*Femme*," Woman, and Dominique was "*Fille*," Girl.

The last night, the curtain fell and with it descended a vexation within Dominique. Back stage, both actresses washed off their make-up. FEMME went back to being Fanny Ardant, the acclaimed French star. FILLE went back to being Dominique, not quite a shooting star and almost just make-up powder rising into oblivion.

Months after the show, she couldn't sleep. She'd get up in the middle of the night, turn on the bathroom light, and recite her lines from the show into the mirror.

FILLE *(facing FEMME, who is still looking out at horizon)*
You scare me.
(takes step closer to FEMME) I never asked to be your likeness.
(another step closer) I never asked the Maker to make me in your image.
(another step) I never asked to spend my whole life carrying your features.
(another step) I never asked to be young when you are already old.
(another step) I never asked for you to grow old before me.
(another step) I never asked for you to die first.
(pause)
I never asked to hear your voice again. *(bumps into FEMME)*
I never asked to remember your scent. *(thrusts more deliberately)*
I never asked to feel your hands. *(thrust)*

I never asked—*(thrust)*
I never asked—*(thrust)*

Dominique took off her nightshirt and underwear. Naked, she ran her fingers over the faint bruises on her sternum and just above her pelvis, where she had "thrust" into FEMME in the show. She could almost feel Fanny Ardant's shoulder and hip ramming into her, as she thrust against her fixed body, pinned to the stage like nails. She could almost hear her own voice, pealing, screeching, her face both humid and icy, her armpits clutching, her legs stiff, and her tear-streaked face and bare feet on the cold stage floor. It was bliss.

*

Everything changed for Aimée with Dominique. The Seine was made of buoyant water, not mud. She smiled at things just for being there. Céline was no one, an indistinguishable figure among the others.

"Baby, baby, baby . . ." Dominique was pulling her in from behind.

*

Just as Aimée was turning 17, feeling full of all the things she could do as she was peeling off childhood, Dominique was turning 27 and realizing she was no longer the star she had been four years ago, in fact, perhaps, she never had been at all.

When Aimée turned 18, Dominique asked her to move in with her.

Aimée traced her finger behind Dominique's ear as she was standing in front of the large white bookshelf, looking across the spines, choosing which one to pull out. Aimée kissed her neck, and just then Dominique pulled away. She crouched down and ran her finger across the line of spines and began to pull at the sky-blue hardcover binding of a book wedged in the bottom row.

*

Dominique's mother was a vigorous altruist with a shy polyglot hobby from a Catholic parish just outside of Lyon. She had casually managed to acquire a conversational level of Serbian, Spanish, German, Polish, and Portuguese. Reaching her 30s with an unintentional pact of celibacy while working for the French Catholic organization in Porto, she met the Portuguese university fellow of social psychology at Sunday mass. His regard like a troubadour's guitar without strings, hers, a saint's lawyer.

Together, they gave Dominique her lightly tanned complexion, her almond eyes full of night-time, a full mouth, a sloping nose, cheekbones curving up to her dark eyebrows, her rich brown hair, and her love of any topic or space that could transcend the institutions of religion and academics.

She had been scouted by Mr Pio Pinheiro, who was almost always accompanied by his tall close-shaven black poodle named Gary Cooper, and who would later miss his opportunity to sign the future Porto-native supermodel Sara Sampaio. Mr Pio P. had the necessary soft-spoken elegance to convince the screw-driver-eyed mother and her delicate-livered father that Dominique's godly and mortal call was to be in front of the camera. Nine-year-old Dominique, her parents, and Mr Pio P. took the trip to Paris, where she shot her first catalog ad for a spring collection.

Dominique had the racial ambiguity and yet European pureness to fit the demand for the "third wheel" in many catalog shoots after that.

Whether by chance or prophecy, her mother was sent back to Paris to the Catholic organization headquarters. Her father was hesitant but dropped his position at the university and came jobless as a leap of faith. Teenage Dominique fell in love with the city.

Nine months later, her father opened up his faded blue Book of Saints, cut his wrists, and bled so much that droplets came through the old wooden floor, through the crack in the lighting fixture of the downstairs neighbors, making their living-room bulb flicker for hours before they heard the ambulance.

There was a lot of speculation about the motive for her father's suicide, both psychological and theological, but everyone came to their own conclusion, and Dominique's conclusion was that she belonged on stage.

*

Dominique and Aimée, lovebirds, grabby, giggling, immersed. In the spring of 2013, France had legalized *mariage pour tous*, and Aimée and Dominique celebrated the equal-marriage right with their favorite shared skepticism, making jokes about the history of bartering wives, then kissed in between an anecdote they were remembering, then just kissed for a while, then opened their eyes and knew.

They were officially married the following autumn. They kept it small, went to the city hall, signed their papers and had their friends over for brunch.

"Can you believe we've been together since I was 16!" Aimée was telling everyone at brunch.

"Cougar!" Olivier said and winked at Dominique.

"Hey, I was only 26 myself . . . and it was dark . . ." Dominique grabbed Aimée by the waist and whispered something in her ear, then bit her lobe.

*

In bed, Dominique read out loud to Aimée from her favorite plays. Especially the roles that she'd never get to play on stage, because they were for a man, or for someone younger or older or whiter or darker.

*

The Night Just Before the Forests . . .

*

They were having dinner at home. Dominique took the call. She went into the bedroom. She came out. She sat back down. She ran her fork in the spaghetti, around and around, not catching a single strand.

*

Ever since Dominique turned 40, she'd been coming out of the bathroom saying that she'd started to look like her father, then pulling down on the skin beneath her eyes. It's true that Dominique had become much paler over the years, and her eyes—which once held that rich, dark heat—were now colder and filled with doubt.

Dominique kept assuring Aimée that "theatre was going down the drain" and no one wanted to see real people on the stage anymore, soon it'll be videos and music playing all the parts . . .

"No, baby, you don't get it. At 23, I thought I wanted to be a star—but I don't want any of that. That's not what I want at all. I just want to—feel it—again."

*

Dominique was shouting, "no no NO!" at Aimée, trying to explain to her that she was too good to be in another "student production" as she called it, which meant the playwright and the director were both in their mid-20s. "What do they know about life? . . . And they are telling me where to stand, where to sit, where to 'exit' offstage . . . !"

Her insomnia had turned to parasomnia and she was screaming in her sleep, then falling out of bed. Or else, lying with her eyes open in the dark, as thoughts mummified her body.

*

They had just had sex. Dominique lay in bed sleepless while her wife was full-bodied drowsy. Dominique started talking about Foucault. Aimée tried to listen to Dominique as she explained that Foucault's father had been a surgeon, and that Foucault himself had told this story from his deathbed to Hervé Guibert, who then transcribed it: Foucault was just a boy and his father called him in to observe an amputation in the operating room of a hospital in Poitier. The boy watched his father saw off the man's leg, and apparently it was this that stole the boy's virility from him.

Aimée mumbled in her sleep, "My father likes you very much, you know . . . he's only trying to help . . ."

Dominique was in bed, reading more Bernard-Marie Koltès. The titles of his plays sounded so tender to Aimée, like *In the Solitude of Cotton Fields*, *The Night Just Before the Forests*, *Tabataba* . . . but the lines Dominique read to her out loud were nothing tender, full of revolt and choking fury.

Dominique put down the book, curled around Aimée, who was already asleep, and held her like a doll against nightmares.

*

In their early dating days, Dominique had admitted that she talked in her sleep. *Somniloquy*. Aimée kept pronouncing it as "soliloquy," which Dominique kept explaining was when a character in a play goes to the side of the stage and confesses something.

"Like in Shakespeare, baby . . . where Othello sees a huge eclipse, or Antony the ghost of Cleopatra, or where Lady M can't wash the blood from her hands, you know . . ."

But what Dominique had was not the type of somniloquy where one mumbles to oneself to buy more bread or answer an email, but where one shrieks, jolts, thrashes, and jumps out of bed.

Aimée could not help but think of her disorder as *soliloquy* because Dominique went to the side of her stage, where the light hung low around her, where she stood upon a surface that reflected like a black river, and where she emitted the words and sounds of the hot-eyed animal inside her, frantic for language.

"That's the difference, Aimée! I'm not bad at what I do. I'm a good actress, I know I am. They just don't want me. I could analyze every which way. If I were mediocre, I could just admit it to myself. But I am good, Aimée. I am really good and they just don't want me."

*

Aimée loved to watch Dominique on stage. There, where Dominique was charged, where she was holy. Like that first night when they didn't even know each other and 13-year-old Aimée stared at those dangerously bare thighs. Aimée loved Dominique when she was acting, because then both of them felt like they fit perfectly into the world: Dominique pulsing in the light, Aimée privately watching. Aimée also loved when Dominique was sleeping, not fretfully, but softly, unsuspicious. She could look at her face and see everyone she had been, all the girls and women she had grown through, resting together, curled up into each other.

*

Although she told her father, the doctor, that she didn't want to talk about it, he took both of her hands and told her, as clearly as he could, "She is exhibiting what any medical professional would call alarming symptoms."

And so finally she let her father get Dominique a prescription of the sleeping pills that let her sleep a full night.

In addition, by her father's suggestion, Aimée had to put a lock on the knife drawer and a bell on the door handle of the bedroom.

*

Aimée took it as a good sign when Dominique veered away from Koltès's texts and began reading a Norwegian playwright back to back and taking interest in saints' lives.

*

"What does it feel like, when you are having one of your night terrors?" Aimée asked, putting the cold compress lightly to Dominique's forehead.

"I guess it's like . . . Like someone is going to come, any second . . . and I don't know who . . . but I know it will be unbearable, when they arrive."

*

When Aimée came home from her work at the gynecologist's office, they were all laughing in the living room, Guillaume, Claire, Eric, Olivier, and his boyfriend, Angelo, who had worked on last season's Wajdi Mouawad production.

Claire was leaning on the counter with her butt facing Aimée. She coiled her head around and said, "Hello."

Aimée put her keys down and walked over to kiss Dominique on the lips.

*

"Stop it, stop treating me like I'm stupid because I'm young or naïve or however it is you justify it—"

"I don't justify it—"

"Wait, okay, wait, so you admit it?"

"No! You're being ridiculous."

"Fuck you."

"Oh great, bravo!"

"What am I, some little quiet secretary by day and stage puppy dog by night you got following you around your shows—"

"I never beg you to come."

"Well I want to, how about that, I want to see you!"

"Baby, you want to have someone to follow around, at first it was your father and now me and—"

"That's what you think, *baby*, that's what you really think of me—"

"Wait, Aimée, come on, I'm trying to say that—Benoît's doing what he wants in Thailand, and your sister's set herself up quite nice in London, and your mom's—"

"And you—you're doing what you want with Claire . . . ? Is that it?"

There was a pause between the women.

"So, are we going to play who's more pathetic now?" Dominique said.

Aimée's teeth clenched into each other as her eyes grew humid.

"Dominique, I swear to God . . . if I'm asking you questions and you're lying to me, I swear to God, Dominique!"

*

Aimée stayed in the spare bedroom at her father's. After a week, Dominique called and said, "Please." When Aimée came back to the apartment, Dominique was lying on the couch on her stomach, with her face in her hands. She picked up her head and looked up at Aimée. Her face was pale and bloated, and her hair greasy at the roots.

Dominique sat up and said in a half-voice, "You are the love of my life."

*

They stopped mentioning names and decided to take a trip to Switzerland. The mountains were breathtaking. The whole train ride Dominique was flirty, teasing, joking, nudging. Everything was so beautiful, so unbearably beautiful.

From Grindelwald station, they took the cog-wheel train toward the glacier through a carved mountain, to a town called Lauterbrunnen.

Those mountains, chiseled gray stone, with the white powder waterfall flowing from the top, making the edges shine like granite. With the clouds sitting on the peaks, Aimée and Dominique talked about Olympus and all the gods, somewhere up there, trying to one up each other.

The train passed steadily through its landscape: the pines with their thin-haired needles and the stubby whitish-green firs and the bright spruces, prickling against the slow-moving fog. The churches with their narrow cone hats and rigid metal crosses on top. The clocks on the towers in golden Roman numerals. The white cottages with the brown triangle roofs. There were pastures of cows, some brown horses in the fields, white puffs of sheep, thinner puffs of goats, calls in the distance, a sudden "moo," a donkey haw, a jawdropped "bah!"

The air was almost liquid with its freshness and chill, and as they approached Lauterbrunnen, there was a perpetual sound of running water, the birds calling to each other in the distance, and the vast mountains one behind the other, seeming so close you could reach your hand out of the train and touch the moss.

*

Hotel Staubbach, on the Hauptstrasse, was a family-run lodge, pale-yellow exterior with brownish-red shutters framing each window, and the hotel letters spelled out in the same color on the side of the building.

*

"Die schönen Berge . . ." The receptionist was pointing outside the window and nodding for agreement.

"The beautiful mountains . . ." Dominique translated for Aimée.

Dominique had retained an elementary speaking German from her mother's home-schooling days, whereas Aimée, who had taken it for years in school, still stumbled over completing a full sentence.

Both women nodded at the thin man in a burgundy vest, with the name tag "Klaus."

*

In their room, the duvet, the walls, the floor, all soft colors and meek designs, pastel green, blushing coral, pale plum, skittish teal, and weaving lines of cream. Dominique opened the large window to the panoramic view of the Staubbach Falls and the Lauterbrunnen Valley.

*

Downstairs, Klaus explained that there were 72 waterfalls in the area and gave them a hiking map with dotted red paths like threads of blood lines through the mountainous earth.

If they wanted to see the shops, they were a 15-minute walk downhill.

Klaus advised them to visit the cheesemaker at the bottom of the hill and then to turn left, off the long road, to the cabinetmaker, in case they were looking to purchase some regionally crafted furniture, and then to continue down the road, where they could get to what Klaus proudly described as "a graceful cemetery."

*

They popped into the cheese shop, passed by the cabinetmaker, and headed down the road. The cemetery at the end was pristine, framed by short-trimmed grass so green it could almost tingle. The graves were arranged in neat rows with red flowers planted in between like berries. The stones stood in lines, white and gray and brown, crosses with carvings, every stone corner looked wiped and shined.

Aimée walked ahead of Dominique on the entrance path. Dominique thought of a monologue from *Faust*, in that Polish production she saw last season, where Faust sang to the devil, suspended from his bungee cord on stage:

This life of earth, whatever my attire,
Would pain me in its wonted fashion.
Too old am I to play with passion;
Too young, to be without desire.

There was a petite woman with a white bun pinned neatly above her thin neck, crouching down beside a dark blue bucket and a pale rag. At her feet, an alert brown and gray German shepherd stood tall. She dipped the rag into the bucket, pulled it out dripping, and wiped the tombstones, one by one.

Aimée noted from the dates that most of the people buried here lived well into their 90s. The petite woman herself seemed to be in her late 80s.

"I guess the Swiss Alps hold the key to immortality," Aimée nudged Dominique. "All that hiking, fresh cheese, hand-crafted cabinets . . ."

Dominique stared at the dog and thought of the hiking trails on the map like blood sewn into paper.

*

As the days passed, Dominique silently measured her own dissatisfaction against the contrast of the beautiful landscape.

*

Upon my couch of sleep I lay me:
There, also, comes no rest to me,
But some wild dream is sent to fray me.

*

Dominique was standing in front of the window, looking out absently. Aimée came up to her and put her arms around her waist from behind. She didn't move. She stared straight into the glass, as if her eyes were just windows, unaffected by the sight that passed through them.

*

Someone is going to come . . .

*

Aimée was no longer the 16-year-old girl following in step with her older girlfriend to make sure she doesn't find her too naïve. She was 31 now, but her role as the naïve partner had merely taken on new forms of maturity. After 15 years together, she was well familiar with the cloudy sadness that would take over her wife. It would leave for years, then reappear. But every time it came, Aimée played her role, not daring to enquire more than Dominique was willing to share, timidly on hand and devoted as if Dominique required more blind faith than informed understanding.

Dominique left the window, went to the bed, and lay down in her clothes. Aimée followed her and sat on the edge of the pale floral comforter. She put her hand on Dominique's back, then slid down to her, placing her face loyally into the crux of her neck.

"Get off me," Dominique said.

*

There wasn't much reception in their room, so Dominique was pacing around in the lobby, near the brown leather sofas and the burgundy armchairs, walking around the corners of the wine-toned carpet, beneath the dew-drop chandelier. She was nodding and biting the skin around her nails.

When she came back up to the room, she pinched her lips and squeezed her fists.

"They want me for the part!"

Dominique's eyes radiated such a warm color that Aimée thought she could see her blood coursing through. Just below, her lips were parted and her teeth, left so unguarded in her smile that Aimée jumped up and ran to her.

*

Someone is going to come . . .

Well it happened

Zorka's father died. I overheard my mamka say that Zorka's mamka was unstable and couldn't take care of herself and that Zorka was turning out just like her mamka, and then she turned to me and said I should focus on my studies. Zorka told me that she was getting the hell out, for real this time. I felt invincible with her and hopeless with my family. I said, "Don't leave without me!"

*

More snow came, large flakes, like lamb's wool.

No one saw Zorka for six days. Not even me. I walked all through the Letenské Park, rubbing my hands together against the cold, whispering, "Zorka . . . it's me!"

On the seventh day, the whole building was full of her name. Ms Květa from across the street was yelling, "Fire, fire!" and my brother said, "Holy shit," in English.

The whole hallway smelled like vodka and burnt hair and in the middle there was Zorka's mamka's prized fur coat, all aflame, like a newly landed meteor. My mamka handed me a bucket and

I ran to fill it in the bathroom. All the neighbors took turns running in with cups and pots and rubber boots and whatever they could find to fill with water, to dump on the burning coat.

When the fire was finally put out, it started burning deep and low behind everyone's eyes. "Where's that little devil's cunt?" the heat flickered.

I snuck out that night one more time and walked through the streets, the snow crunching beneath my boots, husking at the dark, "Zorka . . . ! It's me!"

But I only saw a dementia-faced stray cat, and a man who told me I had pretty hair and asked if I wanted to come up and have a piece of his mother's cherry *bublanina* cake.

I guess I had started to feel very different since Zorka had disappeared, as if I was in charge in her absence. So, I looked the man in the eye and said, "If I was gonna get a stranger's dick forced in me, I'd expect a little more than your mamka's *bublanina*, you asshole. Sharpen your approach."

The man sneered and said, "You little cunt," under his breath.

I turned around and flipped him a winter bird, à la Zorka, then began to run. I ran through the streets, feeling the grainy road layered with ice and slush shifting beneath me, the evening air, chilled and liquid, like curtains of black water. I kept running, turning left, down the streets, across the street, across the river, around the trees, past Wenceslas Square, I kept running, feeling Zorka was just behind me, both arms up, middle fingers penetrating the night.

*

Soon enough though, I was far from the bravery of the *bublanina* cake episode, lying in bed, feeling impossible. I closed my eyes and slept, and in my sleep there was this dream: snow. Snow all over the gardens. She's standing by the closed-down carousel. Zorka. She slides off her mother's heavy fox-fur coat and lets it fall down to the snow. She pulls off her red sweater and drops it too. She unhooks her bra and lets it go. Her hands at her sides, fingers knotted, her body's shivering. She's breathing hard and her ribs are showing. Her breasts are pinched and blue.

"Janka," she says to me and she's shaking from the cold, "I d-ddunno w-wh-why I'm such a *malá narcis*. D-d-d-dunno why I d-d-do these things. Ju-just can't be a g-g-good, obedient dog. I-I-I know the whole world w-w-w-wants me to 'S-s-s-stay put. S-s-sit. L-lie down.' But I can't . . . I ju-just want to sniff people's asses."

I reach out to put my arms around her but she turns away from me. Then I see it, on her left shoulder, there are three tiny sores in a row, puffed and unhealed, each one with a tear of blood rolling down.

*

I started to focus on my studies. I recited a passage from Molière for my parents, in French. And a week later, I memorized and recited another from Faust in German. I continued to stuff my memory with classic passages in foreign languages.

My older brother stopped wearing that blue T-shirt that I liked on him, because of the way it hung from his collarbones. He started filling out, it wasn't really muscle and it wasn't really fat, just more of him from all the angles. Before we knew it, he was immense. Not just tall, but beefy, like a stew come to life, he began hovering his shoulders in and hooking his neck down when he stood or walked. Our mother told him in sing-song voice to stand up straight, and our father flapped him on the back and said, "Be proud of your size, Vilèm." One evening, like so many, I was feeling that sunset ripple of anonymous dejection and was eager to go to my room to cry. Just as I was leaving the bathroom, I saw my brother standing in the back of the hallway like a stump, half his face in the shadow.

He asked me if I'd seen his hair gel.

"Haven't seen it," I said.

I reached for the door of my room, but he said my name.

"Jana . . ."

His voice was so timid just then, I couldn't understand how it connected to that huge figure at the end of the hallway.

"Yeah?" I replied, looking at the door knob.

"Jana . . . I think my ears are going to shit . . ."

"Yeah?" I said meekly, still facing the door.

"Maybe it's 'cause . . . I'm like . . . big . . . like, tall . . . way up . . . or something, but . . ." His voice trailed off.

I felt him take a step toward me and I turned my head. The hallway light caught his thick brow pushing out over his thin eyes, which were retreating like a freshly crashed wave.

"Night," he said, then gave me an embarrassed smile. Just the tips of his two crooked teeth showing on his bottom lip.

*

He began studying computer science at the university and got a side job as a security guard in Železčice u Slaného, 45 minutes out, at that production plant that made hospital beds. He got a gray button-down shirt with a dark-blue tie and matching slacks, through which he looped his worn black leather belt. He'd leave the house with his yellow Walkman in his hand and fuzz blaring from his headphones. I was discreetly crying all the time. He was listening to his Pearl Jam cassette. It had his favorites on it, "Jeremy" and "Alive." He got it from his friend, Slavek, who had golden fingers for American stuff. He'd sing under his breath, "Zheremy . . . zeemed a harmless little fuck . . ." Luckily our parents couldn't distinguish an Anglophone syllable from a cough. Once I walked in on him with his headphones on, eyes closed, squirming his arms and clenching his teeth, singing, "Cheyyyy, cheyyy, I, oh, I'm still ah-live!" He didn't see me. I quietly closed the door and ran outside without my coat.

*

Zorka was long gone then, her father buried, her mamka moved out. I didn't know what to do with myself. I started memorizing proverbs at an incredible rate. We got more dictionaries in the house. I got into the high school specializing in languages and impressed everyone by doing nothing but studying, all the time, big books gasping open all around me. My mamka started calling me "The Scholar" and bragged openly about my skills in French and English and German and Russian, all the while I was in my room, learning more and more. My papka was a bit different about it—a layer of discomfort, like coarse hair in a comb, at having a bookish daughter who could only spit out proverbs. He always echoed my mother, "Good job, Janinka!" But something in the way his pupils rolled away when he pushed a smile at me made me want to disappear forever. He observed me the way you look at people who do small tasks with too much passion and precision.

*

I often wondered if he ever wished I'd go blind so that I'd never read another book again.

*

I studied and my brother studied and my brother worked in the evenings and my brother hung out elsewhere and I kept my door closed. For our grades, they were proud. Mamka, dumbfounded with pride for her giant son and brainy daughter. Papka, along-side, agreeing and uneasy. In the end, we looked nothing alike, Vilèm and I. But everyone knew we were the same household because we both walked animal-like, degenerate in our down-ward glare.

*

"*Von nichts kommt nichts*, Papa. Nothing comes from nothing."

*

Then my brother was completely and undeniably a man, with gelled dark hair and his clear eyes ebbing beneath his thick fore-head. When he smiled, you could see his front straight teeth were framed by two slightly crooked ones. It gave him an instant charm. But if he sat too long without smiling, he just looked a bit bloated and simple. He was dating this girl for a while, Karolina, who was studying engineering and also picking up some hours at the hospital-bed plant. She had thin lips coated with a shimmering pink and drawn-on eyebrows that arced over her clumpy mascara-lashes and oily blue eyes. They got married and moved up north, closer to Želevčice. When he came to visit, he didn't go into my room to say hi. He didn't want to disturb my studying, my mamka told me.

*

"*Chacun voit midi à sa porte*, Papa. Everyone sees noontime from their door."
   "Huh?"
   "It means everyone's got their own interests in mind, Papa."
   "Exactly, Janinka!"

Because my door was always closed, it was assumed that I was always studying. I took many breaks from studying to cry. After the crying, I'd go back to studying. At night, I'd lie in my bed and start to recite proverbs for no reason.

Blizok lokotok, da ne ukusish. The elbow's close, but you can't bite it—i.e. it only seems easy.

La nuit porte conseil. The night brings advice—i.e. sleep on it.

The burned child avoids fires—i.e. you idiot.

Then I pulled the pillow from under me and pressed it against my own face until my cheeks chafed with heat.

*

Finally, I decided to have a destiny. I knew Zorka was living hers out somewhere and I wanted one too. I stopped trying to bite my own elbow or burn my face off with my pillow. I clenched down on my tears and pushed myself fully into my studies, then got accepted into the Sorbonne University in Paris.

*

Autant en emporte le vent! The first French proverb I learned. "As much as the wind can carry!" is the literal translation, and I proclaimed it with zeal. It actually means "empty promises." Luckily no one in my family spoke French either. My mother said, "Listen, we don't have the money." I said, "I don't need the money." My brother gave me some. He didn't tell his wife. It was a beginning.

About Zorka, I'd come to the only conclusion possible. She didn't give a fuck-all for me. She never did. She had a destiny, and as smart as everyone told me I was, I had a birdbrain about my own fate. And so, I did like Zorka and went my own way. I said goodbye to Prague, goodbye to my mamka and my papka and Vilèm and Karolina, like I was winter's last snow melting, evaporating back into the sky, to return again as something else altogether, unrecognizable, a different element, a different being. I disappeared and reappeared Parisian.

I'm glad we r alone now

0_hotgirlAmy_0: Hey you.

Dominxxika_N39: I'm glad we r alone now.

0_hotgirlAmy_0: Me too . . .

0_hotgirlAmy_0: *blush

0_hotgirlAmy_0: . . . now I'm nervous again.

Dominxxika_N39: Don't b nervous.

Dominxxika_N39: My real name is Dominika. What urs?

0_hotgirlAmy_0: Amy.

Dominxxika_N39: What r u wearing, sexy Amy?

0_hotgirlAmy_0: Flared jeans. L.E.I.s. with this rose patch on the knee. And a new tank I got at Abercrombie. It's like melon green, spaghetti straps.

Dominxxika_N39: I'm sure u r looking really nice in it.

0_hotgirlAmy_0: *blush

0_hotgirlAmy_0: . . . u?

Dominxxika_N39: I have long dark hair, full, sometimes it hang and cover my eye. I like it when I feeling shy. My eyes are very blue.

0_hotgirlAmy_0: U sound hot. What r u wearing?

Dominxxika_N39: I wearing red dress. My husband got it for me as gift.

0_hotgirlAmy_0: *frowns

Dominxxika_N39: Don't worry, he not home. I have heels on. They are shiny red with long sharp heel. I'm pressing into the carpet.

0_hotgirlAmy_0: O, wow. But just sucks that u have a husband . . .

Dominxxika_N39: My husband travel a lot for work . . .

0_hotgirlAmy_0: Hold on. Brb.

Dominxxika_N39: I sorry to mention him again.

Dominxxika_N39: Please don't leave.

0_hotgirlAmy_0: Back. Sorry. No it's not you. My mom's making dinner upstairs, she's always bugging me about what we wanna eat, I told her I don't care.

Dominxxika_N39: What she cooking?

0_hotgirlAmy_0: Mac n cheese with tuna. She's just like mushing everything together cause she's pissed my dad's still not home from work yet.

Dominxxika_N39: O yes, I remember when I little and my mum so anger with father all time. He was working in Ministry before Russians took over. All sudden, he doing manual labor jobs only, transporting tiles. My mom say he should not be so coward.

0_hotgirlAmy_0: Yeah my mom can't even say anything to his face. She just blabs to me about it, like O he's having an affair. I'm like yeah right Mom, you're not in a movie, he's just staying late to please Mr Sheffield (that's his department manager). It's kind of embarrassing, like you can see how my dad just feels like a moron all the time, especially like in front of other men, like at the company picnic I had to go to, he had these huge sweat stains in his shirt the whole time cause he was so nervous trying to do everything right for Mr Sheffield.

Dominxxika_N39: We have like Mr Sheffield too in my country, before they take notes and make reports for government, now they regular civilian or boss or politician, but still we scared for their previous ties. Sometime I worry about this too and it make me sweaty.

0_hotgirlAmy_0: Totally. My dad's like so nervous all the time and he and my mom are yelling forever, saying they don't have the money for this or for that. So finally I was like, Ugh just stop yelling, I'll get a job! I mean it was just for the summer. At the Marcus Southgate Cinema. Then these girls came from school and they were like, "Nice uniform, Amy." I was getting them their sweet and salty popcorn, but then they started saying, "Gross, Amy, your elbow touched some of the popcorn, don't you have like a scooping protocol?" Then they said, "I'm gonna tell the manager. That's like a health violation." I was so over that job. And when school started again, those girls would like pinch their nose in the hallway and say that I stink like oil. It was the lamest joke ever.

Dominxxika_N39: These girls are like acting on behalf of intimidators I am sure. They are enforcing scared feelings, it is to contain your individual power, so you not get too outspoken.

0_hotgirlAmy_0: Yeah they are total bitches, I don't even care. With their boyfriends from the football team, and in the locker room after gym class, they're like omg you're so lucky you're going to prom with Jared cause he has the biggest dick. And then they looked at me as if I was even listening, as if I even care, and they said, What are you looking at . . . dyke.

Dominxxika_N39: What is dyke?

0_hotgirlAmy_0: Um. U don't know what that word is? It's like. It means you . . . stare at girls and that you . . . can't help yourself . . . and that it's gross.

Dominxxika_N39: But u r not gross! U r very sexy.

0_hotgirlAmy_0: *blush

Dominxxika_N39: I can see you, you r looking so cute, Amy.

0_hotgirlAmy_0: *embarrassed

0_hotgirlAmy_0: I wish I could just come to Prague. Milwaukee sucks.

Dominxxika_N39: Actually I not in Prague exactly. I live in Želevčice u Slaného, like 45 minutes in car north and west from city.

0_hotgirlAmy_0: What's it like there?

Dominxxika_N39: Prague is very exciting. When I there, I feel like I am in Paris walking around like such modern woman, but Želevčice is very quiet and not much for people, only hospital-bed production plant and very quiet fields.

0_hotgirlAmy_0: Same here! Milwaukee is a total yawn.

0_hotgirlAmy_0: Maybe I can come over there & keep u company while ur husband's away.

Dominxxika_N39: I like this. U can wear your cute jeans.

0_hotgirlAmy_0: And u can show me around . . .

Dominxxika_N39: Yes, we can take walk on road together, if we walk far, past big production plant, on the right big green field, it go so far back, it touch the sun when it setting. On the right, another big green field, leaf tips touch sunlight too and like million little pieces of gold, u feel rich! It is quiet like boredom but it is also beautiful. And I could hold your hand, outside, when there is wind.

0_hotgirlAmy_0: *huge smile

Dominxxika_N39: There is little chapel here, it is pale yellow and has small bell to ring on roof. It built in 1913.

0_hotgirlAmy_0: That's cute.

Dominxxika_N39: One time, my husband take me with him to Litvínov, one hour north, for work trip, and there I visit St Michael's church, also yellow, but little bit sour color, but very beautiful.

0_hotgirlAmy_0: We could totally go there. I have my driver's license!

Dominxxika_N39: Wow, you are a very free person then. My husband do not want for me to drive.

Dominxxika_N39: Do you know Archangel Michael?

0_hotgirlAmy_0: No. Who's that?

Dominxxika_N39: He is important angel. He was against Satan. He is defender. Also, he help souls at hour of their death.

0_hotgirlAmy_0: He sounds kinda creepy . . .

Dominxxika_N39: He is very powerful. He try to help. Sometimes he whisper to humans little advices . . . He come in moment when you think I cannot live life no more.

0_hotgirlAmy_0: Oh.

0_hotgirlAmy_0: I kinda get that . . .

0_hotgirlAmy_0: Cause once . . . in chemistry class, Jared had to be my lab partner . . . In the back, they were passing notes and laughing. I was just keeping my eyes down. Just like waiting for class to be done. For the bell to ring. For everything to be over you know. But I could feel it coming. The piece of paper. It was being passed, down, then down, then down, then they tapped me on the shoulder and gave me the note and I didn't want to take it or unfold it or read it, but I just did. It said:
WHY DON'T U ASK JARED TO PUT HIS BIG DICK IN UR CUNT SO U CAN STOP DYKIN OUT ON ALL THE GIRLS IN CLASS?

Dominxxika_N39: This is not very good advice.

0_hotgirlAmy_0: It was so stupid. Like they thought they were gonna make me cry in class again. It's this game they have. Whatever. I guess it happened then though. I heard a whisper like what you were saying.

Dominxxika_N39: Archangel Michael whisper to u?

0_hotgirlAmy_0: Well I mean I dunno if it was Archangel Michael or whatever. But it did really feel like someone else was saying something to me, not like when you tell yourself something in your head. It was definitely someone else. This voice, kinda low, but strong, whispering to me: Don't cry. Don't cry.

0_hotgirlAmy_0: It was just . . . yeah like I said, it was really strong. I could really hold onto it. Then when the bell rang, I didn't even feel like going to the bathroom and locking myself in a stall. I guess I didn't feel . . . anything. I just went to my locker to get my social studies book, and then went to my next class.

Dominxxika_N39: This may be Archangel Michael.

Dominxxika_N39: But I am little jealous. I want to whisper in your ear . . .

0_hotgirlAmy_0: *blush

0_hotgirlAmy_0: What would you whisper in my ear?

Dominxxika_N39: How I want to touch u.

0_hotgirlAmy_0: *megablush

Dominxxika_N39: Can I . . . touch u?

0_hotgirlAmy_0: Um . . . I'm kinda shy . . .

Dominxxika_N39: U r very cute. Do not be shy, sexy Amy.

Dominxxika_N39: I just touch u with my fingertips. Ok?

0_hotgirlAmy_0: Ok . . .

Dominxxika_N39: I'm sorry my fingertips are little cold.

0_hotgirlAmy_0: That's ok . . .

Dominxxika_N39: My husband turn off heating when he go.

0_hotgirlAmy_0: He sounds like an asshole.

Dominxxika_N39: Shh . . .

Dominxxika_N39: Do you feel my fingertips? They touching waist of your jeans. They slowly stepping under your shirt and walking up to your belly button.

0_hotgirlAmy_0: That tickles. Kinda.

Dominxxika_N39: U want I stop?

0_hotgirlAmy_0: No. It feels nice too.

Dominxxika_N39: Your skin warm. They walking up your stomach. Do you feel them?

0_hotgirlAmy_0: Yeah.

Dominxxika_N39: Where u want me to touch u next?

0_hotgirlAmy_0: Um . . . dunno.

Dominxxika_N39: I take 1 finger . . . where can I put it, sexy Amy?

0_hotgirlAmy_0: Um . . .

Dominxxika_N39: Tell me, where can I put my finger . . .

0_hotgirlAmy_0: . . . in . . . my mouth . . .

Dominxxika_N39: My fingernails are red, like my dress.

Dominxxika_N39: I put my red fingernail on your bottom lip.

0_hotgirlAmy_0: I'm . . . tasting . . . your finger.

Dominxxika_N39: I feel ur tongue, warm and wet, it slide around my nail. Take my finger in ur mouth.

0_hotgirlAmy_0: I open my mouth . . .

Dominxxika_N39: I slid finger in slow, slow, into your mouth.

0_hotgirlAmy_0: I'm . . . licking . . . it . . .

Dominxxika_N39: Suck on my finger, sexy Amy.

0_hotgirlAmy_0: I'm sucking it.

0_hotgirlAmy_0: Up and down.

Dominxxika_N39: I put finger deeper.

0_hotgirlAmy_0: Yes.

0_hotgirlAmy_0: All of it.

0_hotgirlAmy_0: I can feel your knuckle.

Dominxxika_N39: Suck me.

0_hotgirlAmy_0: I'm sucking you.

0_hotgirlAmy_0: Put your other hand down my jeans.

0_hotgirlAmy_0: Put your fingers inside me.

Dominxxika_N39 has gone offline.

0_hotgirlAmy_0: U there?

Tears and saints

Jana came home from the medical trade show, set her keys down, took her heels off, opened the window, lit up a Gauloise Blonde, and smoked it, leaning out of her window.

She felt the corner of a business card etch into her stomach through her blazer pocket. She leaned back, slid her fingers into her pocket, and pulled it out.

THE BLUE ANGEL

Bar à vin.

It was the card Mr Doubek had given her, a stark blue-black with the letters embossed on the paper. No telephone, no website, just a street address. *Rue de Prague.* Prague Street. She flipped the card over.

9 pm.

*

She had finished the early dinner she had made for herself, the last piece of an oven-heated quiche Lorraine with a salad of lamb's lettuce and cherry tomatoes, and two pieces of toast with margarine. She drank a full glass of water. Then made tea.

Then poured herself the rest of a bottle of Brouilly, then considered making another cup of tea, but she knew she was not craving that taste or consistency, but could not pinpoint what it was her palate desired. She decided to ignore the craving, pulled out another cigarette, opened the window, and lit up the Gauloise Blonde.

As she smoked, she felt the craving, more of an agitation, like fibrous threads being pulled through her muscles. She found herself mumbling:

To inhabit a habit, our bestowed skill,
It replaces happiness with will.

It was from one of the passages she had memorized in her youth. This one from Pushkin's *Eugene Onegin*. She remembered clearly now, standing with her gray socks on the carpet so that each of her toes touched a maroon curl in the carpet's design, looking up at her mother, and reciting the passage in Russian. The next week, she went back to French.

These endless stanzas, aphoristic sentences, and smug proverbs she had memorized in her scholarly youth began to flutter in her mind as if someone had just opened a window there.

She unzipped her skirt and pulled it off her body, then took out a pair of midnight blue trousers. Coat off the hook, heels back on, keys in hand, Jana slid the blue card into her trouser pocket.

*

To sigh and furl with eager thought:
When will the devil end your fraught!

*

She walked down Rue Monge to the next station, so she could get one cigarette in before getting on the metro. Passing her, people chatted with voices above them, like birds. The fabrics they were wearing folded, wrinkled, blew back in the breeze. Jana took out her packet of Gauloises Blondes, pulled out a cigarette, lit it, and slid the packet back into her purse.

She passed these people, as if behind a glass wall, where no one saw her, and if they did, she was just an unperceivable mistake in the scenic exhibition of their lives, a misspelling in their autobiography. But they were to her, as well, a scenic exhibition, a dreamy mass of ways of belonging, which she was not a part of. It was a languorous experience of her loneliness, to be an observer of a world for which she was both too special and not special enough.

*

Qui s'excuse, s'accuse. Who makes excuses, himself accuses.

*

She quickened her pace—9 pm if he had meant it sharp—and veered toward the green metal railing holding up the pale-yellow sign of the metro, flicked her still-burning cigarette the way she had learned to in Paris, and descended the damp, oil-stained stairs of the metro.

In the mouth of the entrance, she heard the echo of a microphoned voice. She tapped her metro card and walked through the turnstile toward the voice, which was not so much singing as speaking with moments of melodious bruising. She turned left to go northbound, and went up a flight of stairs then turned onto the platform. There, next to the vending machine, a woman was holding a microphone with her sallow, shaky arm, the wire of the microphone twitching as she shifted side to side and spoke-sang. At the top of the small amp into which her microphone was plugged, there was a paper cup taped with slick brown packing tape.

The woman was waddling to the music, her hair thin, almost wet, brushed back and gathered limply with a blue velour scrunchie, revealing patches of her pale scalp. She spoke the lyrics out, pulling at certain words, as if trying to make them sing. Every time a person passed her on the platform, she gave them a wink, and continued speaking melodically.

"You, who loved me so
Well yes, a while ago
I was a different woman then
Had an apartment near Madeleine . . .

We kissed on Rue de Paix
You said I was your *bien-aimée* . . .
You played the violin, those days
You were *exceptionel*!
But then . . .
You went to Hell."

Jana was slightly taken aback by the lyrics, but no one else on the platform seemed to be bothered by their narrative. The woman tapped her right foot emphatically four times, then raised her other hand, palm wide open, and swung into what seemed like the refrain. "Oh la la . . ." she spoke. "Ooohh laaa laaa," she sang. "Oh la la!" she proclaimed. "Ohh l'la," she admitted.

Two young women, tourists, with tan complexions and pitch-black hair, stood on the platform. One wore a jean jacket with stylish tears, the other a mid-waist fuchsia coat bearing multiple zippers, at the cuff, waist, breast pocket. They watched the woman and swayed their heads playfully to the singing, not understanding a single word. Then the jean-jacketed woman, with her slippery dark hair crimping over the collar, reached into her orange leather purse and took out her iPhone, the plastic cover with a pouch in the shape of a wine glass filled with purplish liquid oscillating as she moved her phone. Aiming the camera at the singer, she snapped a couple of photos, then her friend unclipped her large magenta wallet, scraped out some coins, approached the woman, dropped the coins into her paper cup and returned to her friend.

"*Merci,*" the woman winked, then picked up where she'd left off.

"We never had a child, that's fine
All right it was a fault of mine
I started drinking too much wine
And then you went to Hell.

You were a Jew, that's true
We shared *une vie à deux*
And now—just me, with my chagrin,
And you, in Hell with your violin."

Jana glanced at the two women, who were listening to the singer, blissful for the sounds of the French language, as if the music was foretelling a romance awaiting them in the city. The singer tapped out another count of four, then just as she began swinging into her refrain, two shrill lights came from the dark tunnel and the train shoved into the station.

Jana and the two women stepped into a metro carriage.

"Oh la la . . . !" the singer's voice echoed as the doors closed.

Inside the carriage, Jana glanced over the jean-jacketed woman's shoulder as she flipped through filter options for the photo she just took. She stopped at one, showed it to her friend, who replied, *"Claro, querida!"* with an adorned, vowel-stretched Portuguese.

*

Jana got out at Ledru-Rollin metro stop, as did the two women, who walked up the stairs in front of her, then turned onto Rue du Faubourg Saint-Antoine and walked off into the noise and lights. Jana turned the other direction, away from the circulation around Place de la Bastille that was always alive, people drinking on the steps of the opera house, then walking down the steps and turning discreetly into the graffitied wall to roll their joints.

She walked down the street, then veered left, looked up and saw that she was on the correct street: *Rue de Prague*. Here, there was no one. The road felt detached, reluctant to be walked on. The trees shadowed the pavement and the apartments leaned back, out of the light.

She walked gradually, spotting the street numbers, 2, 4, 6 . . . Then she saw it, a couple of doors ahead. A discreet-looking exterior, black-painted façade, two large windows also painted in black, and a wooden door as dark as the rest. Above the door, there was a blue glowing infinity-like symbol. As she came closer, she saw it was the electric-bulb glass body of an angel, lit up with blue as if with the hottest part of a flame.

*

Das Herz luegt nicht. The heart does not lie.

*

She felt around, but the door had no handle. She put her ear to the wood. No sound came from the bar, no sense of movement, nothing except for the neon blue angel above her head. L'Ange Bleu. The Blue Angel bar.

She drew her hand out warily and gave the black wood a push. It did not budge. She pushed harder, her forearms tensing, but it was like pushing against a wall.

*

Lož má krátke nohy. A lie has short legs.

*

Mieux vaut tenir que courir. Better to hold on than to run.

*

She pushed again. Then again.

*

There flames a desolation, blazing . . .
. . . Yet, Lord, Thy messengers are praising.

*

9 pm.

·Jana slammed the door with both palms.

Come on, what did you expect? She could hear Zorka say-ing somewhere. *You let your cunt get duped like that, Janka?* She thrust her palms into the door. *Is that it, Miss K—?* She heard Mr Doubek's voice chime in. *Do you have a gullible cunt, Miss K—?* There was something behind the door. A rasping thing. An echo. Zorka's laughter. Not only. And Mr Doubek. Chuckling. Yes, they were inside, laughing together. There was saliva in the corners of their mouths. Their laugh was stretch-ing toward each other, becoming one mouth, and the whites of their eyes began rolling around and around, circling the globe— *Is that it, Janka? Is that it, Miss K—?*

Jana rammed her shoulder against the door and the wood stunted her flesh.

The groan, however, did not come from her, but from the gutter.

*

It smelled warm, a spoiled dampness. Jana turned around and saw, at the curb on the sewer grid, a pile of stained and faded blankets, inside of which there was someone, breathing. She ran her eyes over the creases and dips within the blankets, trying to find the head or the feet but saw instead a set of charred fin-gertips sliding out from beneath the sodden covers, toward her.

There was another groan, then the full hand was present, smudged and bloated, flaking at the fingertips. It lifted and turned and curled in, and then did it again.

"*Donnez moi une pièce, madame,*" the voice said. Give me some change . . .

It was neither a man's nor a woman's voice, with an accent that seemed dug up like a long-buried vestige.

"J'en ai pas . . . désolée." I don't have any . . . Jana said without thinking.

"Madame . . . S'il vous plait," the voice said again, more demanding, more unearthed.

Jana instinctively pressed her purse into her hip and shook her head.

"S'il vous plait, madame!" the voice groaned so fully that the blanket shifted and twisted.

S'il vous plait . . . ! Cil ooomm shay . . . The begging voice was stretching in sound. *Il roumm shii pay . . . Liiroum shdii! Lak rimi shhhffff . . . Lak' rimi Shifdi! Lakrim eesi finti!*

Until the phrase found its home and, all at once, Jana remembered something.

*

Lacrimi şi Sfinţi was the first collection by Emil Cioran, the Romanian philosopher, that Jana had read. She had almost taken up Romanian for him, despite his blatant anti-Semitism, which he later retracted, becoming an à la mode nihilist in France. His lines like metaphysical threats or ancestral grudges, she kept them as company, as companionship, as a sense of self-justice— she recited them out loud the way Zorka flung her middle finger up toward the daylight.

Tears and Saints.

Just as she was coming back from her memory, a weight vaulted her from behind. Her body was on the ground. Her eyes closed and inside of them, all black water.

*

Jana had been jumped and pinned down by the kids. There were four of them.

"Baba," one of the kids said to the lump. Jana turned her head and saw it was a boyish-girl, dark stringy hair, a big purple-and-red-striped sweatshirt with Mickey Mouse patch at the center, ballooning over her thin torso. She was sitting on Jana's legs. Jana squirmed at the sight, trying to get the girl off, but she couldn't budge her in the slightest.

Jana flipped her head to the side. A flower-clip, hanging off another child's cropped hair. The grip that was holding down Jana's arm had scraped knuckles and on its meager wrist, a clunky white-and-pink plastic Hello Kitty watch, sliding down against her hand, too big for the child. Jana tried to pull her arm out from beneath the girl's hold, but her shoulder muscle rolled back and stuck—it was like her whole body was beneath a layer of cement.

"Baba," a third child with greasy curling hair said over to the lump.

This child's huge blue-and-white-striped overalls bunched over her short body. At the chest pocket, Bugs Bunny was giving a thumbs up and smiling with his two front teeth pushed out. The girl looked down at Jana with a teething concentration. From her dirt-streaked neck hung a necklace she had most likely strung up herself from a leftover cable and a clear plastic keychain with "TOYOTA" written in red. The girl itched her collarbone with her free hand. At the top, Jana saw a temporary Spider-Man tattoo, blue and red, already partly worn off.

"Baba . . . ?" said the last child.

Jana's eyes darted to the voice. She looked the oldest or maybe it was the way her Spice Girls T-shirt hugged her chest. Across the shirt, all five Spice Girls were jutting their colorful outfits one way or another, the girl's prepubescent breasts pushed out against their heads. A candy ring stuck out on her index finger, lint and hairs covered the partly licked cherry-red candy diamond.

"Babička, can we?" she asked.

"Can we??" the others repeated.

The lump shifted with a deeper groan.

And so, together, the children worked like a harmonious team as they held Jana's shoulders and wrists and thighs and waist and rolled her over onto her stomach with impersonal ease, unaffected by her squirming and twisting. The belt of her coat was untied, her blouse pulled out, her trousers unhooked and unzipped. The Toyota-necklace girl clasped her Spider-Man-hand over Jana's mouth, as Jana muttered and spit and tried to bite her flesh. Two of the other children helped push Jana's face against the cement, until her teeth dug into her cheeks.

Spice Girls Tee pulled out a worn beach towel from beneath the layers of blankets on Baba's sewer grid, a whirl of purple and magenta, ragged with threads and small holes at the corners. Across the towel was Aladdin on his magic carpet, holding Princess Jasmine to him at her waist, and in big teal letters it said *A Whole New World*. The girl took the corner of the towel and shoved it into Jana's mouth until the tattered fabric stuffed against her tonsils, and absorbed her scream.

All together, the children began to wedge their small hands beneath Jana's stomach, getting at her trousers and pulling them down to her thighs. They grabbed her underwear and pulled that down too, the elastic rolling on the flesh of Jana's buttocks, bunching with her trousers.

Jana was choking on the towel when the kids all huddled in closer and began lulling in unison, "Shhhhhhh . . ."

"MADAME," one of the children whispered. "I'm a piece of shit."

"Me too . . ." another hushed.

"Me three . . ."

"Me four, madame."

"We are unhappy here . . ." the first pouted louder.

"We're homesick . . ." another murmured.

"We just wanna go home . . ." the fourth voice trembled.

The children began whimpering, trying to find their words. Then they grabbed hold of Jana's buttocks with their small hands, taking handfuls of flesh and pulling her butt cheeks apart. "We wanna gooo hoooommme . . . !" they whimpered even louder as they stuffed their noses into the open flesh between her butt cheeks. They pushed and pressed against each other's messy heads, trying to squeeze farther inside.

"WE WAANNNAAA GOOOOO HOOOOOOMMME," they sobbed into her anus.

Home

Aimée was watching TV on the couch when she noticed the light-blue hardcover book sticking out of the bottom shelf of the white bookshelf. She walked to the rows of books and crouched down and grabbed the corner with her fingers. She gave a tug and the book slid out from its tight spot.

Aimée sat right down where she was, leaned her back against the bookshelf, opened the book and began to read.

Next to her elbow, in the space where the book had been, a trail of blue smoke began to seep out, just barely brushing across her skin.

As she turned the page, the paper rubbed against itself, like a throat cracking in mid-breath.

The blue trail continued groping its way along her arm, around her shoulder, against her neck . . .

PART TWO

Gejza and Tammie

Gejza parked his truck on their driveway, on Argyle Avenue, the one lined with red bricks and a yard sprinkler he'd installed himself. It was almost summer. He was sweaty. His wife, Tammie, was still at the nearby public high school, no less than 10 minutes up, past Johnson Controls and right below Bayshore shopping mall. Tammie was a petite woman who always wore "creative" tops, where the neckline veered to one side or a zipper allowed a two-inch opening to occur at the bottom seam. She taught French classes at the high school and had her graying-blond hair cut into a childish bob that she wore with a thick fabric-covered headband as if she were Godard's mod ingénue, refusing to age.

One of the reasons she even fell for a Czech immigrant construction worker at the time, was that, instead of whistling at her, he had said, "Oh la la!"

Gejza had always worked with his hands—he had been labeled a laborer from boyhood. But even during the brownest polyester years of communism in Prague, he still lived his little life as if it were a French film. His older sister, Marja, however, lived hers more as an experimental screening. Whereas Gejza walked down the listless street with a private poetic gait, Marja kept her right hand in her pocket, acute and suspicious, as she found certain trees, like birches, incredibly funny, and others, like pines, brought her to tears. On one of Marja's school trips, doused with Soviet socialist values and allusions to State-building, they were going to help plant apple trees. On the way to the farm they had to cross over train-tracks. Marja lagged behind and lingered too long over the tracks and almost got run over by a train. Even Ruzena, the girl with the lazy eye, saw it coming. But Marja was looking at a patch of grass that leaned into the metal rail with such sumptuousness that the girl could not bring herself to part with it.

When one of the older boys retold the story in Gejza's presence, the consensus was that, perhaps a girl that was slow in the head should be run over by a train. Gejza drifted away from the group, broke a low branch off an oak, then came back with a focused calm, raised his branch high as if he were simply bearing a flag, then started whipping the boys in the heads with it.

Although the episode only left them with some lashes on their cheeks and upper arms and necks, Gejza and Marja's parents decided that their weird daughter was having a bad influence on her normal little brother. They explained that having one off child is enough. Opportunity coincided. Gejza was sent away to an apprenticeship, to learn construction. Their parents focused on Marja's one asset, her looks. The thin-nose, spark-eyed, fluffy-haired girl grew into an attractive woman in the 1970s, where her quirks were suddenly decade-appropriate, and she caught the eye of a square-jawed, handsome, hard-working Slovak, and for a moment Marja was just right in her doses. They married.

But in their first year of marriage, Marja suddenly began to speak her mind and act her will in a way that surprised even her. She couldn't quite find the balance between what she should resist and what she should bend toward, so she ended up twisting in all the ways that proved to those around her that she was a cripple of her gender, not quite a righteous woman, and not wholly a defunct one.

*

Her husband broke down the bathroom door and grabbed Marja's flailing legs into his chest, pushing her up, and reaching one hand high for the rope's noose.

*

After Marja tried to hang herself in the bathroom, it was unanimously decided that she needed electricity. And so, a couple of sessions of shocking did it. Marja was fixed. Voilà.

Then their first and only child, a baby girl, was born.

By this time, Marja's little brother, Gejza, was long distant, in America, after getting a chance ticket to come over, passing as the son of his employer.

And now, long after, Gejza was an American citizen, married to the local high school teacher, Tammie, living in Milwaukee, Wisconsin.

*

Gejza hadn't heard about his sister for decades. But when he got news that she was recently widowed, left all alone with one daughter, a problem child, unmanageable, with nowhere to turn . . . Gejza talked it over with Tammie and they decided it was the right thing to do. Besides, Tammie had this thing where she couldn't have children. And she liked spinning the stand-up globe on the table next to the TV and watching where her finger would land. The last few times, it was Madagascar and she thought perhaps a child would come to them from that region somehow. Then this promising kid, for whom Tammie had a special fondness, just fell over dead one track meet, one of those inexplicable heart attacks. Star athlete, star scholar. He was her favorite student in her intermediate French 3 class. Weeks later, when she spun the globe, her finger kept landing in water. Tammie cried sparingly and said she knew it wasn't her place, but she just didn't understand why the world wouldn't explain itself a little more, why certain children couldn't be born and others just dropped down dead.

To cheer up their spirits the couple went out to eat at Taco Bell, but midway through their taco menus there was some sort of fight in the kitchen, where a teenage girl stormed out from the back, her long braids swinging over her shoulder as she pulled her visor with the restaurant logo off her head, screaming, "Ain't nobody wanna see your *ugly-ass* dick," and, "Never axt you for no raise," then flung the visor like a Frisbee at the manager, who was just rushing out from behind the cashier station, in his blue polo shirt and shiny name tag. He got nailed right in the forehead, then screamed, "Dammit, Djamilla!" Then the cops were called, and Gejza and Tammie got a voucher for a free meal.

The next morning, they had the same idea, to sponsor Marja and her daughter to come over to America and live with them.

*

Marja arrived more gawky than Gejza imagined her, with her cream blouse collar laid neatly over her brown-and-tan sweater, tucked over her knee-length brown-checked skirt, with a laminated pink belt hooked at the waist. She had the same bird-eyes and fluffed-out hair, with skin that looked unfolded and refolded already. Her daughter was 16, long-limbed, with a pale complexion and pitch-dark hair cut short, sitting jagged on her head, the trail above her neck slightly longer than the rest. Her face held stark black eyebrows over two dense eyes like iron nails. She had light denim jeans on with two worn holes revealing her bony knees, a loose black T-shirt that was made for a large man, rippling down her torso, and over that a man's white shirt, the kind that would usually be worn starched to the office, but the girl's was wrinkled, one sleeve bunched up at her skinny elbow, the other hanging low over her fingertips.

The flight had been long, but it seemed that mother and daughter were operating on some sort of peace treaty, as each spoke to Gejza in Czech individually, never acknowledging each other's presence.

*

Tammie helped to enroll the girl at the local public high school, got her some after-school tutoring for her English, and put her in her Basic French class so that Tammie could keep an eye on the girl in this brand-new school.

To celebrate their first week in America, the four went for dinner at McDonald's, where the girl took bites of everyone's food and licked her wrist that she kept putting in the ketchup she squirted out for herself on her tray. Tammie listened patiently and every time Gejza tried to translate for her, she politely waved her hand, and mouthed, "It's fine, I'll just listen."

At home, they continued their discussion about who should live in the garage space Gejza had just finished converting into a bedroom, and who in the guest bedroom in the house. Marja was a discreet claustrophobe, and kept having visions of a dark-headed, blue-eyed woman in a fur coat slumped in the front seat of a car in the garage, dying of exhaust fumes. She explained to her younger brother that she thought the place was cursed. Not like American cursed, vengeful ghosts or resentful zombies, but cursed in the Eastern way, by one's own inevitable fate. So she said that her daughter should take the garage room, but under one condition:

"I don't want you to get a venereal disease like the Americans. They look very clean, but they are very dirty." She gave her daughter a firm nod, then her daughter rolled her eyes at her mother, reached inside her own T-shirt, and pulled up her bra strap.

Marja grabbed her daughter's chin and pulled her face in. "Zorka, I'm serious!"

Zorka pursed her lips together and flapped her mother a kiss, keeping her eyes taut and sly.

Marja lifted her hand and whacked her palm against Zorka's cheek. Zorka winced but when she opened her eyes they were fully cocked. Both Gejza and Tammie flinched and grew immediately polite in their unease.

Marja turned to her brother and said in Czech, "She destroyed our mother's beautiful fur coat, by the way, and of course I love her, she's my daughter, but I'll never forgive her, I hope you know."

*

Waiting,
waiting,
waiting.

Are u there?

Dominxxika_N39: Are u there? Amy?

0_hotgirlAmy_0: Yeah I'm here . . . Where did u go last time?

Dominxxika_N39: I'm sorry sexy Amy. Internet cut off.
I cannot stop think about u. My husband come home and
he cut internet. Now he left again for work. I climb on
roof and reconnect internet to satellite dish.

0_hotgirlAmy_0: U went on the roof to fix the satellite dish?
For real?

Dominxxika_N39: Yes this is real.

0_hotgirlAmy_0: I guess I thought . . . u like . . . got weirded
out by what I said . . .

Dominxxika_N39: No, no, my sexy Amy! I was so sad all
week I want to scream a million screams, but I stay quiet.
I wait for my husband to leave so I can climb on roof and
fix internet connection.

0_hotgirlAmy_0: Oh.

0_hotgirlAmy_0: I just wish . . . he hadn't done that. I mean I really wanted to talk to you this week and u weren't online . . .

Dominxxika_N39: What happen this week?

0_hotgirlAmy_0: Whatever, it's no big deal.

Dominxxika_N39: Big deal to me, please tell.

0_hotgirlAmy_0: I mean . . .

0_hotgirlAmy_0: It's just. I've been thinking about Archangel Michael.

Dominxxika_N39: He whisper again to you?

0_hotgirlAmy_0: Maybe . . .

0_hotgirlAmy_0: I dunno.

0_hotgirlAmy_0: It really doesn't matter. I just thought you didn't like me anymore.

Dominxxika_N39: I do like you anymore! Please believe me.

0_hotgirlAmy_0: I guess when you stopped talking to me. Then the thing at school, so . . .

Dominxxika_N39: What thing at school? I am very interested to hear.

0_hotgirlAmy_0: It's kinda hard . . . to talk about.

Dominxxika_N39: O my so-cute Amy, I here and listen so much for you. Please share the hard thing at school with me.

0_hotgirlAmy_0: Just. Other stuff. With the girls.

Dominxxika_N39: Yes?

0_hotgirlAmy_0: I was wearing these sweatpants for gym class. We had to play softball. And it was my turn to bat.

And they were taking extra long, between them, the girls
I mean. One of them was pitcher and the other, behind
me, the catcher. They were looking at each other and
I could feel something was up. And our gym teacher,
Mr Brooks (who's also the football coach), he was like,
come on girls, let's not take all day here. So she wound
up her pitch and threw the ball and I swung and I hit it,
and—the girl behind me, the catcher, she just, um . . .

0_hotgirlAmy_0: . . . she . . .

0_hotgirlAmy_0: She pulled down my sweatpants.

Dominxxika_N39: This is strange gesture in circumstances.

0_hotgirlAmy_0: She pulled down everything—like everything, like my underwear too. And everyone saw.

Dominxxika_N39: This is clear violation! What Mr Brooks
do as responsible leader?

0_hotgirlAmy_0: He just acted like nothing happened! I mean
I dunno, maybe he didn't see it, it was kinda quick. I pulled
them back up right away, so . . .

Dominxxika_N39: He is surely pretending blindness as
strategy to maintain prescribed hierarchy.

0_hotgirlAmy_0: That's what I was thinking too! He had to
have seen it! But I dunno, he just started yelling at me
to run to first base, and everyone was yelling at me too,
and I dunno, in the moment, I just totally zonked out,
I just . . . ran to first base. Then I could hear this hooting,
"Let's get Amy all the way!" And Mr Brooks was yelling
out "Keep running, Amy!"—so I dunno I just started up
running again. Then everyone was shouting "First base!
Second base! Third base!" "Mmmmyeah go all the way for
me, Amy!"

Dominxxika_N39: I know this pressure system.

0_hotgirlAmy_0: . . . You said Archangel Michael comes in the hour of your death?

Dominxxika_N39: This is true.

0_hotgirlAmy_0: Well, as I was running, and everyone was yelling, and sticking their tongues between their fingers, well, he was whispering to me . . . I felt like I was blind maybe. Everything was quiet. And white.

Dominxxika_N39: What Archangel Michael whisper?

0_hotgirlAmy_0: . . . He was whispering:

0_hotgirlAmy_0: "Go online, Amy, go online . . ."

0_hotgirlAmy_0: When I came home, my mom was bitching at me for skipping school again. Cause I'm getting a D in gym class now cause I skip classes or I just stand in the corner and don't participate. She's like, Amy who gets a D in gym! It's gym! I don't even talk back anymore. I just wait for her to be done, then I say I gotta do my homework, cause in my head, he's still whispering to me, and cleaning up the noise all around me, so it's quiet and white. He keeps saying, "Amy, go online . . ."

Get ur freak on

The school bus picked Zorka up on the corner of Dexter Avenue and 24th Street. She waited there with another girl who was a sophomore, long blond hair, thick bangs. Sometimes the girl wore jean-shorts and a sweatshirt that said "Abercrombie & Fitch" across the chest, which to Zorka looked like the name of two scientists who had conceived an anti-virus. Then she wore a baby-blue T-shirt with the word "GAP" written on it, which Zorka deduced to be an acronym for some sort of government service. On warmer days, she wore a melon-green tank-top, with pink bra straps crossed beneath the tank's straps, and faded blue jeans with a flower patch at the knee. Zorka wasn't sure what to make of her then.

Soon enough though she got the hint. True capitalism was all about names on stuff, on clothes, on notebooks, on cars, on backpacks, on shoes. Tammie bought Zorka a powder-rose zip-up top that said "Hollister" on it, and a pair of flared l.e.i. jeans. When Zorka tried the outfit on, the jeans bagged oddly right below her buttocks, and the zip-up drew everyone's eyes to the patched letters that puffed out in awkward angles around Zorka's flat chest.

Zorka said thank you, went back to the garage, undressed, and put her own clothes back on.

*

It was a big high school with a web of groups and subgroups, and yet Zorka could not quite be placed into its network. Her figure beneath the layers of men's shirts had promise—long legs and a straight neck. Her face too was clear, dark brows arching up, strong pupils, no pimples, high cheekbones. But her oddly cropped hair, with a nuanced duck-tail that she let grow until some called it a mullet, made it impossible to call the girl "hot." A couple of the punk kids tested out the potential of this girl to belong to their group, but when she said, "Get lost, hedgehog," they gave her space.

Zorka was not a geek, and she was not a punk, she was not a goth, she was not smart or stupid, she was not hot or ugly, she wasn't a prude or a ho, she was a fully fledged loner, and by the spring of her junior year the Columbine shooting had happened, and some kids started whispering at her when she passed, "Don't shoot us!"

Meghan told Kaylee that she heard the girl hated Americans and America, and that she was military trained because in those countries they start the army when they are children. Kaylee agreed and was grateful we now had metal detectors. But then at lunch, the whole table was taking turns guessing how deformed Zorka's breasts might be if she always wore such baggy shirts. Meghan said that one boob was most likely a totally different shape from the other. Then Kaylee said that one of them was definitely like a little flappy pancake. The discussion continued until it was decided that they were closest to goat-teats, just then

Jared said, "Hey, what if they're not real. I mean, what if they're like bombs?"

*

Gejza had installed a TV in the garage and Zorka stayed in for hours after school, watching the cable channels, MTV, and VH1, every now and then getting off her bed, dancing to the music with her fists and elbows, then lying back down.

*

Tammie was making popcorn for their movie night. Her regular movie-night schedule was primarily "French films," her favorite genre. She was eager to watch the last Truffaut she had not yet seen. She had been eyeing the VHS at Blockbuster, the jacket cover of Fanny Ardant leaning over a young Gerard Depardieu, both troubled and aroused, but Tammie decided it was important for Zorka and her mother to improve their English and gain an understanding of the American culture, so she put off renting *The Woman Next Door* and opted for *Sleepless in Seattle*, *It Could Happen to You, Jerry Maguire* . . . She selected films she thought represented America for its character of hope and strong values, films where children set up adults, where adults meet on planes and show up at each other's doorsteps wet from the rain, where women say "I love you" and men say "I love you" back.

Zorka understood that phrase "I love you" from the rest of the mumbling, and would snuff "bullshit" under her breath whenever she'd hear it because she had never in her life, ever, seen a man and a woman say "I love you" to each other, where it wasn't a threat or something you do in the hallway to show your neighbors you are reliable tenants.

Still, the films played with Meg Ryan and Tom Hanks, with Nicolas Cage who won the lottery and gave half to the waitress and then they fell in love, Tom Cruise, Renée Zellweger, single moms who get saved by do-good attractive bachelors, Hugh Grant rambling in a British accent, scene changes with tinkling piano music, Richard Gere pensive, concerned, Julia Roberts a sex worker who charmingly shocks the upper classes. Then everyone laughing, even all the old people, who are clean, their gray hair well brushed, rings on their spotted wrinkled fingers, pearls in their ears, lipstick to the ridges of their lips, perfect rows of prosthetic teeth, looking around at each other, smiling and patting each other's thighs.

*

Do you like sad music?

*

Zorka snuck out regularly in the evenings and walked up to the tall thin electric poles around the railroad tracks where there were foresty patches, just beyond where the road turned. She waded into the branches until she was submerged and hidden. She sat down in the dirt and put her arms around her knees and her hands into the two holes of her jeans, stared and listened. There was the sound of tires over the road, a car making a slow turn around the corner, its headlights brushing through the branches. The wind rustled through and the sky, like a pool of dark ink, trembled above as if having to hold up its own liquid. Another car passed, with its windows down, the music pulsing with the fussy voice of Britney Spears singing against the reverb.

Then the car turned, taking the song with it.

Zorka sunk her head between her knees and closed her eyes. She thought it was still that same pop song stringing through her head, but the rhythm pulled and stretched with every round, the voice seemed unsteadily full again. It was her mother's voice, singing that old Czech song about love she used to sing as if telling mercy where to find her . . .

Ach, není, není tu

She used to sing it to Zorka like a lullaby, and even though the song was more for her, she still held little Zorka against her chest, her legs noodling as she tried to stand up, Marja kissing her little girl just above the ear, baby Zorka giggling toothless with a full heart, and Marja singing:

". . . What is plowing without a plow. . .

. . . Loving without kisses . . .

. . . They are always giving me what I do not love . . .

Ach, není, není tu . . ."

*

When Zorka came home from the forest, she grabbed the remote and pressed power. Missy Elliott was pumping her knuckles at the screen, just above the MTV logo, then opening up her hands, one long white fingernail at a time.

I told you not to be weird

Yeah, the last time someone called me loony, he got a quick one in the eye socket—Ludek. It was my last month in Prague before it all went to shit, Ludek was right outside our school and he whispered it at me, so I just balled up my fist, punched him in the eye, and kept on walking. He lost his sight in that eye for the day and his head puffed up, and of course his ass-kissing mama freaked out and marched right into school, and my papka was dead already so my mamka was code red beneath her quiet and respectful widowhood. While Ludek's mama was lamenting about her baby boy's eyesight, my mamka completely stole the show, curling in, weeping, then springing out her hand, slapping and scratching me like a wild cat, screaming, "I told you not to be weird!"

The principal and Ludek's mama got her off me and I shrugged and told her in my good-girl voice, "Sorry, Mamka."

*

Then there was our geography teacher, Mr Bolshakov, who was always bringing the topic of Jews into lessons that didn't concern them, and kept calling up Isaac for oral reports on the Transnistrian territories, that little Romanian boy with his dark curly locks and round caramel cheeks like a gypsy-cherub. I told Janka he probably wants to fuck Isaac and she said, "No way, he hates Jews," and I said, "Duh, Janka, hate's like a globe that spins all the way around, that's why men go exploring islands full of dark-skinned peoples, and why they all wanna take naps on women's soft boobs and then smack them, they fuck what they hate." Janka took her time with her thoughts. She said I got a perspective on life that's looking for trouble so it comes around for me and proves me right.

Mr Bolshakov himself was an implant from the Soviet Bloc, and now that the Soviet tanks were gone and we were all proud Czechs, we didn't like him much anyway. But, somehow, he served as one of the commissioners for the oral exams of the *maturia*, the final exam at the end of high school to get into university.

Mr Bolshakov had a Czech wife and a nice house and he was untouchable. He continued things in the old way—bribes, cash and gold preferably—he didn't care much for promises or favoritism, he just wanted to get it in the real and wrap it up in his yellowing newspaper from the 1980s, when this was still his country, and stuff it in his old army boots.

I knew 'cause I broke in and had a little peek for myself. I was curious about that top-dog *Rusky*, what can I say. I found where he kept those old army boots (in the closet, below his trousers and shirts, predictable dumb-ass), I pulled out his stash, but then he came home unexpectedly, had to think quick, so I slid myself under the bed.

I was pressed like a chicken breast between the floor and the low metal springs, waiting for him to leave, except that he kept muttering around his bedroom, then he sat on the edge of the bed and the springs almost collapsed my gut, and whether it was the powers above having a go at me or just his afternoon routine,

Mr Bolshakov started rubbing himself off, emitting ointments of moans, all the while the springs pushing in and out of my gut till I thought I'd wet myself or shit myself or split my spleen. But he finished off and stood up and finally left the room.

I slid out of that space, then felt it coming, so I pulled the bed cover down and vomited onto the sheet, then closed the comforter over that spot, ha ha.

Then I went back to those army boots and reached into my pocket and got out the matches.

*

Before the police or the school got whiff of it, I ran back to our building and pulled Janka into the bathroom with me and locked the door. She knew I'd done something irreversible. I said hush for a minute. We were squeezed in against the toilet and we waited in silence to hear if there were any footsteps in the hallway. There weren't any, so I unzipped my jeans and plunged my hand in and fished about in my cunt and pulled it out for show. Ta-da, I showed Jana the tight wad of money wrapped in plastic.

Janka said, "He's going to kill you!" I said, "No one can kill me, I'm already an angel!" Then I kissed her. Janka said, "Where are we gonna hide this?" I said, "Where else?" and stuffed that money-roll back into my cunt.

*

Never never never, not under no circumstance, never be ashamed of yourself, Janka!

*

It was just one of those days when too many things happened at the same time. Mr Bolshakov found himself alone with me after class, pinned me to the wall and pulled a fork out of his pocket, trying to whisper with his onion-breath that he'd scrape my little cunt out. "Whoever said it was little," I huffed back. "I got a fatty, Mr Bolshakov!" He pinched his eyebrows, what a dullard, so I grabbed the fork out of his hand, stuffed it in my jeans, gave him my signature two-finger salute, then got the hell out of there!

Yeah, I was running, thinking of my mamka actually, that she might even be a little delighted to have an extra fork in the kitchen 'cause she was always complaining how the neighbors were stealing our silverware. But when I got home, Mamka was not in the best of moods, her fingernails were already itching at her woolen skirt. Then she saw me and her mouth reeked of loathing. I pulled out the fork and said, "Here, Mamka, a present for you." She grabbed the fork out of my hand and started screaming about how the police had come around for me again, and in the name of mercy couldn't I stop with my shit and be less defunct. I said, "Listen, Mamka, I am a fallen angel." She started chasing me with the fork, and I thought oh fuck. I ducked and jumped, and still managed to flip her off ('cause, come on), then she screamed "you *malá narcis*!" and then I screamed back "I THOUGHT I WAS THE LOVE OF YOUR LIFE!" and then I could hear the neighbors coming out into the hallway to see what was up. I was running around our small apartment, bouncing from corner to corner 'cause Mamka had a fork like a machete, and she was serious. I reached beneath the sofa to where I knew Mamka kept her vodka bottle, then flipped open the closet and grabbed her prized fox-fur coat and she howled, "You put that down, you put that down," but I sprinted to the door and down the stairs and I was gone.

Mamka must have run to the window just then. She never had good aim, in all the years I'd known her, but I was running in one direction, past the neighbors' faces like a lie, crunching over the snow, cold slapping at my cheeks, when I heard the shriek, it could only belong to one person—my mother. Before I could turn around, I felt it, like some cold metal beast clenched its claws into my shoulder. It knocked me to my knees and my face slumped into the snow. I was pushing myself back up, saying to myself, get up, Zorka, get up. I reached my hand around to my shoulder and felt it there, the fork, stuck deep inside my flesh. I wriggled it, and almost vomited straight up. Come on, Zorka! I held my breath, grabbed that fork, and pulled that motherfucker out. It spat a perfect arc of blood into the snow. My shoulder felt like I just pulled a grown wing outta my body. Holy shit. Holy shit, holy shit. I picked up Mamka's fox-fur coat and got on running.

After that, well, I only came back once—some days later—and it was night-time. I doused that fur coat with the whole bottle of vodka; then I left it to burn in the hallway, fuck and *adieu*.

*

Say hi to the boys, the river and the forest.

*

Then it struck me like an alarm. What have I done? I mean about Jana, you know. Years have a way of speeding up at a certain point. I thought either I'm gonna kill Mamka or Mamka's gonna kill me. Guess that's when I started asking for angels. You wouldn't understand.

Anyway I had the dream. Never saw children that had a lethal buzz to them like that—except for Jana maybe, ha. Lucifer's kiddies—my kind of crowd. So, yeah, I made a wish. That's what dreams are for.

And maybe it was selfish. But they don't call me the Malá Narcis for nothing!

The short of it was I was scared I'd never outgrow my misgivings. I'm all alone and I'm a piece of shit, I kept repeating. I was asking for help.

Woke up to the smell of apples and oranges.

It's a secret

0_hotgirlAmy_0: Don't tell anyone.

Dominxxika_N39: I will not gossip or speak of it, this I am promise! Please tell me . . .

0_hotgirlAmy_0: *smile

0_hotgirlAmy_0: I'm gonna whisper it to u . . .

Dominxxika_N39: My ear is ready for ur whisper.

0_hotgirlAmy_0: *I* . . .

0_hotgirlAmy_0: *love*

0_hotgirlAmy_0: *you, Dominika.*

Dominxxika_N39: O Amy.

Dominxxika_N39: O my Amy!

Dominxxika_N39: O my beauty, my angel, my sexy girl!

Dominxxika_N39: I love u so great I have not find words to say, if I say it, I have to say it million times, like million rosebuds, like million leaf tips, like million gold reflections in the quiet field, I love you Amy I love you!

0_hotgirlAmy_0: *mega smile

Dominxxika_N39: I want u, sexy Amy.

0_hotgirlAmy_0: Me too . . . I want to look into ur blue eyes. And touch ur dark hair. And I want to . . . do so many things . . . ! All day long, I don't care, like at all at all at all. I don't even care. I just wanna go home and go online and be with you.

Dominxxika_N39: When I alone and my husband double-lock door, so I no go out, I put one arm around other and I feel u there, inside my embrace.

0_hotgirlAmy_0: I am I am I am!

Dominxxika_N39: I get so sad, because I am locked inside and cannot see u and cannot be with you. I want to feel u for real and be with you for real.

0_hotgirlAmy_0: We can be, we can! Archangel Michael is on our side. He's guiding me to u every day. And I even looked on the map. And like if I fly into Prague, we can meet up. From Vaclav Havel Airport I can take the 119 bus to Nadrazi Veleslavin, then take the A subway 5 stops and get off at Staromestska, it's near the old Jewish cemetery on the map. Will u meet me there? No one will see us. Will u?

Dominxxika_N39: Yes! Yes yes! But how I get out? U don't understand, Amy. Every night I dream u are outside door. I can hear u and I can feel u on other side of door, but it is lock and I cannot get out and you cannot get in. When I awake, I want to tear down wall with my nails. But my sexy Amy, how can I explain to u how I live? My husband put iron bars on window because he is suspicious. And door frame he make of iron too. It is impossible. Even if I put fire to door, it is only I who burn inside.

0_hotgirlAmy_0: Don't do that!

0_hotgirlAmy_0: Archangel Michael will help us! I'm sure he will!

Fight the dyke

There was a good half-year when Zorka was not aggressive or hostile, just a bit distant and pensive. She was doing her homework, not walking out of school, not flipping off the hall monitors, not yelling back and forth at her mother, not skipping dinner to sit in the forest.

But then Jared brushed against her in the hallway as she was getting her history book out of her locker, and she snapped around, grabbed his hand, and slammed it in her locker door. It happened so quickly that the boy couldn't even yell out, he just stood there with a blurry face, holding his slammed hand at his wrist, with his mouth gaping silently. Then he started shaking his hand out and shrieking, "You fucking psycho!!" Jared pushed Zorka against the lockers and all the kids backed up and a couple started chanting, "Fight the dyke, fight the dyke," then a teacher came out and the students scattered. Jared showed the teacher his hand, already white and throbbing, with the red indent of where it was slammed. "She broke my hand!" he exclaimed in a cramped voice.

Jared's hand was indeed broken, the principal updated Zorka and her mother, who sat in his office with Gejza translating and Tammie with her eyebrows scrunched and high with concern.

The principal was a tall round-faced man with a blue-toned suit. He proceeded in a measured voice, asking Zorka to explain what had happened.

Zorka was sitting with her chin down, looking at the desk legs.

"He touch me," Zorka muttered.

"Touched you . . . Do you mean, in the hallway, Zorka, just then?"

"Yeah."

"Did he . . . go under your clothes?"

"No," Zorka said.

"Did he use his hands?"

"No."

"Well, it seems to me that what you are describing is a classmate who happened to bump into you in the hallway, is that correct?"

Zorka looked up at the principal.

"Not correct," she said. "He touch me."

Finally, Marja caught up with what was being discussed and she shrieked out, "Narcis!" Then Zorka looked back and yelled something in Czech, then Gejza got between them and the two women were hushed.

"I'm sorry, Zorka," the principal continued, "I know it's unpleasant sometimes when someone bumps into us, but if we were to react violently to every person in life that accidentally—"

"Not accident!" Zorka said.

Marja yelled something at Zorka and Gejza repeated it in a hushed voice and Tammie bit her nail. The principal took a breath and leaned back on his swivel chair. He looked directly at Gejza.

"Perhaps you can translate this for Zorka and her mother. It is very important. Violence, of any kind, is not tolerated *in America*, not to mention in a public high school where children come to learn in a safe environment."

Gejza nodded. Tammie added, "I'm so sorry for this."

"She can't just behave the way they do in . . . *the Czech Republic*." The principal pronounced the country with caution, wondering if he was saying it all right.

"Well, this is not the way we act—" Gejza was trying to explain when the principal cut him off with his hand. Then nodded.

"I hope you understand that I'm responsible for the safety of every student who goes to this public school."

*

At home, they cut off Zorka's cable, then they just took away the TV.

*

. . . the boys, the river and the forest . . .

*

Tammie talked to the principal and Jared's parents on Zorka's behalf, and the police were left out of it. Zorka got a month of detention and the family paid for the boy's medical bills.

*

In detention, Zorka spent the first couple of days staring at Deandra sitting diagonally in front of her, wearing loose track-suit bottoms, white K-Swiss sneakers, and an oversized white shirt that had a blue-and-red "Tommy Girl" written on it. Next to her was Deandra's girl, Tiff, taller, small-waisted, wearing tight dark jeans with a thick belt, leaving a gap at the back where her red shirt didn't quite tuck into her jeans.

Zorka kept staring until, finally, Deandra turned around and said, "What's the matter. You ain't never seen a black person before?"

"Yes I have," Zorka replied.

"So what's your problem?"

"You look like rapper Missy Elliott."

"You kiddin' me?"

"No, I know you are not. I say you look like."

"Hell, nah, yo Tiff, check out this Spice Girl over here calling me Missy 'cause she can't tell no difference between us black folk!"

Tiff leaned over and turned toward Zorka.

"You think she look like Beyoncé?" Deandra said, turning her thumb to Tiff.

"No," Zorka said.

"Well, we think yo ass look like a Russian Spice Girl."

"I am not Russian."

"Shh," the detention monitor said and all three girls turned to face forward.

The detention monitor walked up to the three girls and nodded at each one. They all lowered their heads back to their homework and began to write. As the monitor walked back to the front of the class, Deandra snuck her eyes back over to Zorka and Zorka slid her eyes down at Deandra.

*

When the detention bell rang, Zorka walked straight up in front of Deandra and Tiff and stood at their desks. "So . . . I can hang with you now?"

Deandra looked up at Zorka, then over at Tiff, then burst out laughing. "Tiff, am I going crazy? Am I losing it, or is this Spice Girl over here be askin' us if she can hang with us?"

"Dee, I think that's really what she be askin' tho."

Deandra looked Zorka up and down. "Okay, Spicey, tell me, why you wanna hang with us?"

Zorka thought about it. Then she shrugged. "'Cause you are like—revolution," she said.

*

It's true that most people referred to Zorka as "Carrie" or "Psycho," but both Deandra and Tiff had their share of names as well. Tiff had a soft-spoken lisp and acne scars on her cheeks, and in middle school her grandma made her carry around the Bible and it became a game to try and make Tiff use God's name in vain or say a cuss word. To this day, Tiff never used a cuss word, even if Dee threw them around as easily as she threw her fists around whenever anyone had a problem with the fact that Tiff was "her girl."

*

. . . there's fire . . . in the windows . . .

*

Big pieces, little pieces—

"We can't go to my house. But Tiff live with her granny. You can come over. But we gotta take the bus," Deandra said.

The three girls took the 14 bus Southridge bound and got off at Cesar Chavez Drive and walked the rest of the way.

"Otherwise it's two buses," Tiff explained, "and that'd take over an hour."

Deandra added that, once they got a car, they could be there in 15 to 20 minutes tops.

Cesar Chavez Drive was definitely in the Latino neighborhood, Zorka observed. Across the street from the bus stop was a Taqueria Los Comales and a church-type center, tan stone with two-pronged towers and, built into the exterior, two golden tubes with a golden-shaped flame at the top, between which the letters spelled out La Luz Del Mundo, the Light of the World.

They walked past 20th, 21st, 22nd . . . up until West Lapham Street to a long five-story apartment building. The exterior was lined with grainy cement between each floor. All the sliding windows on all the floors were identical, in between each window a bit of brown-red wall. The yard was punctuated with a series of oblong-trimmed shrubs, which looked as if they were embarrassed by the building, hunching into their own twigs.

Inside, the floor was thin and somewhat rubbery, spotted with flecks of brown, and the matching maroon and brown carpet led to the elevator. They went up to the fifth floor, took a left, and went to the last door near the window facing the building opposite.

"My granny's still at work. So no one's home," Tiff said, unlocking the door.

Zorka walked around the living room and picked up a photo of a young man, about 16, wearing a track uniform, shoulders wide, the muscles pushing out of his smooth dark skin, his face even, with eyes looking far, far out.

"He's super fine," Zorka said.

"That's Ray-Ray," Deandra said. "He dead."

"Shit." Zorka put the photo down. "Total shame!"

"For real," Deandra continued. "He *was* super fine."

"He got shot?" Zorka asked.

"Girl, you need to update yourself on some shit, seriously. You killing me with this racist feedback."

"What?"

"Not all dead brothers be dead 'cause they got shot."

"Oh okay," Zorka replied. "I understand."

"Ray-Ray was a star athlete and good grades, academic. He was gonna go to Harvard or some shit like that, plus he was fly as fuck. All the girls be chasing Ray-Ray . . . like even the white girls don't know what to do with theyselves when Ray-Ray come around . . ."

Tiff came back in with a two-liter bottle of Sprite and three glasses, and Deandra got quiet. Tiff stopped and looked at Deandra. These girls could feel each other's emotions like drops in the same river.

"Spicey just be askin' about Ray-Ray . . ." Deandra admitted.

"It's fine, Dee," Tiff said. She set down the glasses and untwisted the cap to the Sprite. The bottle hissed. Deandra reached over and said, "Here I'll do it," and took the bottle in her hand and started pouring everyone a glass.

Tiff looked up at Zorka. "Ray-Ray was my big brother, so . . ."

"I sorry, Tiff," Zorka said. "I say to Dee, he look so super-fly, I am sad to hear."

"Man, I remember how all the girls be crushin' on Ray-Ray, that's when Tiff was all skinny and didn't even pay me no attention, ha—Tiff don't even remember too! But I saw Tiff right away, my heart near damn burst open right then and there!"

Deandra looked over at Tiff. Tiff caught her eye and dipped her chin gently down, smiling privately to herself.

"I saw you . . ." Tiff said quietly.

"Nah, you didn't, I was like acting up all the time in front of you and you ain't even be turning your head—"

Tiff looked over and gave Deandra a self-conscious smile, then bit her lip and looked down as if she'd have a laugh, but just stayed smiling.

Deandra gave a proud one-sided grin and said, "Anyway . . ."

Her face was warm and drifting for a second. It floated over to the photo of Ray-Ray. Then when it landed she picked up her thought.

"He was gonna get a scholarship, like first Milwaukee public brother to get a full ride to an Ivy. 'Cause he was smart too. Keeping his grade up. Plus he was the only freshman on varsity and by the time he was a junior—shit, that boy could sprint that final stretch! There was this white kid, Jacob somethin', he clocked in at like 18 minutes something, like 18:42 or something, for the 5,000 meters, at the Washington Park meet, right? Well Ray-Ray fuckin' shaved that kid, broke the goddamn record PERIOD, 18:08, right? That's the photo, it was in the papers, like front and center, with them big letters, 'RAYMOND THOMSON, THE LIGHTNING BOLT.' We all be going to them track meets just for him, to see him run—well, 'cept for me, cuz I had my eye on Tiff, ha!—but yeah it was like magic, I mean he was like floating across, but his legs cutting through the air . . . But then he just drop dead. Right in front of all our eyes too. It was at Jackson Park, the one between Forest Home

Avenue and Jackson Park Drive, and 43rd cuts it off on the west, you know which one I'm talking about? Anyway it was the two-mile run, and everyone was waiting around the intersection of 43rd and Forest Home and the flags were all set up and shit, and of course who do we see on that home stretch but Ray-Ray sprinting his last yards, like a bullet with his chest out and his legs slicing the air in front of him, he was coming toward us like the goddamn Messiah!"

"Don't say that, Dee."

"I'm sorry, Tiff. But I'm serious, Spicey, that boy was like holy when he be running, you could feel it."

Deandra looked over at Tiff. "Anyway, maybe I shouldn't be running my mouth 'bout it."

"No, it's fine. I mean, she wanna know."

"What happen?" Zorka asked, swallowing her Sprite.

". . . Nobody knows," Deandra picked up. "Like even those smart-ass doctors at that Mount Sinai Hospital couldn't figure it out. Ray-Ray just grabbed his side, hunched down, and collapsed. Then he wasn't moving. Coach ran up and he was like pushing every one away and the other runners kept coming in and some ran around him and others stopped 'cause no one knew what was going on, and Coach was saying to Tiff and her granny, 'It's gonna be okay, just give him some space.' 'But he ain't movin'!' 'Give him some space,' he kept shouting. Then the ambulance came and they were shouting for everyone to BACK UP, and they got out that machine with the wires, and cut his shirt open and taped them wire-ends on his chest and stomach and they were shouting, 'CLEAR,' and Ray-Ray's chest jump up, as if he wanted to get up and run, but then it fell back to the ground, and Tiff's granny was getting in a fight with Coach and one of them ambulance men, 'cause they was pushing her away, and she kept saying, 'THAT'S MY BOY THAT'S MY BABY BOY'—And . . ."

Deandra glanced over at Tiff and stopped.

"I'm sorry, Tiff. I didn't mean to get into it like that. I'm sorry . . ."

"It's fine, Dee. Yeah, Ray-Ray was real special. Not just 'cause he was my brother, but I mean for the community too. Everyone was like, well Ray-Ray can do it . . . don't matter what . . . You know? Made everyone feel like, we can achieve whatever we want, and like if you be working for it, like reading and doing your homework, then training and practicing, you gonna get it, that's how it was. It's like what they say at church be all riding on Ray-Ray 'cause he made it happen like that."

"But why you not study and practice like Ray-Ray and get big scholarship too?" Zorka asked.

"Nah, see here's where you don't get it, Spicey." Deandra stood up and walked to the window. Then she turned around, ". . . 'cause you ain't black and you ain't even American, so you way off if you think I'm just gonna read those white-ass academics and white-wash my goddamn brain so I can get a fuckin' C+ in their history class where we be learning 'bout our presidents and the Louisiana Purchase and the Great Depression and shit, but ain't nobody gonna talk 'bout what the fuck their white asses did to *my people* . . . And ain't they real content with themselves, hoardin' us into Section 8 housing and detention centers, *'keeping the streets safe,'* white folk all 'Tough on Crime' but they just guilty as fuck about history, stashin' us away so no one sees what they done."

"Dee, relax, she just asking . . . she don't know," Tiff said, walking over to Deandra.

Deandra took a step back and turned toward Zorka. "Like seriously, I don't know what kind of fucked up shit went on in your country or whatever, and I'm sorry 'bout that too, but shit's real here. Like it's not history, it's now."

Zorka was looking into Deandra's soft round eyes, willed and faithful. "History is now," Zorka repeated.

*

After Raymond's funeral, Tiff's grandmother would open her prayer book and sit by the window as usual, except Tiff could see by her mouth that she wasn't reciting the prayers or reading from the Bible. She was just mouthing to the clouds, "Give him back."

*

"Blessed be the God and Father of our Lord Jesus Christ, the Father of mercies and God of all comfort, who comforts us in our affliction, so that we may be able to comfort those who are in any affliction, with the comfort with which we ourselves are comforted by God."

*

Deandra hated it when things got too serious. She'd always pull up her tracksuit bottoms and let out a laugh.

She kicked Zorka on the ankle with a smile. "Besides, ain't you supposed to be a dyke anyway?"

"Come on, Dee, don't use that word," Tiff said.

"I'm just playing, I mean, ain't none of my business if you into girls, unless you got a problem with it, then it's my business, but—I mean, come on, girl, what's up with your hair?"

"It's no good?" Zorka asked, touching her hair.

"You got like a mullet thing going on . . ."

"This is dyke hair?" Zorka asked.

Both Tiff and Deandra burst out laughing, covering their mouths and bending over to their knees.

Finally, when the laughter subsided, Deandra spoke. "Nah, it's cool, girl. Keep your hair like that. But everyone gonna be thinking you into girls, that's all. Are you?"

Zorka thought about it. "Yeah," she answered.

*

"For we walk by faith, not by sight."

*

Tammie had an old student of hers who was now the manager at the Marcus Southgate Cinema on 30th Street, so she pulled a few strings and got Zorka a job there on the weekends, switching between collecting tickets and indicating the direction of Theatre 1 or Theatre 2, or working behind the concession stand, asking customers if they would like sweet or salty popcorn, or a combination of the two, and if they'd like to save 50 cents by getting the menu with the large Pepsi.

At first Zorka was embarrassed and tried to make fun of her job to Deandra and Tiff, but Deandra sang out, "*She work harrrrd for the money, so haaaard for it, honey!*" and Tiff said, "You get to see some films for free then?"

Zorka snuck in Dee and Tiff whenever they wanted to see a film, and always gave them the large sweet-and-salty popcorn and two Sprites "on the house."

Tiff told Zorka that if she really didn't like her job she could ask her granny if they were looking for anyone to help out part time with the cleaning in the building where she'd worked as a custodian.

*

When the manager caught on to Zorka's favors, he pulled her aside and told her that he didn't want to have to call the police about this.

"'Bout what?" Zorka said.

"About you getting your friends into the cinema for free to do drugs."

"They don't do drug, they just watch film . . ."

"All right listen, I'm doing this as a favor to Tammie . . ."

"Why?" Zorka snuffed. "You fuckin' her behind my uncle's back?"

*

The police brought up Zorka's alien status and hinted that she was still a guest in this country and should behave accordingly, otherwise she'd risk deportation.

*

When Zorka came by the cinema that summer, they already had some blond chick working the cash register—Zorka recognized her from the bus stop. Just when Zorka was gearing up to make fun of her goody-good look, Deandra pointed discreetly in her direction and said to Zorka, "She a dyke too, by the way."

Zorka looked her over carefully.

"Oooo, you like her, don't you," Deandra continued.

"No, she is simple looking."

"Nah, girl, you totally crushin' on that Mickey Mouse club over there."

"Shut up."

"I'm a go over there and tell her that you wanna get with that."

Zorka pulled on Deandra's T-shirt, whispering, "Stop, I kill you, Dee, I swear! I do not like her, I just looking."

Deandra stepped back and Zorka let go and Deandra began smoothing out her T-shirt. "Damn, girl, why you stretch out my shirt like that. Whatever, I don't need to play no Mickey Mouse matchmaker for nobody."

She shrugged her shoulders so that her T-shirt would fall right again. "But she is kinda cute tho."

*

"For you formed my inward parts; you knitted me together . . . intricately woven in the depths of the earth . . ."

*

A couple of months before graduation, Zorka decided she needed a new look. She went to Goodwill and bought herself a tight pair of black jeans, a tight black T-shirt, and a men's leather jacket. In the end she looked like a rock 'n' roll scarecrow. She didn't want to layer up her skinny body, she wanted to show it off now, like a blade. She spotted a used push-up bra with the black lace on each cup bunched and fraying. It was 75 cents. She bought it. For the first time, she felt that her breasts rose out of her shirt, like two knuckled fists.

Then she snuck Gejza's electric razor and shaved her head.

*

There were black buckets of flowers outside of the Pick 'N Save grocery store, so she pulled a thin bouquet of soft pink roses wrapped in clear plastic and a magenta ribbon and walked off.

The Union Cemetery was between North 20th and Teutonia Avenue.

She crossed the street into an open plain of grass, with graves spotted throughout the green like handfuls of stones thrown upon the earth. As she walked uphill, the tombstones were arranged with more disciplined intent, in rows, by twos, no longer slightly crooked, but upright and all looking in the same direction. Tall cedar trees and ash trees covered the graves with netting shadows. Zorka spotted an old woman carrying a dark blue bucket uphill with a gray German shepherd walking behind her.

"Excuse me!" Zorka shouted at her.

The woman turned around and set the bucket down, the dog stopped at her side. She put a hand up to her brow to cover the sunlight and peered out at Zorka.

"How I find a grave, please?" Zorka shouted, her voice curving up, trying to be as polite as she could shape it to be.

The wind blew a piece of the old woman's hair out of her bun and the white strands flailed at her ear. The woman lowered her hand, picked up her bucket, made her way downhill toward Zorka, the brown and gray dog walking at her shadow.

"Well, it depends which grave you're looking for . . ." the old woman said.

"My brother," Zorka replied without thinking.

"Oh I'm sorry, sweetheart. What was your brother's name?"

"Ray-Ray. I mean, Raymond Thomson."

The woman looked at the pink roses then up at Zorka's shaved head.

"Sure, I remember him. The runner. Nice boy . . ."

"He was super fly," Zorka said, nodding solemnly downwards.

"You're his sister?" the woman asked with a slight squint.

Zorka shrugged.

*

Zorka got Tiff a necklace she stole from Claire's and Deandra a Tommy Hilfiger leather wallet she pulled from the Burlington Coat Factory in Brown Deer and placed a 20 into it. She wrapped the presents and took the 14 bus, got off in front of the Taqueria, and walked to the gray and red building on the corner of Lapham, pulled hard on the glass door that jammed, then stuffed the package into Tiff's granny's mailbox.

*

"Leaving? I'm sorry but that's the dumbest shit I ever heard. Wait till you graduate at least!" Deandra said.

"I do not wanna graduate."

"Come on, Z! You ain't dumb, I know it, so why you playing it like that?"

But Zorka didn't answer. Instead, she sniffed loud.

"Shit, Dee," she mumbled. Then the tears began to form in her eyes.

*

Zorka hummed a tune as she walked, the meaning distant from the melody, the melody a glaze down her throat.

It was like music for a silent film, where a woman turns the corner and the light dilates and we see with her eyes what will become love at first sight. Except this was music for a silent world, where a woman walks onto the stage and the sky dilates and we see with her eyes what will become—

Czechoslovak Radio, Wednesday, November 22nd: Wenceslas Square, 12 o'clock and 10 minutes. It's hard to guess how many people are here ... tens of thousands of citizens ... They're expressing their longing for democratic changes in our society ... The singer Marta Kubišová, who had been banned from appearing in public for nearly 20 years, will sing her best-loved song, "A Prayer for Marta."

The singer sang her prayer a cappella, give us back our peace, give us back our governance, give us back our decency . . . her voice expanding into the hollow between the mass of heads and the sky.

*

Radio Prague: Can you remember how people reacted when they heard the song?

MK: I was very high above those people, but friends told me that all the people were crying and pointing upwards.

*

Green duffle bag in hand, the one Tammie had gotten her in the hope that she'd join the soccer team, Zorka raided her uncle and aunt's money cache, a coral-colored fanny-pack tucked in the back of a sock drawer.

*

It was only when the bus crossed the state line that the murmur of memories created a soreness of unidentified longing, like for Ray-Ray with his holy lungs, running through the woods. She pushed her teeth together and smeared her face with her palms, then turned completely to the window and watched the pines passing in rows.

*

She had spun Tammie's globe one last time before leaving. She placed her index finger on the spinning surface like a needle to a turning record and listened to her nail run across the grooves of continents.

"Tell Tammie, I'm going to call the cops myself and get that girl deported."

"Marja, you're no longer her legal guardian, she's 18."

*

On the Amtrak train to Pittsburgh, a man wearing a dark business suit sat across from Zorka, looking at her suspiciously.

"What?" she said straight at him.

". . . How old are you . . . ?" he asked.

Zorka unzipped her jacket and squeezed her cushioned tits.

"I'm a porn star," she said, then zipped her jacket back up.

The man went back to reading the paper as Zorka continued to stare full-force at his forehead until he folded up the pages, put the newspaper in his briefcase, got up, and switched seats.

From Pittsburgh she kept going east, one train then another. In the stations, she studied the railway map, brushed her teeth in the bathrooms, paced about the halls, eyeing around for predators, then slept in the plastic chairs, curled up over her duffle bag.

*

The train pulled into South Station in Boston and she decided to stay a moment and have a look around the city. She got onto Summer Street and walked straight toward the flow of water. The river was curling beneath the arches of the bridge and cresting out, toward the tree-lined banks, glimmering at the sheer skyscraper with its reflective windows absorbing the sky above.

Zorka watched the water's surface unable to rush itself as much as the current insisted, folding into its own burden, and thought of Jana. That serious girl with the puddle-colored hair and slate-gray eyes. She picked up a pebble and chucked it over the bridge into the river.

"Agnus Dei and the Jans!" she screamed and pinched some air-guitar chords at her gut.

It began to drizzle.

*

Zorka stopped by a 7-Eleven to get a bottle of Sprite and some of those spicy Cheetos she liked even though they turned her fingertips neon orange. The guy at the register was looking at her. She clocked him a couple times, putting his features together in her head. Short brown hair with a side parting, the front slightly flipped up, his two eyes curved down toward his big ears, just in line with his long beakish nose, thin lips shaded by a bit of stubble . . .

As Zorka was slipping the bottle of Sprite into her jacket, he called out, "Hey," but didn't move from behind the register.

Zorka grabbed the bag of chips and began to walk around the small aisle toward the door.

"You can take whatever you want, I don't give a fuck," he said.

Zorka stopped.

"My name's Paul," he said. "You from out of town?"

Zorka gave him the middle finger.

"Oh yeah, I heard of that place. It's hot over there . . . full of flames . . ." Paul laughed and took out a pack of Marlboro Reds from behind the counter and chucked them at Zorka. "On the house," he said.

Zorka caught the pack and put it in her jacket pocket and began to leave.

"Wait, hold up. You ain't even gonna tell me your name?"

Zorka stopped and thought about it. "Zorka," she said.

"You got a place to stay, Zorka?"

Zorka shrugged.

"You wanna place to stay?"

"Not looking for rape," Zorka replied.

The man laughed.

"Yeah me neither. Shit's gross," he said. "Wait, hold on—hold up. Look. Just hear me out. Like take me, right: 36 years old, working the cash register at 7-Eleven, most people'd think, that dude's a fuckin' loser, right? Bet when people look at you, they don't see the truth neither, do they? You ain't a loser and I ain't a loser."

*

One could have called it a chance meeting. Paul was just filling in this shift for his younger cousin, Ben, who worked the 7-Eleven after school. Financially speaking, Paul was not a loser. He lived in a pale-yellow house with a teal-and-purple-painted porch in Jamaica Plain, off the orange line on Bardwell Street in south-east Boston, which his uncle had left to him and Ben after he got diagnosed with prostate cancer and tried to move down to Florida to take it easy for a couple months, but seizured in the airport and died near the baggage claim. Ben's mom was living in Dorchester with another family, and Paul's family had moved to Florida after his uncle's sudden death, thinking, life's too short. They called Paul from the baggage claim area, whispering into the phone.

"Why you whispering, Ma?" Paul said.

"I love you, Pauly, you be a good boy."

"What the fuck, Ma, why you saying that, what's going on?"

"Don't swear, Pauly."

"I'm sorry."

"I'm putting your father on the phone."

"Okay."

"Pauly?"

"Yeah?"

"It's your father."

"I know. What's up with Ma?"

"Pauly, we're okay, we're just—" His father stopped speaking and a muffling sound twisted in the phone.

"Pa . . . ? You crying?"

His father sniffed.

"Can I be honest with you, Pauly? You a grown man now so I can be honest with you."

"Yeah?"

"We're scared . . . We don't wanna . . . go . . ."

"Go? Go where?"

"You know, Pauly. We don't wanna . . . die . . ."

"DIE?! You think 'cause Uncle Hal drop dead all the sudden that it run in the family or something? I'm sorry but it was Uncle Hal's time, that's all. It ain't your time and you know it. So just relax, okay?" His father sniffed again into the phone.

"Maybe you're right . . ."

"Take Ma to the beach."

"I will."

"Get some vanilla ice-cream in a cone."

"I will."

"I love you, Pa."

"We love you too, Pauly!" his father said into the phone, then he heard his mother yell out in the background, "I love you, Pauly! Tell Pauly I love him and to be a good boy and to take care of Bennie!"

*

Ben was 20, a computer science student at the community college in Roxbury, and working at 7-Eleven part time. Paul had a series of his own start-up businesses that he ran from home, one always failing and another succeeding, each idea growing from the decay of the previous. He used to freelance on

Rentacoder.com, then built himself up as the Goldfinger, so-called because he could solve a client's coding problem in no time and always billed reasonably, then moved on to bigger clients who reached out to the Goldfinger with an emergency project here or there.

Since the house that Ben's father, Paul's uncle, had left them was big, with spare bedrooms, they decided to rent out the rooms to make extra cash.

*

In the two-story house lived Paul and Ben, Rico from Texas, Kimberley from Vermont, who hated when people called her Kimmie so Paul called her Kimmie, a French girl with rusty-brown hair and freckles who everyone called "the French Girl" 'cause she had only recently moved in, and now Zorka, who Paul announced should be called Zoro 'cause she always wore black. Zorka said that anyone who called her Zoro would get kicked in the nuts and/or pussy. She said it with such a straight face that no one called her Zoro, except for Ben, who wasn't there when she made the announcement, and promptly got kneed hard between his legs and doubled over, confused.

*

Zorka shared a room on the second floor with the French Girl, who was working at the European Wax Center on the crossroads of Beacon and Harvard. When Paul told Zorka she needed to get a job, she told him she didn't have a high school certificate. Paul said, "Not a prob!" and the next day she had a high school certificate. "You can pay me back when you get a job." Zorka took the thick piece of paper and inspected it. Then she let out a laugh. It was the first laugh he had seen from Zorka.

"I finish with honors!" Zorka exclaimed.

"Yeah, I figured . . . why not, you know. I'm sure you would've finished with honors anyways . . ." Paul said and gave her a wink.

*

Rico was different from the rest of the guys. He was short and chubby with smooth tanned skin and no facial hair except for a couple of wisps on his upper lip. He was from the Philippines but moved to Texas when he was three. Now he was studying comparative literature at Emerson College off Boylston Street in front of the Common and he was there mostly on scholarship. Rico was a shy guy. Three times a week, he worked as a cashier at Whole Foods in Brighton.

*

Zorka and Rico would sit together on the teal-and-purple porch of the house, Zorka smoking, Rico twisting blades of grass between his thumb and forefinger.

"I know career," Zorka said. "It's like doctor lawyer cash-machine."

Rico laughed. "No . . . careers don't have to be like 'doctor lawyer cash-machine,' it's like, how you want to interact with the world."

"I wanna . . . fight, maybe."

"Fight for what?"

"So people don' give me shit." Zorka looked at Rico. "You dunno shit about shit!"

"Oh yeah?"

"Yeah."

"Come on, Zorka, I'm a short, chubby, brown trans kid. You wanna know what getting shit feels like?"

While Zorka was thinking about her career, Paul got her some shifts at the 7-Eleven and Rico got her books to read during her shift. Mostly poetry books, which looked easy to Zorka because they were short lines and only a page or two. For the first time in her life, sitting behind the cash register and watching the gas pumps hung with their noses in the machines, Zorka felt a sort of calm. She didn't want to pick a fight. She didn't feel angry. She just wanted to sit and read and think and look at the sky negotiate its blues and whites.

She decided she wanted an aesthetician's license like the French Girl, so the French Girl gave her her books to study and led her through some of the waxing tutorials at home. She'd sneak back some supplies from work, heat up the wax, and show Zorka how it was done. The French Girl gave her lessons on waxing—upper lip, chin, armpits, bikini line, butt-cheeks, butt-crack, anus . . . Zorka took to waxing right away. It was methodical and intrusive and she liked that. Her favorite were Brazilians, which she imagined onto those prissy private university girls with a personal sense of accomplishment.

"I make their pussy look like a blind eye. They never see, what do they see, they see nothing."

*

Since the French Girl was completely waxed already, compliments of the job, and they had already done Zorka, and Kimberley said, "No way," and Rico had no hair 'cause he was Filipino, Paul volunteered Ben.

"Oh come on, Paul, I ain't gonna get waxed!"

"Sure you are. Zorka needs to practice."

"But I don't want to walk around with legs like a girl for a month—no 'fence, Rico."

"It'll be good for you, Ben. You too stuck on appearances anyways."

"You kiddin' me? They gonna beat the shit outta me—"

"Ain't no one gonna touch you. If you think hair on your legs makes you a man, then you can draw the hair back on," and he threw Ben a black Sharpie.

*

Ben walked around with smooth hairless legs and hairless armpits for all of that warm autumn, and something in him changed. He started coding programs just for fun, then getting curious about people who were different from him, then he crashed an MIT party where he met a girl to whom he explained that his hairlessness was a sacrifice to his sister getting her aesthetician's license.

"That's partly endearing," the girl said, "and partly super-weird."

But something about his easy way of listening and his dark bowing eyes kept the girl there.

"So you wanna tell me your name?" Bennie said with a smile.

"Nidhi."

"That's cool. I like that name. My name's Bennie. Or Ben. However you wanna say it. Nidhi, what is that, like Indian?"

"Yeah . . ." the girl said. Then, after a pause, she said, "You don't go to MIT, do you?"

"What makes you say that?" Bennie replied.

Nidhi let out a laugh.

"Just your manner of speaking, Bennie, that's all."

"Yeah, I know, right. I'm actually doin' a double, MIT/ Harvard, because I couldn't decide so I thought why not, you know. It's like at a buffet when you end up putting a chicken drumstick and a slice of meatloaf on your plate 'cause you can't decide, and it looks weird, but it's not too bad, actually."

By winter, Bennie and Nidhi were dating and Zorka got her aesthetician's license and started waxing at the European Wax Center, where it was considered a point of expertise for the woman who was waxing you to have an accent. Part of the European touch.

*

At times, Rico and Zorka mumbled to each other with clunky Russian accents like Boris and Natasha from the *Rocky and Bullwinkle* cartoon, the tall female spy with sharp eyebrows and a tight smile, and the shorter agent with two evil mustache wisps. Other times, Rico read her poetry from his classes. Zorka kept saying, "I don't get it," to all the poems, except Anne Sexton. She got that. She wrote intrepidly about all the things "no one wanna see" as Zorka put it, like menstruating, masturbating, wanting to die, addictions, incest, cheating, begging . . .

*

All My Pretty Ones

*

Anne Sexton lived and wrote in Massachusetts, Newton, Lowell, Boston. Some of her poems could be a walking tour. One that would lead nowhere, but gave you firm instructions. Like "45 Mercy Street," up and down Beacon Hill, Back Bay, Charles River . . .

Anne Sexton got home. She poured herself a glass of vodka. She put an arm into one sleeve, then the other, of her mother's heavy bristled fur coat, she slid them off her fingers, one by one, her rings, she went into the garage. She locked the door. She got into her car and started the engine, then closed her eyes and leaned back.

*

Ghosts . . .

*

Rico took Zorka to Anne's grave at the Forest Hills Cemetery in Jamaica Plain.

*

My Friend, My Friend
The Fury of Abandonment
The Fury of Earth
The Fury of Sunrises
The Fury of Sunsets

*

Rico spent every Christmas with his family in Houston. That year he invited Zorka to come down with him, and so they got into his midnight-blue Toyota Corolla, and began their road trip south-west, down past Hartford, New Haven, Krispy Kreme,

Wendy's, the 95 to the 78, around New York, past Hershey, past Harrisburg, then on the border Zorka rolled down her window and yelled out, "PEACE OUT, PENNSYLVANIA," and Rico honked twice.

They continued down through Maryland, the long 81 down into Virginia, through the George Washington and Jefferson National Forests. Zorka took a small invisible hat off her head and said with a bow, "Khello, Mr Presidents, how you do . . ." and Rico burst out laughing.

Past Roanoke, Blacksburg, Firestone Complete Auto Care, La Quinta Inn, Kingsport, "What up, Tennessee," Rico saluted, "the gays are comin'," at which Zorka began to sing the new song she made up as their talisman for driving through the South: "gay as fuck, wish us luck . . ."

Knoxville, down the 75, around the corner of the Chattahoochee National Forest, through the tip of Georgia, then onto the 59 into Alabama. Rico was tapping on the steering wheel. Then he reached over and turned the radio up and Zorka began to swivel in her seat, singing along to the lyrics with a thick pronunciation while rolling her window down.

"Missssssssyyyyyyyy!" Zorka yelled out into the passing field. In the distance, a cow responded "mooo."

*

They stopped for the night at a Super 8 Motel, the coral exterior with the yellow sign holding the dilated orange-red 8 popping out of the wood. The woman with the name tag "Candice" gave both Rico and Zorka a long look, then slid the paperwork over and handed them the key.

"Enjoy your stay," she said, uninterested in her own sentence.

They parked their car and went up the stairs, past the ice and snack machines, to the second-level rooms, 5B.

In the room the carpet was the color of mashed potatoes and the two twin beds had quilted comforters with square patterns in mauve and turquoise. On the wall was a watercolor painting of a bouquet of flowers and another of a large seashell.

*

They drank a couple of beers then turned on some music and Zorka danced around while Rico read. They talked about what Rico wanted to do after he graduated. He said he wanted to go to grad school. And to Paris.

"You wanna go to Paris, Zorka?"

"Yeah, sure, Rico. Maybe French Girl can take us. *Zhe parl an pu fransay, vou savey.*"

"You got a good accent . . ."

"Shut up."

"Ha, well no less discreet than your accent in English."

"Yeah, this shit suck big time. Wish I just have no accent and speak like you."

"No way, Zorka. It totally works for you."

"'Cause I know how to verk it . . ." Zorka dipped down, touched her toes and rolled back up.

*

They woke up in the middle of the night to yelling in 5A.

"I fucking knew it . . . !" a man hit his palm on the wall, right above Rico's bedside lamp.

"You don't know nothing," the woman yelled back. "You too busy with your goddamn self to know something . . ." The woman began to over-enunciate her words. "You an embarrassment, William don't want to see you, he tell me he don't want to see his daddy no more, you got him getting knocked 'round in school 'cause of you and he just a kid . . . comin' home with a black eye, got his nose bleedin'!"

"Oh I'm a embarrassment? Who the fuck you think pay all your bills?"

"Fuck you, that shit's called child support and it's for Willie to get his notebooks and shit for school, you asshole, it's for him to get his fuckin' hepatitis B shot!"

The man hit the wall again. The seashell watercolor swiveled on its hook.

"I ain't 'fraid of you, Mitch."

There was some pacing, then the room became quiet. The bed next door creaked shyly as each person got in it. Not long after, the couple was asleep.

Zorka got up, fixed the seashell painting, and got back into bed.

*

In the morning, they checked out, got back on the road, past Birmingham, stopping at Denny's for a late breakfast. Zorka got extra hash browns and covered them with a thick swirling layer of ketchup. They continued on the 59, crossed into Mississippi, past Laurel, past Hattiesburg, right to the tip where they could see the water, then drove on the 12 into Louisiana, Baton Rouge, Big Head's Bar-BQ, Goodwill, then the 10 to Lafayette, Beaumont, straight to that southern tip of Texas, into Houston.

"Home Sweet Home," Rico said and parked the car in the driveway.

*

When Rico and Zorka came through the door, Rico's mom was spraying vinegar on the countertop and wiping.

"Oh, take off your shoes." Rico pointed to the neat row of shoes by the door.

"Honeyboy!" Rico's mom came running into the hallway with her arms wide, her right hand still holding the vinegar spray.

"Hi, Mom," Rico said and gave her a hug.

"This is Zorka."

"Khello," Zorka said awkwardly.

"Come here, honey."

Rico's mom pulled Zorka down to her level and gave her a squeeze. "Are you hungry? I hope you're hungry."

*

Dinner reminded Zorka of those New Year parties she'd had in her building as a child, with the long table of plates of food, and her and Jana sitting under the table, whispering.

On this table: a ceramic pan of beef in a thick brown sauce with sliced green peppers, plates of cold cuts, ham, turkey, pastrami, a large aluminum pan filled with slices of pork belly, cubes of crispy fried pork, a square plate of sweetened cured pork, piles of glass noodles, dishes topped with halves of boiled eggs, shrimp, a macaroni chicken salad, bright-indigo rolls, pastries in all colors, pink and yellow and green, rows of meatballs, and finger-sized fried rolls with bright-orange dipping sauce, white rice with sliced chives, glistening barbecue skewers, white bread puffs splitting at the top . . .

She wondered if she lifted the tablecloth and crawled underneath—would Jana be waiting for her?

*

"You can call me Perla," Rico's mom said.

She went around the table, ". . . and that's Tita Karen, that's Tita Baby, that's Weng-Weng, that's Pinky, that's Joseph, that's Bongbong, that's JJ, and this is my husband, Bruce."

Everyone waved as she said their name.

There were photos of Rico and JJ, his younger brother, in frames all over the walls, around which looped silver and gold tinsel and vines of Christmas lights. There were two stuffed Santa Clauses hanging from each corner and a lit-up snowflake the size of a head in the window.

Perla said something to JJ in a different language and JJ picked up the cellophane-covered remote control, turned off the widescreen TV, and came back to the table.

"Your language is nice sounding," Zorka said.

"Thank you, honey, that's a nice thing to say," Perla replied.

"Rico, why you never speak your language?"

"Rico doesn't really speak Tagalog," JJ said.

Rico pinched his lips. "Wish I did . . . I mean, I understand it. I just can't really reply in it."

"You know when we came to America, Rico was baby," Bruce said. "Two years old. I was veteran and Perla work nursing . . . Well, we were too busy. We didn't take time for Rico. We try to make life here as quickly as we can. By the time JJ come, we were settled. JJ go to Sunday school, and we take time with him. That's how it was."

*

"Oh, honeyboy looking so handsome!" Perla said, admiring Rico from across the table.

Rico's insurance wouldn't pay for his hormones or top surgery, but his family passed around the hat, so to speak, and two Christmases ago, his present was a thin envelope wrapped in forest green paper with gold stars and a big sparkling blue ribbon. When he opened it, it was a check.

*

"You still playing *Pac-Man?*" Rico asked.

JJ pushed Rico on the shoulder.

"That was like 1,000 years ago!"

JJ showed Rico and Zorka the new *Grand Theft Auto* on the widescreen.

"It's a game where you steal cars and drive them . . ." Rico explained to Zorka.

"That legal?" Zorka asked.

"Only in video game," Bruce interjected, looking at JJ.

*

While Rico and JJ played *Grand Theft Auto* together, Zorka walked around the wall of photos and stopped in front of a middle school photo: Rico had to be nine years old, he had sleek black hair in two long braids, a boat-neck purple shirt with a purple bow on the shoulder, and wide lip-gloss-covered smile. There was a banner on the bottom of the photo that read: "Erica Joy Yee."

"Oh, that's a funny photo," Perla said behind Zorka. "Rico wanted to wear his favorite blue T-shirt and big red shorts, but I kept saying wear this dress, please, you look so beautiful in it, please—so he do it for me and he let me brush his hair out and braid it nice and neat like this. I just wanted him to look so beautiful for his school photo, you know. That was, of course, when we all call Rico 'she,' when we not yet understand, you know . . .

"Anyway, he did it to make Mama happy, and Mama was happy . . . ! But then I see Rico come home and he take off his backpack and he undo the braids and he change real quick into his blue T-shirt and his big shorts and he run around like a cloud, so free and light. I tell you, I took my two hands and I put them to my face and I say, 'Perla Perla Perla, are you blind?' Rico was happy in his blue T-shirt and his wild hair. Why I want him otherwise, I ask myself. I want Rico like this all time, running around so happy and comfortable and proud."

*

"My ma is fuck-up," Zorka said. "And my pa is dead."

"I'm sorry, honey," Perla patted Zorka's back.

Zorka shrugged, then looked away as if waiting for Perla to take her hand off.

"I want for you to be like a cloud also, Zorka," Perla continued, her hand still on Zorka, "for you to be happy and comfortable, and proud."

*

Perla hugged Zorka and Zorka let herself be taken and held and her eyes looked around the room, not knowing where to rest. As Perla held her, Zorka looked at that middle school photo of Rico in his purple dress and long braids, then she saw Ray-Ray running in the background like the Messiah, and behind them a clearing, and in the clearing a circle of poles with carved wooden horses stuck in mid-air, then a voice so devoted and reaching that it used to scare Zorka, the voice beneath the earth, behind the door, from the sky, whispering, "Zorka . . . it's me . . . !"

*

Before they left, Bruce said, "Hold on," and Perla came down the stairs in a rush, holding a 20 dollar bill.

"Honeyboy," she handed the bill to Rico. "Treat yourself."

Whenever Rico came home, his parents always gave him a 20 as a parting gift. Rico took the bill and kissed his mother, then his father, then gave them a hug each.

"See ya, Rico!" JJ yelled from upstairs, then ran downstairs and stood in front of Zorka. "See ya, Zorka."

Zorka lifted her hand to her chest and awkwardly waved to the boy. Just as she was getting ready to put her hand back in her jean pocket, Perla held out a 20 dollar bill toward her.

"You too, honeygirl," Perla said. "Treat yourself."

*

Rico got accepted to Yale for a graduate program and Paul and Ben threw the biggest party they'd ever thrown. Zorka drank too much of the grainy rum punch and kept hugging Rico, saying, "Don't go!" then running back and saying, "Go, go!" She made out with the French Girl and they fondled each other a bit on the porch until Ben snuck up on them and took a photo, then Zorka chased him around and pinned him to the ground and said, "Next time I wax your pussy, by the way, this is no joke, Bennie!" But when things calmed down, Zorka slept in Rico's bed, pressing her forehead into his back, with her arms wrapped around his resting body.

The day after Rico left, Zorka went into the empty room and sat down in the middle, mindlessly tracing the wood grain in the floorboards with the tip of the switch-blade she had stolen from Slavek's papka back in the day, with the thin snake coiling across the metal handle.

She gave her two weeks' notice and announced that she was taking her savings and moving to Paris with the French Girl, who said she'd get them jobs waxing somewhere and Zorka could work on her French.

*

Paul drove them to the airport and said, "You family now, so don't do nothing stupid to each other and if you do, just say you're sorry. Take care of each other."

*

The Truth the Dead Know

Malá Narcis

Jana was keeping count of the days, 92 since Zorka had set fire to Mr Bolshakov's boots, stolen his cash and peaced out, then snuck back and left the burning fox-fur in the hallway as her salute. The fire had left the whole floor charred and the occupants like wolves against her mamka, who discreetly packed up and left in the early morning a couple of days later. Still the girl continued to be the central topic of discussion, the neighbors exchanged their opinions, inserted their expertise, summoned up examples from literature, hearsay, history, and deliberated on the appropriate form of punishment, until the topic of Zorka became the communal means of speaking about integrity in this day and age and the protection of our vulnerable youth.

*

"She should have been put in a youth detention facility long ago."

"She belongs in jail, end of story."

"I'd drag that girl by her hair into a cell and turn the key myself!"

"I'd lock her up by her ankle with a thick metal chain."

"Like in a dungeon?"

"No, inside the house."

"It's a shame when girls choose to become criminals instead of women."

*

. . . She's sitting on the floor, in the corner, with the heavy chain on her ankle, in her flaming red dress, the one I gave her, and she looks absolutely beautiful . . .

*

"Well, it is not easy to give our young people democracy."

*

"Unlock me!" she screams, her fingers scratching at the metal ankle brace.

*

"It's true that if we don't catch them as children, we'll be paying the price years later . . ."

*

"I can't unlock you, honey," I explain to her calmly. "If I unlock you, the first thing you will do is go on the computer."

*

"Unconventional cases call for unconventional methods."

*

"I won't!" she's crying. "I promise I won't go online!"

"At that age, you can already tell the type of women these girls are becoming."

I kiss her on the forehead, always, before I leave for work. "I love you, my darling," I tell her, every morning when I leave and every evening when I come back home. "However," I must explain this to her, unfortunately, daily, "darling, despite your own efforts, you are a liar."

One evening, my love looks a little different from usual. "What have you been up to, my one and only?" I ask her. She says, "Nothing, I have been sitting here in the corner, waiting for you to come home. I haven't even stood up to use the basin you left me to urinate or defecate. I've just done both things in my underwear. Forgive me."

I touch her cheek gently and I tell her it's all right. "Let's get you cleaned up, my love," I tell her as she is lifting up her red dress and I get down on my knees to help take off her sullied underwear.

The last thing I remember is that I am crouching and reaching beneath my wife's red dress . . .

When I open my eyes, I can feel right away that my trousers are down, so is my underwear. I am lying on the ground, on my back, that is certain. I try to sit up, but I can't move my arm or my leg, even my head is pinned. I roll my eyes around and see the children, dirty faced, holding me down and smiling. When children smile from above, it is very disconcerting. Then a voice erupts from their gaze.

"Missing something?" a girl-voice says. She's wearing a big red bow on her dark cropped head, the hair jagged around her face, and her pupils are dense and pitch.

She's standing above me, her eyebrows tilting like knives, and she's holding something in her right hand. I squint and focus until I can decipher what the object is. It is, indeed, my cock.

"That's my cock!" I shriek.

"Bingo!" the girl says. "You want it back? Or should I toss it?"

"No, no, don't!" I plead. "I want it back!" She wiggles the thing above me.

"Buh bye, buh bye," she is saying in a high-pitched voice and wiggles the thing away like a fleeting bird.

"Wait! No! Wait, I said I wanted it back!"

She stops the bird's flight and my cock quivers, then settles into stillness.

"Okay, mister," she says, "but you give a little, you get a little, that's how it works. Plus, you've chained your wife to the house. That's a major red flag, you know."

All the kids begin to nod.

"But how else am I supposed to monitor her use of the world wide web?" I try to explain.

"We understand your concern," the girl replies. "That's exactly why we decided to take your dick, mister. How else are we supposed to monitor what you do with it?"

"What do you mean? I don't even do much with it. I urinate and I wash it when I wash myself and all right, I also touch myself from time to time, but we don't even have sex anymore, my wife and I. When I get home and unlock her, she always says that her leg hurts and that she's not in the mood . . . What if I give you my word, that I promise not to do anything disrespectful with my member!"

"Words are like dreams," the kids say in unison. "Dreams are like angels. Angels know when you are lying . . . even when you don't know yourself."

"But I'm not lying!"

"Listen, Mr D, let's just say I'm Snow White and I just woke up and I'm really pissed off. See what I'm getting at?"

". . . No . . ." I'm looking around and all the kids begin to smile in succession like a circle of budding tulips.

"Hey don't worry 'bout my friends, Mr D, it's a whole different ballgame for them. They're pretty homesick, you know. For me and you, well, this is just a dream. For them, it's a diaspora. Apples and oranges."

Then the lanky girl takes my cock and puts it in her blue hoodie pocket and takes out a shiny red apple and hands it over.

"Wanna bite?" she asks.

". . . No . . . thanks . . ." I'm trying to tell her, but my voice is shaky. Then the apple is pressed against my lips and her hand's gripping my head.

"Take a bite, Mr D."

Now I'm chewing and the kids are giggling around me.

"I have a friend in Paris . . ." the girl is explaining, ". . . all you have to say is . . . *I knew your friend, the Malá Narcis* . . . got it?"

I start to nod, but I can feel the apple chunks tickling my throat from the inside. I'm inhaling through my nostrils, trying to cough. The girl is reaching out her hand for me again, holding a sky-blue handkerchief, silky and limp in her fingers.

"Here you go, Mr D, mind that cough . . ."

The street named Prague

Jana lay face down, her trousers bunched right below the curve of her bare buttocks, her blouse pulled up on her back. White flesh in the darkness.

Although her body was still, her two butt-cheeks began to pull apart. From the crevice, a chatter came. The kids began crawling out, first as voices, then as bodies.

Back on the street, pigeon-toed and shy, low noses and hunched shoulders, they shuffled against each other in front of the Blue Angel bar, then began to draw up their chins, looking around.

They spotted Babička on her sewer grid, walked over to her, and crouched at the blankets, rummaging inside to curl in closer.

Then the pile on the sewer grid settled and lay calm. The lump as a whole squeezed together even tighter and tighter, their bodies condensing into each other, until the limbs and blankets began to dissolve into a blue tint, thinning into the evening air.

*

Janka . . . it's me!

PART THREE

Aimée

For the past two years, Aimée had had the sensation that she was being followed. Not by a person, but by a color. She dropped several cobalt-rimmed dishes, then cut her index finger on the fish-scale-blue knife blade she'd got for her birthday years ago. She'd thrown away her dark blue bathrobe, painted over the brine-tinted hallway of her apartment with an objective gray, and stopped smoking Lucky Strike Blues, then Camel Blues, then Gauloises Bleues, then all cigarettes, as tobacco began to taste blue to her. She began staring at her own bruises, suspicious of their shape and movement within her skin.

But all of this, as her father suggested when she confided in him, could be explained by her own desire to draw meaning from the world around her, reveal structure and repetition to hone her sensation of chaos. She could not disagree. She wavered between apathy and panic. At its excruciating pace, time vexed even the dust. So maybe she did want the company of connotation. But it wasn't just her eye picking up like-colored objects, nor was her mind giving her patterns to soothe its agitation. She was definitely being followed by a bright-blue cloud.

The first time she saw it was on the plane back from Portugal. Her head kept toppling over between sleep and wakefulness, then she leaned back against the seat and pulled up the window blind. There, among the white clouds was a solid blue one, thicker than the others, almost furry in its color. She leaned into the window, her nose against the fat plexiglass panel. The blue cloud leaned toward her.

At home, she got in the habit of mulling around her apartment, checking the street from the living room window by the bookshelf, pacing between the couch and the TV, going to the door and squinting at the corridor through the peephole.

*

It was a couple of weeks after the plane ride. She had taken time off work. The doorbell rang. The man at the door stood with his Interflora vest, holding a bouquet in dusty lavender paper. He handed her the flowers and she said "thank you" and he went back down the stairs. There, among the thick waxy green leaves were four stalks of ink-blue hyacinths. Inside the bouquet, the card was a wall-white with an indigo trim, and the writing, a rehearsed cursive. *Our thoughts are with you.* Signed, *Olivier & Angelo.* Friends of Dominique's.

She went to the window and when she looked down, there on the street, the blue cloud was hovering by the lamp post, looking up.

*

Meu Deus.

Time passed and her father made frequent visits. He told her she could take a longer leave from her job, she could even move in with him if she needed to. But she went back to work, and even began looking forward to those administrative tasks that filled eight hours of her day with purpose.

The evenings and weekends remained difficult. She felt both too exhausted to take up any activities, and too anxious to have nothing to do. She kept the TV on, the volume low, crime shows and talk shows and American re-runs dubbed in French, culinary tips, politics, history revisited.

There were months when she was getting the knack of it, worktime: filing, typing, scheduling, welcoming patients during the day. Having dinner with her father twice a week. Ruminating around the rooms to the sound of her washing machine spinning, looking out the window at the lamp post, glazing over at the TV images, glimpsing at their smiles and shrieks, hugs, chases, couples having coffee face to face, old people patting each other on the knee, a silhouette walking out the door . . .

*

Night-time, the TV is laughing. Aimée's brushing her teeth, she spits and looks up at the mirror. Her eyes trace a bulging blue vein down her neck.

*

Why did you bring lemons, miss?

She got up from the couch and walked unintentionally to the peephole, peering through into the empty corridor to the neighbor's front door, then toward the right to the edge of the wooden stairway.

At the railing, the thick blue cloud was rolling upward. She watched it crawl to the top and there it turned and began feeling its mass toward her door.

*

"Hello?" her father responded.

"I'm sorry, Dad," Aimée said. "I know it's late . . ."

"Aimée? Aimée. It's going to be all right," he said drowsily. "You're just having a tough day."

She was nodding her head to the phone. Two tears streamed down at the same time.

"Why don't you go to sleep and tomorrow it'll be better."

She continued nodding. The tears rolled over her chin and down her neck with a cold consistency. She whisked her hand at her throat and looked at her fingertips, expecting to see a blue liquid. But it was just the smear of a transparent tear.

". . . Aimée . . . ?"

"I'm here."

"You can take one and a half of the white ones tonight if you want."

"I'm fine, Dad. I have to go . . . I work early tomorrow."

"Everything's going to be all right."

There was a pause on both ends, then her father spoke. "Goodnight, Aimée," he said. "I love you."

The phrase tilted itself against the moon and fell over the edge.

*

Aimée made a decision. She stopped paying attention to the blue cloud, she stopped seeing her friends, and she stopped remembering. That's how the year passed.

*

Where shall I pin it?

*

The Monday after the medical trade show at Porte de Versailles, Aimée was walking to work down the wide street, dark suit in hand. Her father had told her he could do it himself, but she insisted, saying the dry·cleaners near her work was better. Above Monceau Park, men with pinned ties and Italian socks, pre-teens precociously groomed and styled, signature backpacks, rosy cheeks, and runway sneakers, pedaling themselves with one foot on their slick metal scooters to school. Aimée passed the Portuguese Embassy and fished out her ring of keys with the white plastic badge. At the sliding doors of the clinic, she scanned her badge on the black box and walked inside. Youssouf, the guard, was already poised at his post. She said, "Good morning, Youssouf," and went to the welcome desk, putting down her purse by the ergonomic footstool below. She reached over and turned on her computer, then went to the sliding closet in the carpeted hallway. She hung up her coat and her father's suit, took the lab coat off its hanger and fit it over her blouse and buttoned it up. She bent down and took out a pair of heels, took off her loafers and put the heels on, then walked back to the welcome desk.

"How was your weekend?" she asked Youssouf.

"Oh, it was fine. Took the kids to the zoo on Saturday. Weather was nice and warm, wasn't it?"

"Yes. It was."

"How was your weekend, madame?"

Saturday had started off promisingly for Aimée, but just as she began motivating herself to go out, it was noon and the day had already begun to sag. She changed back into her house trousers and a worn T-shirt and watched the day pass from the window, telling herself she'd go out tomorrow. When Sunday came, however, she closed the curtains and convinced herself it would rain.

All day, the sun shone broadly in the cloudless sky.

*

Aimée pushed her swivel chair closer to her desk and continued going through the phone messages from the weekend.

The doctor came in late. His first patient, Mme Mercier, was the type of woman who expressed her annoyance flirtatiously, which Dr Christian Coste cultivated, so no one was too dismayed by the 45-minute setback. Aimée organized the incoming lab results and updated two patient files, and made another appointment for poor Mme Blanchard who had another yeast infection.

At lunch, she logged out of her computer, went to the closet to hang up her lab coat and put on her jacket, and took her father's suit in her hand.

The dry cleaners was a small shop between a café and a supermarket. The woman recognized her and they exchanged hellos as she prepared her ticket. Just as Aimée moved to hand the suit to the woman, she checked the pockets to make sure they were empty. The left one was flimsy, but the right had a stiff rectangular piece inside. She reached her fingers in and felt the edges. The business card was thick, dark as her father's jacket, the letters embossed into the paper.

She angled the card toward the light and read the letters.

THE BLUE ANGEL

Bar à vin.

Rue de Prague

She flipped the card around and shone it toward the light as well. There, in the empty space was a scribble in blue ink. She tilted the card right and left to read it.

9 pm, it said.

She put the card in her pocket, handed the suit over to the woman, and took the ticket.

*

Four evenings in a row she thought about it as she sat on her couch and watched the TV screen flash. Friday, she had dinner with her father. Her eyes lingered on his knife and fork as he diligently cut his steak and matched the piece with a couple of green bean halves before putting the combination into his mouth.

Then it was Saturday. The morning felt no different than the night and by the time the afternoon came, she felt the day dripping off its face. She began to clean, to dust, to vacuum, to refold her towels and change the angle of her chairs.

Her gaze landed on the large white bookshelf. She went down the rows of books until she got to the last shelf near the floor and stopped at that blue hardcover book, sticking out of its tight spot again.

She went to her closet, slid her hand into her coat pocket, and pulled out the card.

The Blue Angel bar

Aimée walked up the stairs of the Ledru-Rollin metro. At the top, she glanced around for context. At her shoulder, Le Faubourg Café, its low-lit terrace half-filled with conversation. Across the street, the big supermarket Monoprix, and diagonally Générale d'Optique, with various pairs of glasses on display. She turned back around and walked toward the square blue P parking sign, continuing on Avenue Ledru-Rollin, away from the collective evening of others, into the dimming street that less and less people occupied.

She veered left at the Biolam Laboratory and spotted the path. Prague Street.

The road felt muted. Parked cars. Faint lamp posts. The trees, tall and bare, intervaled along the pavement, reluctant witnesses.

She eyed the door numbers as she walked, 2, 4, 6 . . . Then she saw it, a couple of doors ahead. The façade was completely black, with two square windows at each side, both painted over in black, and in the center, the door, as if no door, but there it was, as charcoal as the rest. Above it, the blue symbol glowed neon. An angel.

Aimée gave the dry black door a push, and it separated from its frame and slid heavily open, revealing two long blue curtains upon a curved railing around the doorway, the hem bunching at the floor. The door shut behind her and she slid her hand through the parting, pulling one side of the curtain open.

*

The place was small, both cluttered and somehow spacious. Ahead of her, there was a long counter on the right with four high stools in worn, dark leather, behind which were shelves of bottles of wine, all in dark blue glass. On one of the bar stools, a man in a gray suit was leaning over his glass.

To the left were small round tables with wooden chairs, all occupied by people, face to face across each table, a glass of dark wine in front of them or in their hand. Their bodies leaning in, nodding, listening, their eyes only on their companions' in an overcast concentration, mouths loitering within their voices, speaking as if they had been speaking for so long they were no longer doing the speaking.

Across the top edge of the wall crawled blue fairy lights, faintly holding onto their color. As Aimée followed their string, the lights flickered, then settled in their glow.

Beyond the soporific clientele and the man leaning at the bar, was a small dance area. The walls there were painted a bright blue, as well as the floorboards, as well as the ceiling. A small glinting disco ball hung self-consciously from a plastic gray wire in the middle, slowly turning in the empty space. Two speakers, also painted an opaque blue, were perched in each corner, filtering a steady stream of melancholic music. Jacques Brel's voice crooned through an anxious string orchestra, exclaiming with romantic exhaustion.

The volume of the song was not louder or softer than the bar chatter, all the voices balancing inside each other, moving forward together, a clock's hand.

The bartender, a tall dark-skinned woman in her 30s with a tightly curled afro and a thin nose, held a yielding surveillance over the crowd. She glanced over at Aimée and tilted her head.

*

Aimée made her way to the bar and sat down on the leather stool. She looked down at her watch. 8:51 pm.

*

"*Vous desirez?*" the bartender asked as if giving condolences. What would you like?

Aimée looked at the row of identical bottles, then said, "Red wine, please."

The bartender pulled a corked bottle off the shelf, uncorked it, and poured Aimée a glass. She took the glass, but her head drifted to the right, toward the figure sitting beside her.

The man in the gray suit lifted his glass and nodded at Aimée.

*

The song was ending and another one taking its place, the soft repetition of piano chords, then the voice of Françoise Hardy, sing-speaking in crestfallen heartache.

"It's nice music here . . ." the man said in broken English.

Aimée wasn't sure if he was speaking to her or to his glass.

"You like sad music?" the man continued.

Aimée looked over at him and squinted.

"I do," the man replied to his own question.

He tilted his head up toward Aimée. "Do you know about loneliness?" he asked.

*

The music changed again. There was a heavy chord of an organ, then a man's voice pushed fiercely through the reverb. He sang a couple of lines, then cut himself off, whispering abruptly, "*Je t'aime!*" The organ squeezed and expanded.

"This is beautiful song," the man said, turning back to his glass.

"It's Léo Ferré," the bartender inserted as she wiped the counter again.

"Leyo Feray," the man repeated as he looked deep into the remaining wine pooled at the bottom. "I try to remember."

"*Je t'aime!*" the singer shouted out again into the mournful music.

The man took another sip, then began to cough. As Aimée turned toward him, he reached inside his jacket, pulled out a sky-blue silk handkerchief, and drew it toward his face.

The string of lights began to flicker again. The curtains shook as if the door on the other side had been opened.

Aimée looked down at her watch. *9 pm.*

The stool to her right was empty and the bartender was wiping its place clean.

The bloodstream

The Zentiva representative was younger than Jana had thought it likely for such a company to send to an important sales meeting. He looked not long out of university, her brother's age just before she had left Prague. The rep shook the Frenchman's hand, trying to squeeze it and smile at the same time. He thanked him for the thoughtful exchange at dinner but before he could finish his own phrase he added that he did not want to insist, but he felt it was important to underline that Zentiva delivers high-quality, cost-effective pharmaceuticals for the international markets, all their generic medicines have tested extremely well in relation to the original branded drug in the bioequivalence clinical studies, the active ingredient releasing into the bloodstream at almost the identical speed and quantity as the brandname medicine. Jana translated for the client as the Zentiva rep interrupted her, adding that they are the guaranteed ideal supplier of choice, then stumbling over a couple more statistics about their respiratory and central nervous system pharmaceuticals.

The client listened to Jana, then shook both of their hands and told them he had a generous amount of information to consider.

*

As the French client walked toward the main street to get a taxi, Jana shook hands with the Zentiva rep and told him she thought the meeting went well. The rep exhaled in relief and shook her hand again with gusto.

As she walked away, she imagined him on the plane tomorrow morning, back to Prague. She saw him fumbling with his seat belt and trying to close his tray. She saw his knees, awkward in the dry suit fabric, lean right, left, trying to find their place in the allotted airplane seat space. She saw the back of his ears, oddly clean, the habit he inherited from his grandmother of rubbing the corner of the towel there after he washed. She saw his head turned toward the window, watching the clouds squeeze from one form to another, like slow-beating hearts, and sitting there, trying not to wrinkle his business suit, watching the sky, the smile on his face, so unprotected, extempore.

*

Have you seen my hair gel?

*

Jana kept on walking. It was, no doubt, one of the sloppiest pitches she had ever interpreted and she was near certain his offer would not be considered any further.

*

Her shoulder hit the man's.

"*Prominte*," the man said in a hurried Czech. Beg your pardon. As he stumbled off, the top of his eggish head reflected the moonlight.

Jana caught her balance and looked up. Above her, the salient blue light shone from the electric angel.

*

Her hand was pushing at the black wall, which parted and became a door. Inside, the blue curtains were being drawn open and Jana's legs were moving her forward toward the bar, where she was now sitting on a stool. She glanced to her left. The blond woman was looking down at her watch.

"It's 9 pm," the woman was saying to her wrist.

*

The doctor that's speaking at the Global Plastics round table, that's my father . . .

*

". . . He has a way of thinking about limbs," Aimée was speaking to her watch at the bar, "like there is no barrier between our bodies and medical supplies, like there is no physical movement we cannot find a way to simulate."

The bartender set a glass of wine down in front of Jana and she reached for it, parting her fingers and sliding the stem into their crux.

"I don't want to simulate my body anymore . . ." Aimée continued.

*

"Do we know each other?" Jana asked the woman.

The lights began to flicker again. Aimée straightened up and looked over at the woman sitting next to her, lingering on her face.

"I was hoping we did," Aimée replied.

*

"Aimée de Saint-Pé," the woman pronounced for Jana. "Would you like to dance with me?"

*

They made their way to the dance area, their bodies somehow delayed from their stride. The disco ball turned gradually above their heads and the melancholic music played on, voices yearning, beckoning, regretting . . . It played through their thoughts like an itching of memories.

Jana looked at the blue walls around her, then at the blond woman at her side. She realized that she had no idea how to dance to such a slow, languorous song. Her shoulders began to sway as she studied the woman. Aimée's eyes were closed and her torso twining to the verses.

*

. . . N39 . . .

The lights snowed down onto the tops of their heads.

Jana's hands lifted and settled on the woman's waist. She stepped in closer to her. Aimée reached around her as well. Jana could feel her blouse wrinkling beneath her gliding palms as she went up her back, then settled upon her bare nape, each finger closing in a bit of heat. The woman's hips were grazing against Jana's and her breasts leaning into her own until the two women were face to face, their breath mixing together.

The song began melting into another one, in which the strings creaked and the quivering voice of Jeanne Moreau sang an ode to the troubled sky.

The music moved them together and they let their eyes float within each other as if down a river.

*

The taxi drove past the Madeleine metro stop, taking a slight left up Rue Tronchet.

"Right up here," Aimée said and the taxi slowed to the curb in front of her building.

The two women stepped out and the taxi drove away.

Inside the building, Jana walked behind the woman, hand on the wooden railing of the stairway.

The woman turned around and smiled into the darkness, reaching her finger down to the lapel of Jana's coat.

*

Liné

The key clicked and Aimée pushed the door open. The light switch flicked, she was undoing her coat, and Jana, glancing around, her fingers untying her own coat belt, her eyes gazing at the powder-colored couch, pitch-black oval coffee table, TV screen, rug, picture frame, and then settling on the large white bookshelf, each row full of books, a stuffed mouth.

"You like to read," Jana said, approaching the shelf.

"Those aren't my books," the woman answered and reached out to her, taking hold of her wrist. "Come here . . ." she said as she pulled Jana back into her own body.

*

Aimée's hand was hooked into Jana's as she was leading her down a hallway.

*

The forest sweats its leaves and the stems of flowers break and moisten at the fissure.

*

In the bedroom, the bed made, the curtains drawn, only the half-open door lets in a cut of light.

*

"Are you afraid," Aimée whispered, "to kiss me?"

Jana was reaching up to take hold of the woman's face, leaving the woman's question unanswered, covering it up with her movement, she tilted her head into the darkness until she felt her lips touch the woman's.

The woman opened her mouth and grabbed at Jana's breath.

*

The woman's hand was on Jana's stomach, wedging under the waist of her trousers, her fingers unclasping them and pulling the zipper down. Her hand was working beneath, reaching into Jana's underwear, then inside, to where her middle finger pushed into the soft flesh, rolling her fingertip around the ballpoint and smiling at her and whispering, "Does that feel good?"

Jana moaned with her mouth closed and the woman slid her index finger down along her slit toward the opening, circling the place within Jana where she could, at any moment, go deeper.

*

The woman was lowering herself to the floor, pulling Jana's trousers down, then her underwear, ringed at her ankles. She reached one arm around her legs and grasped her thigh, the fingers of her other hand opening up the slit, then she lowered her warm tongue inside the folds. Jana's knees softened, but the woman clutched the flesh of her thigh as she pushed her face into Jana's wetness, letting her tongue rub down from the top of her slit toward her opening.

Jana held onto the woman from above, squeezing her shoulders.

*

Aimée stretched the muscle of her tongue, inserting the tip into Jana's opening and licking the rim as Jana gripped her shoulders tighter.

*

Jana was reaching down toward Aimée's face, pulling her up now and kissing her, her fingers running through the woman's mouth, Aimée's tongue weaving through Jana's fingers.

*.

Aimée was on top of Jana on the bed, her flexed hand in between Jana's legs, sliding her fingers into Jana as her thumb circled the outside.

*

"Come for me . . ."

*

Aimée's knuckles were rimming the opening with each jut, and Jana swerving into her clutch.

*

"Come for me, come for me, come for me!"

*

The blue vapor seeped from the large white bookshelf, gathering itself into a cloud and moving down the dim hallway toward the opened door of the bedroom.

U there?

Dominxxika_N39: Sexy Amy . . . ? U there?

0_hotgirlAmy_0: I'm here! I'm here!

Dominxxika_N39: O I so happy u r online!

0_hotgirlAmy_0: Me too! I've been going on like every chance I get! But u're never there!

Dominxxika_N39: My husband is hang around so much since he get back from business trip. Now he gone but he come back soon.

0_hotgirlAmy_0: Did he lock the door and windows again?

Dominxxika_N39: Yes . . .

Dominxxika_N39: And . . . he . . . chain me . . . to bed post . . . on my ankle.

0_hotgirlAmy_0: WTF?! Serious??

Dominxxika_N39: He just get sweaty and nervous. But do not worry, my beauty, I drag whole bed to the doorway, and chain long enough for me to use living room computer.

0_hotgirlAmy_0: Omg. We gotta get u outta there.

Dominxxika_N39: Lock and chain is iron. This is not possible.

0_hotgirlAmy_0: It is possible! Stop saying that, we'll figure out a way.

Dominxxika_N39: I'm scared . . . there is no way. I cannot break free and meet you at Jewish cemetery anymore.

0_hotgirlAmy_0: That doesn't matter. I'm coming.

Dominxxika_N39: What?

0_hotgirlAmy_0: I'm coming to Prague and I'll get up to Zelevcice and I'll save you!

Dominxxika_N39: This is high ambitious plan.

0_hotgirlAmy_0: I have almost 800 dollars in my savings account. And my mom is always forgetting her wallet around the house. And I'm gonna be 18 next week.

Dominxxika_N39: Your birthday? O my beauty, my love, how I want to wish you happy birthday with my kisses.

0_hotgirlAmy_0: You can. You can!

0_hotgirlAmy_0: I'm getting outta here and I'm coming to Prague! I'll take out the 800 next Tuesday. Then use my mom's credit card to buy the ticket for Friday. Which is also my birthday. So, whatever, no one can stop me, I'll be 18.

Dominxxika_N39: O my dream, I am waiting for you!

0_hotgirlAmy_0: Send me your adrs. And the times your husband is away each day.

Dominxxika_N39: O you are such brave girl!

0_hotgirlAmy_0: I love you, Dominika. And Archangel Michael told me, it's all going to be all right.

Dominxxika_N39: I love you million times from my throat, in my eyes, and on my fingertips!

0_hotgirlAmy_0: Don't lose hope! One week!

Dominxxika_N39: I will touch your whole body with mine and I will hold you in my arms and you will be my angel.

Someone is going to come

"They want me for the part!" Aimée and Dominique were jumping up and down, holding onto each other.

*

The play was at the prominent Théâtre National de Chaillot near the Eiffel Tower, in their epic Jean Vilar auditorium, seating 1,250, moreover it was that famous Polish director, the one who, a couple of years back, did Goethe's *Faust* vertically, meaning he hooked all his actors into rock-climbing ropes. It was about mortal gravity, and the devil. The critics loved it.

For his next production he decided to simplify. He was suddenly done with concepts. It was his theatrical homecoming. He wanted good actors. He wanted to feel that feeling when you watch someone experience something, breath by breath. Instead of backing up, he longed to get closer. And so the Polish director went with none other than Jon Fosse, the Norwegian playwright hailed as the contemporary Beckett, the purified Ibsen, the master of silence.

It's true that the Odéon Théâtre de l'Europe in the Left Bank, one of France's six national theatres, already did Fosse's *Dream of Autumn*, appropriately last autumn. But quite frankly, both Chaillot and the Polish director thought that they could do Fosse better.

They chose Fosse's very first play, *Someone Is Going to Come*, about a man (HE) and a woman (SHE) who buy an old house in the middle of nowhere so that they can get away from everyone and everything, and be alone together. As soon as they get out there, though, the anxiety begins between them that someone is going to come by. The man assures the woman that they are finally alone now, no neighbors, no friends, no distractions, they can relax, and just . . .

SHE
A beautiful old house
Far away from other houses
and from other people

HE
You and I alone

SHE
Not just alone
but alone together
[. . .]

HE
And no-one is going to come

But then, someone comes. A younger man to whom this house belonged in fact, who had sold it and moved into a more suitable place for himself, ironically becoming their nearest neighbor. He came by just to say hello and see the house . . .

*

"They want me they want me they want me!" Dominique was clenching her fists.

Aimée put her arms around Dominique.

They were kissing now.

They were on the bed now.

Through the window, *Die schönen Berge*, with those 72 waterfalls and the braggart gods in the clouds.

*

They went out to dinner that night at the restaurant called Oberland, recommended by Klaus, who urged them to try the potato rösti. Dominique even put on her favorite heels that she was always packing and never wearing, the shiny leather pumps.

*

Although the younger man, the previous owner of the house, is the only one in the near vicinity, his visit unravels the anxiety further. He could come back at any time and say hello again. He could invite them over or invite himself over. And did one of them, within the couple, secretly hope that someone would indeed come?

*

On the train back, Dominique fell asleep in the crux of Aimée's shoulder.

When she woke up she said she had had a dream where she tasted something sweet, so sweet . . .

"Do you ever taste in your dreams?" she asked Aimée.

*

". . . so sweet, like honey, but somehow . . . bitter . . . at the end."

Then Dominique told Aimée about Homer's *Odyssey*, when Telemachus, Odysseus' son, is depressed after failing to find his father, and Helen comes to him and mixes a substance into their wine so that ". . . all sense of woe delivers to the wind."

*

I Am the Wind

*

Dominique started rehearsal, and she was a completely different person it seemed, always in a whirlwind of her thoughts and ideas and explanations.

"It's my favorite Fosse play," she kept adding when she explained what she was working on, "excluding, of course, his most recent, *I Am the Wind*, but that's for two men stuck at sea, and the casting is not flexible apparently, they *have to* be men, because *only men* can be lost souls, women—women are ghosts . . ."

*

One afternoon, after having lunch with her father in the 16th arrondissement, Aimée passed by Café du Trocadéro. On the terrace, she spotted Dominique sitting with Claire, two espressos on the table. Dominique was speaking with so much light in her face and Claire was listening with delicacy, sliding her hand up and down Dominique's forearm.

*

"It's not like that, Aimée . . ."

Dominique explained that Claire was doing the make-up for this show as well.

Aimée bit her tongue and dreamt that she was trapped in a car sinking into the ocean. She was pounding at the windows but they wouldn't break. Then she looked over and in the passenger seat, buckled in, already unconscious, was the platinum blond scalp and freckled face. Claire!! She was shaking the body. Claire!! Where is Dominique?

*

Dominique's 42nd birthday was in March. They invited everyone over and Dominique wore her favorite heels with a new tight-fitting wine-colored dress, the fabric sleek, almost rubbery, with a heart cut out at the chest.

"Hope I'm not too old for this dress . . ." she mumbled to herself in the bathroom.

Aimée snuck up behind her, slipping her hand up her skirt, whispering, "You make me so wet . . ."

Dominique pulled her hand out and readjusted her dress. "Baby, please . . ."

*

Dominique took her pills and slept like a log. Aimée sat up in the darkness and leaned over toward her. She kissed Dominique on the mouth very lightly, so as not to disturb her, then licked her own lips, trying to see if she could find the sweet taste.

*

"I'm not going to explain myself every time I come home!"

*

Aimée closed the bathroom door and pulled down the thick gray towel from the rack. She pushed her face into the bunched terrycloth she was gripping and screamed into the folds.

*

"Baby, baby, baby—guess what? I have a surprise for you . . ."

*

Dominique was rehearsing the whole end of spring and early summer, but they decided to take advantage of the small holiday before the opening night as a treat for all the hard work—for the show and between them as a couple. It was their last chance to be together before the show went into intensive rehearsal for its premiere at the Festival d'Automne in Paris, late September.

Dominique brought up Portugal, she hadn't been in years and Aimée had never been.

"But not the city, I don't want to go to any city," Dominique insisted. So they booked their tickets to Estoril, a resort town in the south of Portugal.

They landed just before noon, slammed the door to their hotel suite at the Albatroz Hotel on the beachside, which they had booked disregarding the price, and ran straight down to Praia da Conceição. The sand was yellow and warm, already filled with color-blocked umbrellas and towels. Children sank their small feet into the swampy sand of the waterfront and shrieked, then fell onto their butts and spotted a shell and stared at it. Groups boozed in the sun. Parents rested. Tan people tanned. Aimée and Dominique dropped their blue-and-white-striped unrolled towels and hurried forth, over the sprawled resting bodies, toward the water, which was rising in its lenient waves, folding toward them, foaming in grays and whites. The women nudged each other forward, saying *"desculpa"* for each other when they stepped on someone's towel edge, then pushing the other again. Around them curved the bumpy mountains, which were thinly coated with the fur of low plants, boulders sticking out this way or that, as the women sauntered right and left, and Aimée slapped Dominique on the side of her thigh and Dominique turned around and managed to flick her back right between her legs. Aimée shrieked and the children on the waterfront turned their heads, but they both ran forward into the water and by the time they were swimming, they were already reaching into each other's swimsuits.

Dominique swam away. Aimée called out for her, but Dominique dunked her whole body under and pushed herself far through the thick water into glimmering blindness.

*

Through the tall open windows of their hotel suite, the sun was setting heavily as if being ground into the horizon, leaving amber shards of light inside the salon on the dark wooden table and the cushioned footstool and the glass-tiled lamp.

*

Their swimsuits lay abandoned and sopping, Aimée's red-and-white-striped bottom and stringy top soaking over each other in a pile on the lime-and-red carpet of the hallway, and Dominique's one black clump in an outline of water on the white tiles of the bathroom floor.

In the salon, Aimée was naked, wet hair on the floral sofa, her hand grabbing the oval coffee table next to it, trying to grip it, her fingertips sliding off. Dominique on top of her, her dark hair letting go of droplets of water down her back as she was twisting into Aimée, kissing her neck, biting her flesh, reaching for her mouth, which fell open and Dominique licked the contours inside.

*

The heavy bronze curtains were pulled to the side, the golden tassels from them swung with each bit of breeze, the palm trees cut into the setting sun.

*

Aimée's head was tilting off the sofa, her mouth open, catching the sky. She was glancing over at Dominique, watching her brim with eagerness. She felt elated by Dominique's breath, by her touch, the wetness of her tongue upon her skin. It was almost like falling in love again. *I forgive everything*, the phrase raced through Aimée.

But when she reached her hand between Dominique's legs, there was a dryness there. Before she could find her eyes, Dominique had pulled Aimée's hand out and flipped her over.

"Shh . . ." Dominique whispered in Aimée's ear, "let me . . ."

*

Aimée's forearm knocked the TV remote and the hotel magazine to the floor, the pages flipping and caving into each other. She was spread over the coffee table, her arms wide and her breasts pressed into the waxed tabletop.

Dominique grabbed Aimée's hips, and pulled her back with a thrust, Aimée's buttocks spread and pressed into Dominique's pelvis.

The ocean rolled and cracked beyond the window, grays and whites, lined with the water's orange rind. A thin amber light cut across Aimée's back.

Dominique took her fingers and began crawling them around Aimée's cunt as Aimée was moving into Dominique's fingers, which crawled down farther, dipping into the crevice of Aimée's ass. Dominique placed the tip of her finger at the center of the tightest hole and began to push inside. One push, one more, and Aimée's anus took her in, the muscle squeezing around Dominique's finger in its silky coated choke. Then she pulsated her finger in that tight space, sliding deeper with each jut.

*

Aimée came in a torn voice and flipped around, reaching out for Dominique just as she was leaning back. Aimée's hands grabbed the air and fell back down to the floor empty.

Dominique was still, going over Aimée's face—her resting cheekbone, the shine upon her jaw, the lenient pull of her throat, her blond hair clinging to her neck, and in the center, the vulnerable dip between her collarbones. Dominique reached out her hand and put her fingertips upon that spot, feeling the fall between the two bones and the thin skin there.

Aimée was peering at Dominique's irises, the black pupils wide, and the dark mahogany around them glazed, but there were thin traces within that rich brown circle that she had never noticed before, they were almost invisible, fine lines of a bold blue. Dominique let Aimée look at every thread of her iris. She could feel her wife going over the incremental colors like a finger over a row of book spines, but her touch couldn't read the stories, it could only grope at their bindings.

Dominique inhaled and broke their gaze. She crawled on top of Aimée, moved some of her blond hair away from her neck and put her mouth there, and lay breathing her humid breath as Aimée swallowed the sky.

The weight of Dominique on top of her felt like a mass of water and she thought of her dream in the sinking car, hunched-over Claire with her blond hair and blue skin, the empty back seats, the bubbles from her mouth. *Where is Dominique?*

*

That night, Dominique slept without waking up or mumbling, holding Aimée tightly in her arms.

It was Aimée who woke up. It was not yet dawn. Dominique was peaceful with a consistent breath. Aimée was surprised she was sleeping through the shouting. It was coming from the window they had left open in the adjacent room. Next door, a couple were arguing on their balcony, their voices carrying into Aimée and Dominique's suite.

She carefully took Dominique's arm off her, got up, and went to the balcony windows. She closed them discreetly, and then tiptoed back into bed.

*

The next morning, there was a knock on the door. Dominique got up, put her robe on, then came back with a plastic bag with her shined leather pumps in them, held together with a large rubber band.

"They shined them for me."

"Are you going to wear them tonight?"

*

Though Dominique had promised no work during their holiday, she convinced Aimée to take a walk for an hour or two, as she just wanted to go over a couple of scenes, that's it, she said, she wouldn't do any more after that.

They kissed in the doorway.

When Aimée left she noticed the skin on Dominique's hand, around the glossy nails, was ripped and chewed.

*

Aimée took a walk down Frederico Arouca Street, then turned north toward a garden she had spotted. She crossed the street and walked past the fold-out tables, one with cheap jewelry and another with piles of books. Between the stone fountain and the span of freshly cut grass was a merry-go-round, the roof a white-and-tan-striped tent, music tinkling and the plastic horses going up and down. Behind the carousel leaned an immense willow tree, the cernuous vines resting on the roof beams, where a row of light bulbs flickered.

When she left the park, she looked at the sign, Jardim Visconde da Luz, and made a note to take Dominique here when she was done rehearsing. On her way around the streets, she spotted bright-red flowers with ridged petals, ones with tiny magenta buds and white eyes, pinkish tiger lilies with yellow-spotted tongues, others with alternating yellow and violet petals, then a daisy patch.

She took the curving road up, past the car rental shop, then saw some people walking with blue plastic bags full of fruit and vegetables, so she followed the track up, then around to the smaller road, Padre Moisés da Silva, into the large covered market. She wandered around the stalls and stopped at the green crate containing a layered pyramid of bright-yellow lemons. She wanted to buy just one to show Dominique, but ended up getting a kilo of them. She got out of the market with her kilo of lemons in a thin blue plastic bag and sauntered across the street to smell an almond tree she had spotted, blooming with its peach bunches of flowers at each branch. She walked past the glass-paned shopping center, stopped to touch the beautiful cobalt-blue painted tiles that covered a façade, thinking of Dominique's irises, then looked at her mobile phone and realized she had been wandering for over an hour. Although she wanted to go back already, she thought she should give Dominique her space, let her indulge if she wanted to rehearse a bit. So she walked back down to the beach, took off her sandals and stuck her toes in the yellow sand. She sat, watching the waves, but couldn't enjoy them. She felt like a punished child, all she wanted to do was go back and be with Dominique, to pull her outside and walk around with her, take her to all these places. She began making angel wings with her feet in the sand, wiping them back and forth, as if they could fly up from her heels. She looked at her phone again. Finally, two hours had passed, and she got up, dusted off her shorts, put her sandals on, and headed back to the Albatroz Hotel.

*

(A knock)

*

Aimée walked up the carpeted hallway, got out her key card, and slipped it into the door. The light flashed green and she turned the metal doorknob and pushed the door open. It slid across the carpet like a crashing wave. There were Dominique's high heels, standing orderly side by side. She put her bag of lemons on the coffee table and looked around. The bedroom door was closed. She took a couple of soft steps toward it, wondering if Dominique was still working. There was no sound in the suite. She tiptoed up to the door and put her ear to it. Completely silent. And yet, she could feel there was someone in there. She waited for a weight to shift.

*

Who's there?
A friend!
A beast!

*

"Dominique? I'm back."

She turned the doorknob and pushed the door open, shushing every bristle of the carpet in its path.

Face down on the hotel linen, the body—

*

Dominique was slumped face down across the bed, still, naked, a plastic bag cinched over her head.

*

No no no no . . . !

*

Aimée, with her arms reaching out far in front of her, grabbing for Dominique. She began to lift her naked body up, but it was heavy and fell back toward the pillows. She stumbled, then turned the body over and let it fall against her, then back down to the bed. Her fingers scrambled beneath the rubber band around her neck, trying to get it off. It snapped and flew across the room. She tore the bag off. Dominique's lips were pale and cracked.

"No no no no . . . !"

She let go of the body and drew her hands to her scalp, then dropped her hands down to her sides.

"Dominique, no . . . !"

She climbed onto the bed and leaned her ear near Dominique's mouth. She couldn't feel any breath there. She put her two fingers on her throat, then to her wrists, but couldn't find a pulse.

"No, no!"

She pulled Dominique's body up again by her armpits and tilted her weight against herself, then slid her clumsily off the bed, then laid her on the rose-colored carpet.

She got on her knees beside the body, then sprung back up again and went to the phone at the bedside, picked up the receiver, her hand shaking and rattling the plastic device against her cheekbone.

She dialed and said *no no no* as it rang.

When the front desk picked up, she tried to say it, but her mouth kept stuttering, "P-p-pa-pa-po-por-por favor por favor-orrh-EMERGENCY!! AMBULANCE!!" The receiver slid from her grip and fell down onto the carpet and bounced. The voice of the front desk clerk was still rattling out, but she was back on her knees now at Dominique's body.

"Okay okay, okay okay," she told herself.

She placed the heel of her left hand just below the sternum, then her right on top, and began to pump, *un deux trois quatre cinq six . . .* until she reached *trente*, thirty. Then she leaned down, pulled the corner of the bed sheet to wipe the cold saliva from Dominique's mouth, tilted Dominique's head back, lifted her chin up with two fingers, pinched Dominique's nose and put her mouth completely over her wife's and breathed one long breath. Her mouth tasted sour and spoiled. She looked to see if her chest was rising. There was no movement. She turned to her again, put her mouth over Dominique's and gave her one long, strong breath, then a second. She looked at her chest. It was as still as the mountains. She put her palm back on Dominique's sternum and began to pump, *un deux trois quatre cinq six . . .* She leaned down, pinched Dominique's nose, put her lips firmly over Dominique's and exhaled, exhaled, exhaled . . .

—un deux trois quatre cinq six sept huit neuf dix onze douze treize quatorze quinze seize dix-sept dix-huit dix-neuf vingt vingt-et-un vingt-deux vingt-trois vingt-quatre vingt-cinq vingt-six vingt-sept vingt-huit vingt-neuf trentre—

"DOMINIQUE!" she screamed.

She leaned down and gave her two more breaths.

Un deux trois quatre—

There was a knock on a door.

She kept pumping.

She heard the beep and the sliding door and the footsteps on the carpet. He stopped at the doorway to the bedroom.

"*Meu Deus . . .*" he said under his breath.

She looked up. He had acne all over his face and his hotel-shirt was slightly untucked.

"AMBULANCE!" Aimée shouted in English.

The young man began nodding but stood still.

Aimée crawled over to him and started pushing at his legs until he stumbled back, then ran off. She turned toward Dominique and put her palms to her chest again and began to pump. Droplets rolled off her and hit Dominique's chest and slid down her ribs. Aimée thought, why is she sweating?

Un deux trois quatre cinq six . . .

"Please, please, please, please."

Another droplet hit Dominique's neck and rolled down into the dip between her collarbones. Aimée drew her hand to her face and realized that the droplets were tears coming from her own eyes. She smeared her cheeks dry and wiped her nose against the back of her hand, then leaned back down and gave Dominique two more breaths.

"Please. . ."

Aimée took two fingers in a hook and pushed them to the back of Dominique's throat, feeling the mucus gathered there, fishing to the right then to the left, but Dominique wouldn't lurch or vomit. She took her fingers out and grabbed Dominique by her shoulders, shaking and screaming at her face.

"DOMINIQUE!!"

The whirling sound of the ambulance filled the street. More footsteps. The manager was pacing, pushing the young clerk out of the way. A dark-skinned woman with bangs, and a blue-eyed, red-bearded man behind her, both wearing forest-green trousers and matching button-up short-sleeve shirts tucked in and belted.

"*Fala Português?*" the woman said, leaning down.

"I don't speak Portuguese!" Aimée yelled back. "We're on holiday here!"

"Please, madame," the man said in a nasal tone, buzzing his consonants. "Please, move aside."

Aimée looked up at the man, but all she could see was the patch above his heart with the thin red snake.

The woman touched her shoulder and repeated, in a more determined tone, "Please, madame, come here, madame . . ." She pulled Aimée up and led her away from the listless body of Dominique lying on the rose carpet.

The man was already on his knees, his fingers at Dominique's neck, then wrist.

Aimée screamed from behind the woman, "I checked already!"

"Are you a doctor?" the woman asked in a soft voice.

"No . . . but . . . my father is . . . I—" she began pushing past the woman, yelling, "I already checked all that, please, please, she's going to die!" The woman held her back by her shoulders. It was almost a hug.

"I understand, madame. Please help us. Can you tell me what medication this woman has taken?"

"It's not 'this woman'! She's my wife!" Aimée screamed, trying to see beyond the woman to what the man was doing on the floor with Dominique.

"I understand. Can you please tell me what medication *your wife* has taken?"

"I . . . don't know . . . I don't know . . ."

The man was unzipping a pouch and getting the defibrillator out. He stuck the wires on her chest, then on her side. Aimée was trying to nudge herself past the woman, looking over her shoulder into the bedroom.

"Clear," the man pronounced in Portuguese and Aimée saw Dominique's body jump up and fall back to the carpet.

The woman was suddenly holding a square packet of pills in front of Aimée's face.

"Are these hers?" she asked.

"Uh . . . yes, they're just . . . antihistamines, they're not . . . lethal . . ."

Then the woman was holding a capless empty plastic bottle of medication, unfamiliar to Aimée, the ingredients written on the label with bulky print, "m"s or "z"s or "d"s . . .

"And this, madame?" the woman asked.

"Clear," the man said again from the bedroom. Aimée jerked toward the doorway. She could see Dominique's chest pulled up, then thrown back down against the rose-threaded ground.

"I . . . don't . . . know," Aimée was saying, trying to get past the woman, who kept trying to get her to sit down.

The woman pulled up her walkie-talkie and said something in a hushed Portuguese. Another man was coming in, wearing all forest green, along with the manager. The forest-green man had a stretcher. Aimée began to scream at the sight of the stretcher. *Afaste-se, madame, por favor,* Step aside, she felt her eyelashes on fire, DOMINIQUE!! *Estapa de lado, madame,* move aside, DOMINIQUE!! Aimée's hands grabbing at things that turn soft, pillows, blankets, towels, WHAT THE FUCK ARE YOU DOING, *Por favor, madame,* GET OFF ME, *Por favor,* DOMINIQUE PLEASE, Aimée's reaching out her fingers, *Meu Deus,* PLEASE DON'T GO, *Por favor, madame!* Then she's gripping through forest-green fibers and thin red snakes, for the body, somewhere, within the leaves of hands, flesh, just beyond the fingertips, Dominique, fleeting across those woods, where rows of trees are scratching out the daylight from her eyes.

PART FOUR

The forest

Before Jan Zajíc, the second student, took the train to Prague and went into No. 39 on Wenceslas Square to set himself on fire, he wrote a letter to his family.

He ended the letter with, *Say hi to the boys, the river and the forest.*

Directions

Dominxxika_N39: At bus stop, there is another road. Road goes up, like hill. On one side, field is only plowed dirt—nothing planted yet. Other side, bushes, one two three four five. Behind, farmhouse. Go up hill, stay on farmhouse side. Metal road barrier soon will break on this side. 500 metres in front of break, three small houses, red roof shingles. Go through barrier opening, follow row of tall trees.

0_hotgirlAmy_0: Okay.

Dominxxika_N39: Then you see wire fence. This is beginning of big hospital-bed plant. Follow fence line, but not touch fence (it is security, maybe electric shock I do not know), just follow fence line. Then it open on another road. So you get on that road. And there, one house, distance on hill, but has blue fence, close to road. This is my favorite fence, because wires are knit close together and when it rain, it make dew-drop pattern in fence like wall of tears. It is beautiful like u.

0_hotgirlAmy_0: *blush

Dominxxika_N39: Follow beautiful blue fence. Then fence end. It look like there is only big forest in front of you. But it is not true. Continue straight. Straight, straight, straight, into forest. Thick trees, dark, wet soil, muddy, be careful. On other side, you see the dirt path. The dirt path lead to my house.

0_hotgirlAmy_0: And which one's your house?

Dominxxika_N39: There is only one house on this road. This is where I live.

0_hotgirlAmy_0: Okay.

0_hotgirlAmy_0: . . . Dominika?

Dominxxika_N39: Yes my beautiful Amy.

0_hotgirlAmy_0: I'm a lil scared . . .

Dominxxika_N39: O my love, I am lil scared too.

0_hotgirlAmy_0: . . . oh.

Dominxxika_N39: But it's ok, my angel. Remember, we are together.

0_hotgirlAmy_0: Yes, we are!

0_hotgirlAmy_0: It's just that . . . I'm really scared.

Dominxxika_N39: O my Amy, you are also really brave.

0_hotgirlAmy_0: Yeah.

Dominxxika_N39: Do not forget to pack ur cute jeans.

0_hotgirlAmy_0: Okay.

0_hotgirlAmy_0: . . . Dominika?

Dominxxika_N39: Yes my angel.

0_hotgirlAmy_0: I'm really, really scared.

The sky

I'm all out of pee now, Mamka.
—why certain children couldn't be born and others just dropped
down dead—
He's whispering . . .

I think my ears are going to shit.
I knew your friend.
You dunno shit about shit
So what is violence?
Her eyes of green venom glowing in the spotlight . . .
Go play!
Even her knees were mesmerizing.
Dominique, I swear to God . . .
I never asked—
you knitted me together
Die schönen Berge
holds the body of the patient in "zero pressure"
No, no, no, no, no
I hope you like sad music.

                    No, no, no, no, no,
        I THOUGHT I WAS THE LOVE OF YOUR LIFE
(Give him back.)
        I don't know what to do with History,
Go online, Amy
        the big one that belongs to all of us
Go downstairs, now.
        and my small one, like a keychain.
. . . wish us luck . . .

        Shh . . . Let me,
        But I can't see you . . .

        Does that feel good?

The dress

Aimée put on the form-fitting black dress that Dominique had picked out for her years ago. Aimée had worn it, to please Dominique, to those social occasions when she was present as Dominique's wife, a cocktail party, after-show party, birthday dinner—but no matter the event, it never seemed to fit her body or the occasion. It was too stiff or too tight, or too elastic, too close to her own flesh, groping through her skin toward her skeletal structure, disapproving of where her limbs extruded, arced, softened, receded, or hinged, insisting its own form and order upon her figure, determined to be more her skin than her own skin, like pencil-lead being pressed into paper, commanding another silhouette, to squeeze out a more natural voice from her waist, a more natural roll from her pelvis, a more natural spiral for her DNA helix, to flick the tongue in her mouth and glimmer the eyes in her sockets and tip the weight toward her toes.

*

Not just the dress, but also. Gestures, but also. Words, but also: nature's will. Pencil-pokes and paintbrush strokes. A dead rabbit flopped next to a branch of tears as plump as green grapes, a rash-red pomegranate spread wide, kernels glistening like siren songs, a lemon rind curling off like the same old story, but also: *nature morte*—still life or life stilled—that woman (in the movies), who knows when to stand in the shadow, and when to let herself be kissed, and when to die off.

*

Every time, the dress demanded, by its curve, its zipper, its thickly stretched fabric, that Aimée be more flirtatious, that she coil and tease like a modern woman while still appeasing her ancestors with a reverence for tradition, that she indulge in her own allure, while regulating it with the permission to be alluring, that she fit in with her sexy contemporaries, stay young enough by growing older to look younger in such a dress, worthy of having a partner in such a dress, worthy of their fidelity, of their eye on you, their hands on you, their mouth on your mouth in the bathroom while the dress digs into your waist and with your eyes closed you imagine that pressure is not the dress, but your lover's grasp, a validating pinch, bestowed—at the end of the night, in their bedroom, Aimée peeled off the dress, her flesh exhaling in a timid claim to its freedom, as Aimée looked down at her skin lined with imprints of the threading, the zipper, the seams, etchings, notes of critique, stipulations from the dress, zipped up and back on the hanger now, and Aimée, left to her own nakedness, looking across the room at Dominique, trying to read her eyes.

*

"Come to bed . . ." Aimée coyed, but Dominique was undressing too slowly and too silently. Aimée got on her hands and knees and serpented across the soft mattress toward Dominique as if she were still wearing the dress, as if the dress could formulate language for her, use her voice to whisper into Dominique's ear, *Do you still want to fuck me?*

*

It was the last time she'd wear this dress, Aimée decided as she put it on, and as she walked around and gathered the faint condolences at Dominique's wake, she realized—it finally fit, this dress, it fit her body and the occasion. It engulfed her and it erased her, it made her a silhouette of just the right woman. A black hole, a lapse in memory, someone else's orgasm, someone else's blood-rush, someone else pumping for life, heart, pelvis, nervous fingertip on the table, restrained, aligned, and polished nails catching the light—the rest of the body, standing up, sitting down, waiting, waiting for someone else's gaze to fill her ellipsis.

Aimée could almost grasp it, the cohesiveness—her, occasion, context—but it unthreaded on contact, strings of feeling, mysterious, as it had been throughout her life: a moment of seemingly unfounded fury or an arbitrary dunk of despair or an erratic spasm of repugnance, at her, the occasion, the context, at the fact that something of her womanhood was failing her like a sickly organ, the mysterious rage whose scream always came out in a wheeze, a sigh, a yawn, her breath unable to grasp the source or reason for the lack of air.

Not continents, but also. Not urine, but also.

*

Not silence, but also. Betrayed by language, we use phrases like tunnels.

*

Years back, when Dominique was rehearsing late and Aimée couldn't stand to be alone inside the apartment anymore, she texted her friend, Mathieu, who told her to come by and have a drink with him and see his cousin, who was a bassist in the jazz quartet playing at a bar near Gare de l'Est. When she arrived at the steps of the terrace, the passageway glowed between the chatting smokers as if, through this doorway, everything between her and Dominique would be okay.

On stage, the blond jazz singer was wearing a tight-fitting black lace dress from head to toe. Aimée watched her sing and thought without thinking, *When she goes home and takes off the dress, what of her leaves her body?* But the thought quickly lost its words and became an unreadable sensation, a prickling of humiliation for that blond jazz singer standing so openly in front of the public in her lace container, betraying something of herself so deeply in the lines of that threadwork pressed into her flesh, souring in the spotlight.

"My cousin says, apparently," Mathieu whispered to Aimée as they watched the singer, "she's sucked them all off in the band, even the bald piano guy!"

Aimée jabbed Mathieu in the rib. "Don't be gross," she said.

"Hey I'm not the one who's doing it, she is—and you're killing the messenger . . . !" Mathieu nudged back, then made an angel with both hands fluttering up as he whistled a small gunshot and let the angel plummet down to the counter, wriggling his fingers and warbling in a cartoonish voice, "Help, help, angel down! I've been shot by a feminist!"

"Grow up . . ." Aimée said and sipped her beer.

"Hey, I'm sorry," he whispered. "I was just trying to cheer you up, you know . . ."

Aimée glanced over at Mathieu without a word. Then, she moved her eyes back to the stage.

"Hey, listen . . ." Mathieu tapped her arm gently. "It'll be okay, Aimée, it really will, I promise. But in the meantime, seriously . . ." Mathieu pointed a low finger toward the stage, "she *does* have a ridiculous rack, right?"

*

Between nature and artifice, there was blame. Herself, or, herself through someone else, or herself through herself through herself, until it became someone else.

*

Dominique's mother and her Catholic face, always wiser than someone else's pain, too wise for emotions and for the body, too faithful to be fooled by mortality—*was this the face she made when Dominique's father slit his wrists over the Book of Saints?*

This woman who had refused to go to their wedding but was now attending Dominique's funeral. *Did death make your daughter a heterosexual in the end?* Aimée tried not to cringe as she exchanged glances with the woman, feeling suddenly irate and stubborn, she wanted to go straight up to her and tell her that this *sexy black dress* that she was wearing was Dominique's favorite in fact, and as Aimée imagined the tense exchange that would ensue, there was a jolt of vengeful innuendo, pleasing her body, a muscular clutch of satisfaction, but after a couple of hard flashes, it was all gone, bravado and purpose, and the rest of her was left, a floppy carcass, held together by the dress, a fistful of sadness.

Sadness being an opaque word, a stone in the mouth.

Sadness like a language dubbed over our lives, to which we are moving out of sync, our feeling swaying outside the lines of our speaking and doing.

Sadness like the eye on a cooked fish, like the eye of her father when he takes off his glasses to look at her, like her own eyes in the mirror when she catches herself without meaning to.

Sadness like the inanimate objects that look as if they so desperately want to be able to say something—that wooden chair with a rounded back, the heart-leafed plant, the top potato in the yellow-netted bag. Sadness like dead matter hoping for voice, and like living matter yearning to be rid of it.

Sadness like the dream, where people are just people and we let them come and go without realizing that in real life, these people are gone, some long gone, and it was only in the dream that they came back, and we did nothing to savor their presence—we just let them—come and go, like perhaps, in real life.

Exactly like that, sadness, that dream, where she is calling on the telephone, you know it's her, ringing, and you don't pick up, where she is outside the door, and you know it's her, knocking, and you don't open—and then you wake up, and you curse yourself and you spend all day checking your phone and opening and closing doors, windows, cabinets, and drawers, a badly dubbed slapstick on rerun.

*

Dominique's mother put her palm on Aimée's shoulder and nodded, then she took her hand off and went down the hallway.

Aimée heard the door close and she glanced into nowhere, as if to seek out eye contact with oblivion, to be released of the sensation of her body, of her shoulders, or at least of that shoulder, the one Dominique's mother had just touched.

"Have you eaten something?" her father's voice asked.

*

Somehow the day had turned into each attendee bringing something or saying something or doing something that was "Dominique's favorite," as if everyone, all together, were pitching in to reconstruct Dominique through the history of her singular tastes.

*

The foil was crinkling like stars fighting to keep their light. Claire was unwrapping the carrot cake as Aimée came into the kitchen.

*

"Olivier asked me to come," Claire said.

"Did he?" Aimée replied from the doorway.

"Yes, he did." Claire gave a half-smile and let her glare thin out. "I brought her favorite cake."

*

"Pethidine—Demerol and Dolantin," Aimée recited.

Claire stopped cutting the cake into squares.

"That would take what—72 tablets of 50 milligrams each, that means you're unconscious within 15 minutes or latest by 50 minutes, given the lack of oxygen provided by the bag."

Claire's brow pinched upward.

"Or Methadone—Dolophine and Adanon," Aimée continued, "300 milligrams, 60-ish five-milligram tablets . . . Or . . . just morphine, that's about 200 milligrams, 13 15-milligram tablets, no, 14 to be sure . . ."

"I don't understand what you're talking about, Aimée," Claire interrupted.

"It's just that there's a procedure to these things, Claire, they don't just happen magically; it's quite meticulous, I mean, you really have to think it through, like how would she know that she'd have to drink something hard with it, Claire, and take an antihistamine so she doesn't vomit it all up, and put a bag over her head—"

"Aimée, I—I'm really sorry . . ."

"Thank you. Thank you for saying that. Did you come here to say that? Is that what you told Olivier you'd like to say to me and he said, you know what, you should come in person and say—just let me finish, even if I am the puppy dog at Dominique's side, the one she shooed and kicked away, the one you are all laughing at, the one who keeps coming back with her wet nose—but she was my wife and I get to be her widow now, and it's my right, it's my goddamn right, Claire!"

"Listen, I'm—I guess I shouldn't have come."

"You guess so? Is that your wildest guess just now?"

"*Mais merde*, Aimée! You know, you're not the only one who—"

"Claire, I swear to God, if you finish your sentence and that sentence is that you lo—" Aimée swallowed.

"You'll what?" Claire said, sliding the cake knife across the table toward Aimée.

*

I never asked—

*

The evening closes itself gently like a storybook, and Aimée takes one of her father's pills and drifts between the covers as if rolling unhurriedly around her eyeball.

The dream unfolds as if it has been waiting for her, and her hand is reaching for the long blue curtains and pulling them open and stepping inside.

The string of blue lights begins to flicker, then jolts to a halt and becomes a blue-lit line around the walls. The customers at the tables are speaking to each other and sipping their glasses, all their voices brushed together, not a single strand sticking out. The bartender is standing behind the bar with one hand on the counter, blue rag, soft palm, wiping in slow circles.

From the blue speakers, an accordion squeezes a solemn chord and the dry voice of Yves Montand tells the story of those who love, those who are separated—

The bartender stops her wiping and looks up at Aimée.

"*Bonsoir,*" she says.

"*Bonsoir.*" Aimée's voice emerges from her mouth as the bartender is putting a glass of red wine on the counter and Aimée is glancing down at her lap, two legs, touching at the knees, sitting upon the bar stool. Her right hand is reaching for the glass of wine, the ridge against her lip, the liquid somehow syrupy and bitter.

The accordion stretches and folds back together, but the sound feels like it's coming from her organs. Aimée is placing the glass of wine back on the counter. She is lowering her eyes, loosely gazing, and there, a small clean hand is tugging on her leg. The little girl is wearing a powder pink baseball cap too big for her head. When she tilts her small face up toward Aimée, a blond princess in a blue gown is sweeping on the front of her cap, beneath the princess's feet in embroidered cursive, the teal threading spells out *Cinderella*. The large beak of the cap shadows the girl's face down to her nose, and at each young-lobed ear, her blond hair is gathered in neat pigtails that balance like sunshine above her ironed cotton dress with an eyelet fringe. The fingertips of her other hand are reaching at the edge of the countertop, trying to get up.

"Here." Aimée lifts the little girl up and places her on the stool beside her.

The girl fixes her oversized cap upward, so that she can see. She looks over at Aimée and her eyes are glittering blue.

"*Děkuji,*" the girl says politely in Czech. *Thank you,* a distant voice translates between Aimée's ears.

When the girl lowers her chin to smooth out the fabric of her dress with her delicate fingers, the baseball cap falls back down over her forehead.

The girl fixes her cap again and looks up at Aimée.

"*Proč jste přinesli citrony?*" the little girl asks in a curious voice. Her eyes are sparkling impossibly. *Why did you bring lemons, miss?* the translation echoes.

Aimée looks down, her hand is gripping the blue plastic bag full of lemons. She lifts it over the counter and hands it to the bartender. The bartender takes the bag and nods one simple nod.

Aimée looks back over to the girl. Her posture is straight and her gaze is fixed upon something just beyond Aimée, her small arm, perfectly horizontal, pointing past Aimée's shoulder to the dance floor.

The disco ball is turning sleepily, sprinkling shards of light onto the blue dance floor, where, in the middle, the naked woman in dark leather heels is swaying to the music. Her back curves right, then left, she is stepping back and forth in her pumps, shifting the weight of her nudity, back of the knees, thighs, the buttocks tense, release, she is dancing, her spine bristling through her flesh. At her nape, the ends of her rich brown hair are jagged like a shriek, sticking out from a clear plastic bag suctioned over her head, held in place with a thick rubber band.

The woman turns around as the music sweeps, her arms floating to the singer's voice. She is looking at Aimée, the plastic bag clinging to the contours of her face, cheeks, eye sockets, between her lips. Her right hand lifts, fingernails dig beneath the rubber band and she tugs the bag off, as if undoing a mask, the plastic peels up, and her hair drops over her shoulders. The dancing woman opens her eyes and exhales through her nostrils, strings of blue smoke.

Aimée is reading her lips as the blue smoke is lacing and unlacing out of her mouth. Aimée is walking toward the woman, reaching out her hand, touching the woman's skin now. She is trying to find her own hand with her eyes. It is inside the woman's hand. And her body, against the woman's body, below the disco ball, swaying to the music.

Aimée lowers her head to the woman's shoulder and her fingertips begin to trace the woman's back, spine, and hip. The skin is a perfect temperature, so conscious to her touch. Aimée pushes her face deeper into the woman's neck until the woman's lush hair falls into her eyelashes and cheeks, the scent of branches. She is tightening her arms around the woman's waist and holding her against her stomach.

Aimée's lips are moving into the woman's throat. "Come for me . . ."

*

Fanny Ardant Fanny

*Ardant Fanny Ardant Fanny Ardant Fanny Ardant Fanny Ardant
Fanny Ardant Fanny Ardant Fanny Ardant Fanny Ardant Fanny
Ardant Fanny Ardant Fanny Ardant Fanny Ardant Fanny Ardant
Fanny Ardant Fanny Ardant Fanny Ardant Fanny Ardant Fanny
Ardant Fanny Ardant Fanny Ardant Fanny Ardant Fanny Ardant
Fanny Ardant Fanny Ardant Fanny Ardant Fanny Ardant Fanny
Ardant Fanny Ardant Fanny Ardant Fanny Ardant Fanny Ardant
Fanny Ardant Fanny Ardant Fanny Ardant Fanny Ardant Fanny
Ardant Fanny Ardant Fanny Ardant Fanny Ardant Fanny Ardant
Fanny Ardant Fanny Ardant Fanny Ardant Fanny Ardant Fanny
Ardant Fanny Ardant Fanny Ardant Fanny Ardant Fanny Ardant
Fanny Ardant Fanny Ardant Fanny Ardant Fanny Ardant Fanny
Ardant Fanny Ardant Fanny Ardant Fanny Ardant Fanny Ardant
Fanny Ardant*

*

Aimée woke up into the gaunt light seeping through her curtains,
her eyes opening and settling upon the face in front of her, still
sleeping upon the adjacent pillow, the eyelashes in a delicate arc,
the faint brow, the loose light-brown hair, fair skin, and those
serious lips, even in her sleep, somehow determined—then
there is a prickling across this woman's face, around her nostrils,
between her brow, and—

Jana's eyelids begin to flutter, then lift.

*

"Good morning," Aimée murmurs across the small white valley
between their faces.

Jana shifts from her pillow, her ear lifting then pressing back into the cotton, sinking with the weight of her head.

Good morning, her thoughts are swallowing up Aimée's voice.

There is something hardened about me, yes. It started before the Soviets, before my birth, before the Jans, before. I was always afraid to kiss you. I don't like melancholia. But I suppose I'm something of that shape. A fleshy grudge. Isn't it funny, yes, what we do, with our freedom. Last night, yes, I was afraid, because I have been afraid for so long, to kiss you. Would you understand something like that?

You said, Come for me.

Even before, do you understand, before my brother started losing his hearing and before Milena was dug up, before my petty life, before the Berlin Wall was built and smashed, before the borders were proclaimed and violated, I don't know if you would understand, I mean before Jesus Christ, before microbes, in the astrological gases, wasn't there something of me, and wasn't that something of me already coming for you?

But then that something got a body and such, and you know, matter and non-matter, to align all that, it takes a lifetime, at best, most of the time it's just us, finding matches for our doubt. But everyone wants to believe. I mean, everything, everything believes.

Even a stone, yes, believes itself a bulb waiting to bloom. Even that stone, the one in the palm of a violent intention, the one that is swung and that breaks the skin of another, even upon contact, the stone believes it has a gentle face that will . . . petal . . . out . . . one . . . day . . .

So I spent my childhood waiting. Waiting for a significant sort of pain like a starting point. To begin. I wanted to finally begin. All that being, without a beginning—girlhood was a too-hot cup of tea I had to keep carrying back and forth without spilling and, of course, the ridges of my hands burnt, a banal inflammation, not yet the Great Pain, the starting point. Womanhood was our solution.

Not just in Prague, everywhere, everywhere, wasn't it? Wasn't it like that for you, too? Our solution to the anxiety of non-being, of waiting to begin. I couldn't wait to have a grown woman's body, do you understand, so life could finally, truly . . . hurt.

I was so ashamed of our kiddy pain, squeaky, clumsy, Zorka and I prowling for credibility, asking when, when would life hurt in a womanly way, all of it, my ambition and my intellect and—the limbs of me that still, despite what everyone told me without telling me, believed themselves to be touchable, though no one touched me, not even to violate me, no one did (except Zorka, and that's a very long story and with her, I had no choice but to play it cool, to be a precious stone, hard-faced, restrained).

But still, I hated that part of me, the very small mouth of me, the wanting mouth, despite all reason, wanting to be touched.

I was a child, then I was brainy, then I was on my own. I'm afraid, yes, that I missed something. That's why I was afraid to kiss you, that you would feel that lack with your tongue, that you would taste it on me. I missed becoming a woman because I spent too much time asking, when will it begin, when, when, and suddenly I was asking, when will it end, when, when, and I didn't savor the way life hurt already, I didn't dare to whimper, but I was scream-ing the whole time, for life, for life, for life, so suddenly, last night, between my mouth and yours—

*

"Those books, in the living room, they're all my former wife's . . ." Aimée began. "What I mean is, I guess I should tell you, just that . . . I used to love someone very much . . . I'm sorry, I didn't mean to start off like that, I . . . I don't know where to begin, but . . . suddenly it was the end and I didn't know what to do with the living I still had left to do . . . without her, so . . . you're the first person I've—"

Aimée pursed her lips together and let them go.

"Me too," Jana said.

"You too . . . what?" Aimée smiled.

"I'm also . . . a little . . . scared."

Party time

Olivier hadn't called Aimée since his messy break-up with Angelo, so when she saw his name on the caller ID she had assumed he was having a relapse and picked up the phone ready to console. To her surprise, his voice was chirpy, joke-spun.

"Come to the party, Aimée!" he heralded.

Aimée was caught off guard, unprepared for her isolation to be challenged.

"I can't . . . I mean—maybe you should come over or we can get a coffee, it's been years and I just don't know these people."

But Olivier explained that it was at his new boyfriend's place, and all his friends would be there, and his boyfriend was turning 25 and Olivier was turning 45 this year, and then he started explaining to Aimée that he just wants one person there to be sincere to him.

"I know I'm being insecure about it," Olivier said. "It would just mean a lot to me, to have you there . . ."

"Is Claire going to be there?"

"No, she's not. Don't worry. Plus bring whoever—by the way, wait, are you—that's it! You totally sound like you're seeing someone!"

"I'm not—I mean, it's recent, so—"

"Aimée, I'm so happy for you, *chérie*, this is exactly what you need! Bring her!"

"I'll think about it, okay . . . ?"

"Please, please, please, please—"

"I'll—"

But before Aimée could finish, Olivier was smacking a flutter of kisses into the phone and exhaling a long "Thank you" with a certain gravity that made Aimée think of her 13th birthday, the way she filled her mouth with air and gusted toward the constellation of flame-tipped candles flagged into thin white frosting of the cake placed on the table by her father's two hands.

*

Olivier had taken the women's coats and the bottle of red from their hands and said "Welcome." He laid the coats on the white-toned bed in the bedroom, which was simply decorated, a sensitive oblong cactus on the floor, next to a lamp, then some bare nails in the white wall, onto which were pinned certain photos of fabric, one grainy blue wool, another a stiff yellow linen.

"So, this is who I've been telling you so much about, this is Aimée," Olivier beamed.

"Hello, Aimée," Erki said in a uniform tone.

Erki was a designer, originally from Estonia. He was one of those whiz kids, a hot new thing who had learned French fluently, spoke Estonian, German, and Russian, and a bit of Finnish. He was raised by a single mom who cleaned houses and took young Erki along to help. Erki got into trouble at school. He got caught kissing a boy, then beat another one up with a rock until his face was unrecognizable.

"Stay away from boys," his mother told him, "and lend me a hand."

She gave him things to sew up and mend. He ironed and washed and folded for her. When there were extra scraps, he made odd things out of them that made his mother laugh.

Even if now he was making more than ten times her salary, he still kept his own place simple and spotless.

In Paris, he'd found himself an entourage he called the EB, the Eastern Bloc, who were the romantic cowboys of their countries' cultural and economic isolation, and put their childhood disparities into fabrics, cuts, and fashion statements. In the folds, seams, zippers, leather, those memories became Western fetish of the failed Communist dream.

Erki stood with reserve, his flat reddish-blond hair parted perfectly in the middle, slicked down just past his jaw and tucked neatly behind his ears. In one earlobe was a thick metal ring, and in the other a stud. His bottom lip stuck out from his underbite. His marigold-colored hoodie was tucked into his high-waisted trousers, looped with a thick leather studded belt, the marigold sleeves overly long, dangling past his hands.

*

"And this is Jana," Aimée put her hand on Jana's back, then slid it around her waist.

*

"*Ot kuda tih?*" Erki asked flatly, in a slightly accented Russian.

"*Iz Czeskaya Republika,*" Jana answered in Russian. "But I live here now," she switched back to French.

"Jana speaks six languages," Aimée added.

Erki nodded and smiled.

"EB linguistics," he added. "Let's get you ladies a drink."

*

After both Aimée and Jana got their plastic cups of red wine, Erki disappeared into the crowd of highly stylized friends, but kept looking over at Jana, sharing an estranged complicity across the room.

As more people squeezed by, Aimée and Jana found themselves in the hallway. Some people were waiting for the bathroom and some were smoking by the window. Aimée slid her hand around Jana's waist, then drew her closer. Jana leaned over and kissed Aimée below her ear, feeling the thin golden earring touch the top of her lip.

"Thank you for coming here with me."

*

Jana had gone to the bathroom when the doorbell rang once. Then it rang a succession of four times, as if someone was attempting to puncture the buzzer. Aimée was leaning against the wall in the doorway, sipping her wine, waiting for Jana to come back. She looked around and caught eyes with Olivier who smiled with a widening gratitude at her, a liquored curl to his lip.

The buzzer jabbed three more times.

"I'll get it!" Aimée shouted into the crowd and went to open the door.

Just as she turned the handle, the door pushed open and the woman almost fell in, catching herself.

She flipped up her head, letting the crown of her lacquered platinum-blond hair catch the light. Her face was tan with soft freckles across her nose. She had purplish lipstick and her furry pale-pink coat was hanging amply open.

She looked up at Aimée and her smile slowly evened out.

"Oh," Claire said at the door.

Claire took another step forward and Aimée took a hesitant one to the right. Behind Claire, another woman gave her a little shove and said, "Come on!" and jabbed Claire to step inside. The woman followed, long-legged in her thick-waisted loose combat trousers with two big pockets at the knees and an over-sized stone-colored bomber jacket open, showing a skin-tight red mesh turtleneck tucked in, beneath which one could see the folds and seams of her leather patchwork bra that pushed out angularly through the sheer top. Around her neck hung a gold necklace holding up what appeared to be a namesake in the middle, but instead of anyone's name, the letters simply spelled out: SUCK IT. Her head was shaved, revealing an even dark stubble, her face pale, with dark eyes, dense pupils, jutted eyebrows, and lipstick so red it looked neon.

The bathroom door opened and Jana stepped out. Across the crowd of people, she saw the two strokes of eyebrows and the hardened pupils. Both women stood still, clasped in their glance. Then the woman opened her blazing red mouth and yelled out in a rasped-edged voice, "Janinka!"

*

Zorka made her way through the crowd toward Jana, as Claire made her way behind Zorka, as Aimée made her way away from Claire, in a direction that would curve back to Jana.

*

"*Jste nezměnili . . . !*" Zorka said to Jana. You haven't changed.

"You know her?" Claire said to Zorka, but Aimée took it as being addressed to her.

"Yes, she's with me," Aimée responded.

Zorka looked over at Aimée and gave her a squint. She opened her mouth and began speaking an accented French. "It's fucking crazy," she said to Aimée, "we grew up together. In Prague. How do you know—what's your name again?"

"I didn't tell you the first time. It's Aimée."

"*Enchantée*, Aimée," Zorka gave a bow and oily smile, then turned to Claire, trying to read her expression. "What? Is this your ex or something?"

Claire gave Zorka a pinched glare. "I . . . used to . . . work with . . . her wife . . ." she replied warily.

"Wife?" Zorka exclaimed, "You shitting me? For real? Fuck! This is like 21-century-lesbian-level-shit—dykes getting married! Could you have even imagined such a thing back in the day, Janka—Wait, hold on, wait that means—Janka, is this your girlfriend? You a dyke too??"

Aimée's face flushed, but Jana somehow cooled very quickly and became focused, untouchable.

"Yeah, I am a dyke too, Zorka," she said in an uninvolved tone.

Zorka flicked Jana on the shoulder, then gave her a meaty thumbs up.

"Dyke-o-rama!" Zorka grinned at the women, then reached out her long arm and grabbed the bicep of a passing girl with two thick braids woven tightly down her scalp.

The girl turned around, and Zorka gazed at her bare lips and large eyes, the pupils medallions and muddy-green, through her left nostril a thin golden hoop.

"Hey, you a dyke too?" Zorka blurted out.

"You'll have to excuse my friend here, she's got no manners," Claire said politely as she traced her eyes over the girl's tight green top.

The girl gave a faint shrug, then turned back and continued making her way through the crowd. At the other end of the room, she looked back again at Zorka, who pursed over a grin at her. The girl gave a toy-smile in return.

"Listen, honey, I'm so sorry, I didn't think Claire would come!" Olivier stammered to Aimée in the hallway. "Honestly, I didn't know!"

*

Jana could hear Zorka from across the room, surrounded by the crowd, with Erki at her side, telling a story about her Hungarian grandpa and how he used to exclaim, *"Lo' fasz a seggedbe!"* A horse dick in your ass!

She was streaming in jokes about Catherine the Great and her supposed fetish for horses and how she had a contraption built for her wherein a horse could be lowered down into her.

"Zorka, I could see you as like this dark stallion," a shorter American guy with a pudgy face and square glasses said.

"With a thick one . . ." Oleg, a tall ghoul-faced Russian in the group added, "just how you like it."

"Yeah, then you could sit on my dick," Zorka replied to Oleg. She glanced over at Jana, then quickly brought her eyes back to the group.

*

Whatever the others in Erki's entourage thought of Zorka, everyone knew that this ragged Czech turned art-piece was his muse. Even Claire could feel that somehow Zorka was becoming sacrosanct, and when the heat of Zorka's attention was on her, she felt the impulse for rudeness and brevity to protect herself. She even started seeing a friend of Erki's, Céline, who sometimes brought a dildo or two in her backpack to clubs, just to have them on hand.

One time, the gang was hanging out in Olivier's living room, early evening, Céline lying on the couch with her head of dark wavy hair in Claire's lap. Claire stroking Céline's scalp and glancing over at Zorka. Zorka picking something out of her teeth with her fingernail. Erki with his arm around Olivier, sharing a joint. The chubby American flipping through his Instagram on his phone. Then Oleg started talking about how fucked up it was that if you don't use one black model in your show, everyone calls you a racist.

"Why don't they," Oleg continued, "drive through every village in Russia," he looked over at Zorka, ". . . and put in one black person a piece."

Zorka flicked the gunk off her fingernail.

"I told you not to fucking say shit like that," Zorka said.

"Baby got a sharp tooth growing . . ." Oleg tried to reach out and finger at Zorka's cheek, but she whacked his hand away.

There was a moment of silence for someone to switch the conversation, but Oleg jumped in again, fretful at leaving things where they were left.

"You spent way too much time in the U S of A, Zorichka, got you bleeding your panties over every boo-hoo word."

Zorka tensed up, but Erki reached out his foot and kicked it between the two, at Oleg's shoulder.

"Shh . . . I'm relaxing."

"Yeah, me too, I'm taking it easy," he adjusted his trousers. "Just saying, Zorichka's acting like a dykey Amal Clooney over here, all high class with her human rights—"

Erki smiled at that and the American chuckled into his phone screen.

"When reality is—" Oleg continued. "Now hold on, don't get pissy, baby, I am too, we both crawled out of the shitty Soviet asshole. And now we're all mixed in with the fancy 'Europeans' and the fancy 'Americans' with their good names and good noses and their fresh cheeks—" Oleg leaned over and started poking at the American's cheeks.

"Aww, you're so cute, my chubby free-world sweetheart," Oleg said in a puckered voice.

"Hey, that tickles." The American squirmed until Oleg took his hand away.

"Sooooo cute especially when they act all proud of themselves for their democratic values and equal rights and their fair-handed politics, saviors of our civilization—awwww, it just makes me want to squeeze their little soap-smelling asses!" He tried to grab at a bit of the American's stomach sloping slightly over his waistband.

"Hey, stop it!" the American said. "I do not smell like soap."

"You totally do . . ." Claire chuckled.

"Don't worry, I like the soap baby smell," Oleg continued, "just, can you clarify one thing I don't understand and maybe it's 'cause I didn't grow up with so many different types of cereal and TV channels and so on, but, like: if you are so afraid of dictatorship, why are you always telling your people what they can and can't do, what they can and can't say . . . getting all nervous about keeping things equal all the time . . . ? Like, in America," Oleg began chuckling, "for every white fag I'd fuck, I'd have to fuck a colored fag too?"

Céline began to laugh into her cigarette, but her breath cut as Zorka pulled the switchblade from her ankle and lunged at Oleg, who jumped up to his feet as Zorka to hers, gripping her hand over the thin metal snake on the handle of the knife, the tip of the blade stopping just in front of Oleg's crooked nose.

Claire let go of the piece of Céline's hair between her fingers. Erki sat up. A click snapped from below and everyone looked down. There, near Oleg's feet, was the American holding up his phone.

"Ah shit, that's such a cool photo!" he said.

"Let me see," Erki said, reaching out his hand.

"Zorka you look so bad-ass in it! Seriously!" the American continued and passed his phone over.

Erki studied the photo. It was taken from below: Zorka, flexed bicep, intense eyes, holding a knife at someone, the blade hiding his face.

Olivier turned to Erki. "You know, we could rent a house, trash it a bit, and just shoot photos of Zorka pulling a knife at whoever other models, just like this, this angle."

Then Erki suddenly stood up. "Oh shit. It's perfect, actually."

"That's fucking hot," the American added.

Erki turned to the American and handed him back his phone, then said in a humorless tone, "Send me that photo. Delete it from your phone. You weren't a dumb-ass and posted it already, were you?"

"No, I just took it. Look, I'm sending it to you now."

Erki stood up and reached over to Zorka. He touched her wrist gently and held it there as she folded the knife back, unsure if she was being defeated or praised. He kissed her on her cheek, then he fell back down into the crook of Olivier's armpit and extended his forearm on Olivier's thigh.

*

Jana watched Zorka slip off and go into the kitchen.

"I'll be right back," she told Aimée.

*

"I wanted to write you," Zorka said.

She was leaning against the sink, pouring more vodka into her drink.

"Yeah?" Jana said.

"I mean, I knew you were in Paris," Zorka continued. "Your brother told me."

"Oh."

"I called your mom and she hung up on me, big surprise. Then I got this friend of mine to snoop up your bro's number. He wouldn't pick up, but then I texted him to say it's me and he texted back saying you were in Paris."

Zorka explained how she had ended up in America, of all places, and that she'd been living in Paris for a couple of years now. She first had a job at a beauty salon, waxing women. She said she liked it a lot. Jana thought it was a demeaning job, but said nothing.

Zorka pulled up a red-lipped grin and stared at Jana. "Anyway, now I guess I do a bit of whatever."

"Whatever?"

"I mean Erki has me modeling some for his stuff, and it's really getting big, so. Janka, it's fucking nuts. The amount of money I get, just for fuckin' wearing some clothes! Talk about the capitalist cow!"

"Who's milking who," Jana mumbled.

"Ah Janka. Come on."

Jana looked up and darted her gaze into Zorka. "Congratulations, Zorka, you seem like you figured everything out," she said numbly.

"Woah," Zorka said, "you pissed at me or something?"

Jana looked into her plastic cup and then took another sip.

"How's your mother?" Jana asked.

Zorka laughed like a memory of laughing, as Jana went over her face.

"Don't look at me like that, Janka, you know I always take it to heart, the way you look at me."

"How do you want me to look at you?"

"Fuck, Jana, I'm serious."

"Serious about what?"

"That—that—I get it, it doesn't take a genius like you to catch on, that you're pissed at me!"

Claire burst in, her pink coat on her shoulders, holding Zorka's stone-colored bomber jacket and reaching it over to her while her other hand held a phone in mid-conversation. "Come on, the Uber's here."

Zorka took the coat from Claire.

"Yeah, I'm coming," Zorka replied.

"I'm waiting for you downstairs," Claire said and put her phone back to her ear.

Zorka stood there, with her coat in one hand. She bit the inside of her cheek, then let it go. "Yeah, shit, I don't really feel like a club, but we promised we'd stop by to say hi to these friends so . . ."

"She's your girlfriend?" Jana asked.

"Claire? Ha, nah, she's like my . . . my best friend, I mean sometimes we . . . have some fun, but nah, Claire and I are just . . . like . . . buds, you know."

With that she began to put her bomber jacket on, one sleeve at a time, then she looked back up at Jana. "Well. Even if you are pissed at me, it's really nice to see you, Jana . . ."

Jana swallowed, preparing for a solid phrase, a brick on brick, but when her lips parted, the voice came out as a breeze, a cotton dress, a sun's ray.

". . . you too . . ." Jana replied.

Zorka lingered her gaze on Jana and Jana watched her with the sense that Zorka was growing taller and taller and she, shrinking back in time.

Zorka sniffed. "So . . ." she said, and began to nod. She flipped her jacket hood over her head and took a step toward the doorway, then stopped, putting her hand on the wall. She turned back to Jana, her hood falling off her shaved head, and raised her left hand to her shoulder, her right hand at her gut, closed her eyes and began cringing sounds as she fingered an air guitar.

"Agnus Dei and the Jans!" Zorka proclaimed.

She flipped her hood back on, pivoted, and walked out.

The party noises were slapping against each other, but in the kitchen it was a solemn display, a modern sort of *nature morte*, with a stack of white plastic cups, scattered bottle tops belly up, glass bottles with dewy labels, squeezed lime slices in the sink, and Jana leaning her back against the counter, staring at the cabinets in front of her with wide, empty rabbit eyes.

Jana blinked into the quiet, grabbed her refilled plastic cup, and went back out into the party.

*

It seemed like months, years, since Zorka and Claire had left the party. Jana was smoking out the window with her hand loosely on Aimée's knee as Aimée was telling her a funny story about Dr Coste from work when Erki tapped Jana on the shoulder. She turned around and he passed her his phone. She looked at the open text message.

"It's for you," Erki said.

Jana read the text stream between Erki and Zorka.

<SHE STILL THERE?>
<Yeah>
<TELL HER TO COME HERE>
<U tell her urself>
<DON'T B A KUNT ERKI>
< ;) >
<PASS HER UR PHONE THEN FUCK>
< Serve & Obey>

She scrolled down farther.

<JANINKA, ITS ME>

<POJD SEM> *Come over here.*
<JUST FOR A LIL>
<PLZ>
<IM SENDING U AN UBER>

There were no more texts after that.
Jana touched the phone screen and began typing back.

<I can't come. I'm at the party.>
<I KNOW. DUH. JANKA PLZ>
<I'm with people>
<BRING HER TOO, WTF. JUST COME>

She looked over at Aimée, then back at the phone. Erki was standing above her, observing. The blue bubbles were appearing in rapid succession.

<JANKA OK IM A FUCKUP>
<BEEN THINKIN ABOUT U LIKE ALL THE TIME>
<CUZ I MISS U>
<JANA>
<PLEASE>
<MY MAMKA'S DEAD>
<Please, Jana, I've said Fuck You to so many people in my life. Please, don't make me say Fuck You to you>

*

It was in the doorway of Erki's apartment, the two women, Jana with her coat on, Aimée with her hand on the door frame, and the conversation couldn't quite find its form, their eyes went back and forth, between their shoes and their hands and their lips. *I'll see you later though?* Jana said. *Later?* Aimée responded, with a disbelief that felt too expansive for one evening. *Yes, later. Can I?* The words were turning their heavy bodies, right, left. *Later, at my place?* Aimée asked, her voice somewhat dulled from the question. *Would that be okay,* Jana replied, feeling her thumb bend into her palm, her forearm tense, her weight shift. *Because I need to go and see this friend,* she was explaining again.

There was a certain relief in the act of going over each other's words, in the doorway, with no utility, there was nothing more to understand, the information was exchanged and the Uber was waiting downstairs, and they were repeating each other's words as if they could each grasp something of each other that they could individually keep, because just then, there was an urge to keep something of the other, because disbelief is expansive especially when the day is turning over its edge, and one can feel their whole lifetime in the words they must throw away at the threshold of a door.

Call me, then, when you're about to leave, Aimée said and reached up and put her hand on Jana's jaw and brought her lips toward hers.

The hallway bulb flickered, then sparked back on.

There was Jana, footsteps going down the stairway.

There was Aimée, fingertips sliding off the handle of a closed door.

*

Zorka was waiting at the curb outside the club with a big red smile. She had her stone-colored bomber jacket open. Underneath, she was only wearing a leather bra top, which sat flatly over her small chest, with her gold SUCK IT necklace dangling, her bare white stomach prickling in the cold, combat trousers loose at her narrow hips, with the Calvin Klein waistband of her underwear showing, and the sleeves of her red mesh turtleneck tied in a knot on her crotch. Jana began to feel self-conscious about her outfit beneath her long camel-hair coat: the dark-blue trousers neatly ironed and her cream blouse with the flimsy collar, open one button.

Zorka took Jana's hand without a word and pulled her past the line. She slid her eyes toward the bouncer, who nodded his head, and both women walked in.

*

Inside, the thump of the music from the various rooms, to the sides and below, throbbed the air while people with their big December coats squeezed by: bristled leopard-print hanging open on their biceps like limping furred wings, long military-green coats with hunchback shoulders and stiff, angular lapels jutting up like scales, puffy snow-white jackets with thick hoods giving a double-headed shadow, sports caps on top of stringy hair like overgrown beaks, or sweaters of thick yarn with sleeves woven too long, hanging like excess flesh. The small bulbs of light hung on the ornate molding of the ceiling were a searing yellow, then there were the tubular rays diffusing humidly from the dance floor ahead.

Zorka led Jana along a red velvet rope, cutting the hallway into two routes, one leading to the cloakroom, and the other toward the main room. After they checked Jana's coat, she stopped and looked up at Zorka. "I hope my outfit's okay for here."

Zorka let out a laugh. "Jana, you always look like a bad-ass, even when your clothes are lame."

Zorka cracked a smile and nudged her until Jana gave a smirk back.

*

The hallway was lined with mirrors that flashed when the light changed, and seemed to be chewing on the faces they were reflecting.

There was a constant flow of people trying to get by, and Jana pulled her left shoulder in, trying to avoid getting bumped. As they entered the opening, a large room with a scaffolding of topless angels still clinging to the old walls, the crowded bar to the right, and at the end, the DJ with her chin to her neck, holding her headphones, the light on her face changing—white, yellow, green, blue. Jana felt a liquid splash on her forearm. It was so icy that it stung. She flinched and looked up. A tall girl looked back at her, dark thinning hair greasily parted in the center, sticking to her temples, her long neck pushing out of an oversized sweatshirt, striped purple and red, at her heart a worn patch of Mickey Mouse's face.

Zorka turned around and saw that the girl had spilled some of her drink on Jana.

"What the fuck," she snorted at the girl.

The girl raised one shoulder and shrugged.

Zorka leered toward the girl and flicked her collarbone. The girl stumbled and spilled some more of her drink on her own sweatshirt.

Zorka took Jana's hand again and pulled her deeper into the crowd.

*

When they got to the bar, Zorka squeezed herself between two boys, then leaned back toward Jana and shouted over the music. "What do you wanna drink?"

"Whatever you're having," Jana replied.

Zorka's grin grew.

When their drinks arrived, they were a fizzy copper color. Jana took a sip, it tasted like a sparked metal and pine needles, as if it had to come from a plant which only grew beneath the snow.

"What is this?" Jana asked.

"Yeah, it's gross, sorry," Zorka said, "but it makes you feel good."

They moved toward the wall with a small ledge at shoulder height, placed their drinks there, and leaned back.

"It was in her tits," Zorka said, with her eyes in her drink. "Mamka, I mean."

"Like cancer?"

"Yeah." Zorka lifted her gaze over the sea of heads and balled up her mouth. "Yeah," she repeated, and let her lips go loose.

"I had no idea, Zorka, I'm really sorry . . ."

"No one knew till the end, when it was too late, you know. She was hiding it and stuff. And the funny thing is, it all went down when I had come back to visit—after all my years away. Man, when I left that house, I seriously thought I'd never see Mamka again, but my uncle Gejza convinced me to come. He said something like, all was forgiven. He bought me my ticket. Didn't catch on to why he was being so generous until I saw Mamka in the flesh. She wouldn't go to the doctor, and was not so thrilled to see my face either. She kept slapping me away, saying no, no, no, no, no. Then she got really sick. We got her to the hospital like dragging a cat into water. Uncle Gejza, who's usually a total softie on all accounts, put his foot down on this one. Mamka was so frail, a boneless chicken, but she still threw a fit, wouldn't let the doctors touch her—remember her fits?"

"I remember. She threw the best fits," Jana said solemnly.

"Yeah," Zorka exhaled, "no one topped Mamka's cuckoo." Zorka crinkled her nose. "Yeah. Fuck. I hated that looney bitch. I hated her so much and I hated my papka for dying early, for leaving me with her, and I hated myself, 'cause she was in me, her genes, her foulness, kept wondering, when I'd go nuts like Mamka . . ."

"You're not going to go nuts like her, Zorka. You're just on fire, you know."

Jana was suddenly at the end of her drink, she slurped the remains with her straw. She was feeling the wall between her thoughts and articulation thaw and become one flowing gesture.

"You're a fallen angel with her wings burning off . . ." Jana continued.

Zorka began to laugh. "There we go, Janka's coming back!"

"I was always here. You're the one who fell off the edge of the earth, remember. And you never even asked me, by the way."

"Asked you what?"

"If I wanted to come with you."

"You kidding? Come with me where?"

"To wherever, wherever you were going, I don't know, you could've asked me!"

"I was going nowhere, Janka! You were the one going somewhere . . ."

Jana felt her eyes fluttering and the music pulsing in her throat. She thought of the kitchen table legs, and her father's razor, and the roll of money and the Vltava and Vilèm and stacks of books, and fur on fire, and three droplets of blood.

"You were my future, Zorka," she mumbled.

Zorka put her hands on Jana's shoulders.

Jana's eyes began to close as she shrugged. "It was a long time ago . . ."

She continued to watch the memories in her mind, the colors of their sweaters, her mamka's scream, the bruises on Zorka's skin, the sky as it moved like secrets above them.

Jana began to squeeze her eyes until spots of light burst into a hollowing darkness in her pupils.

The snowfall. Her tongue. Two fingers spread apart. The top of her head a sleek black, her pitch eyes and her fuzzy way of laughing and her knuckles against Jana's sternum—

Zorka was shaking Jana's shoulders. "Don't get sleepy on me."

Jana opened her eyes.

"Come on, let's get you another drink." Zorka was smiling like a flashlight in the forest.

*

Zorka was reaching, back from the bar with two shots of blue liquid. She handed one to Jana.

"What's this?" Jana asked.

"Tastes like piss, feels like bliss," Zorka said and picked up her own shot glass, clinked with Jana and both women shot the liquid down their throats. Jana shook her head and squeezed her eyes as the liquid went down. When she opened them, Zorka was handing her a new glass filled with sizzling copper liquid.

Behind them, people were pushing their way to the bar. Right over Jana's shoulder, an arm plowed through, on top of the hand an odd tattoo, blue and red, of Spider-Man reaching his arm out to spray his web. When Jana turned around, she saw a girl with short-cropped hair, wearing baggy blue-and-white overalls, one of the straps undone and hanging, at her gut a small embroidered image of Bugs Bunny pushing a thumbs up forward.

Jana made eye contact with the girl, who took her glare as a sign and pulled her bottom lip down, revealing another tattoo, on her inner lip—block letters sewn into the rose-colored flesh, spelling out J A N A.

The girl let go of her lip and it rolled back up.

Zorka pulled at Jana. "Come on."

They went downstairs and made their way through the dance floor, Zorka pulling Jana forward, trying to get to a woman with her head back, her neck open and catching the light, in a tight white T-shirt, with one of her pierced nipples jutting against the fabric. The woman lowered her head, her gelled blond hair shining like a helmet, caught eyes with Jana and smiled.

"Hey you," Claire said.

She reached out and touched Jana's jawline as if she couldn't quite make out where it was, then leaned in and kissed her sweetly on each corner of her mouth.

"It's *sooo* good to see you . . . !" she drawled.

Jana stepped back and turned to Zorka. "I thought it was just us."

"Nah, chill, don't worry," Zorka yelled out in Czech, "she's high off her ass, you won't even notice she's here."

Claire closed her eyes and flopped her head back and began writhing her body in between the strangers around her. Zorka started moving her shoulder angrily to the music, while glancing over at Jana. Jana wasn't sure how to start dancing to this techno beat. She thought about whether she should move her hips, or just bob her head a bit, but when she looked down at her body, she realized she was already dancing, like a muscular helix.

"You got sexy, Jana!" Zorka shouted at her.

*

Jana could feel her phone buzzing in her pocket. She took it out and tried to focus on the screen, squinting as she read the name on her caller ID, *Milena.* Her fingers fumbled over the button to silence the call, then she put the phone back into her pocket.

Some bodies next to her started raising their hands, thrusting their fingers as if pinching the electronics in the music. The bass was getting heavier, and the synthetic rhythms prickled through the room. Jana started to feel like she was a digital tree growing branches. When she looked back at Zorka, she was kissing Claire, both of them grinding into each other, Claire trying to rub herself into Zorka's baggy trousers.

"Hey!" Jana shouted at Zorka. "Be honest, are you out there, jumping all the girls like a horny doe in the woods or what?"

But Zorka didn't hear her, she continued grinding into Claire.

"Hey!" Jana shouted again, pulling on Zorka's bicep.

Zorka took her face off Claire's and looked over. "What's up?" she said.

"I'm not a frigid bitch, by the way," Jana said.

"Yeah, I know," Zorka nodded. "I get you."

Just as Jana was forming her lips to reply, Claire popped up between them, twisting over to Zorka.

"Hi Zebra! Why'd you leave?"

*

Zorka let herself be pulled away by Claire. She gave Jana a sloppy shrug, then stuck out her pelvis and began jutting it on Claire's body.

As Jana turned away from them, she felt a hand on her shoulder. The man's balding head was flashing in the lights, as the rest of his body stood awkwardly within his suit. He held out a phone in his palm.

"You dropped this, miss," he said.

Jana squinted at the man, then lowered her eyes toward the phone in his hand. She took it from his palm and began sliding it back into her trouser pocket. When Jana looked up, there were dancing bodies overlapping to the music like trees in a hurricane and the man was gone.

*

Yeah so, Janka, in the States they made me see a therapist, and those people got some magic powers for real, I went in, soldier style, like, "Fuck you, lady," but she had me in the palm of her hands, I was coiling around myself like a baby snake, telling her all

about you actually, my friend Jana, my friend Jana . . . She even-
tually said, "Where is your friend Jana now?" I said, "I dunno,
she's probably the president of some country by now." She said, "It
sounds like your friend Jana was very important to you." I said,
"No shit, lady."

Later on, she asked me if I loved you. Damn, I was think-
ing. What kind of a fucking question is that? She told me to take
a moment and think about it. I was like, okay, you know what, I will
think about it, lady. I mean, fuck, who asks questions like that to
someone they don't even fucking know, you don't know me at all,
lady, seriously, so let me just think about it, shit. So, yeah, I really
did think about it. Like, I went into my heart and everything and
looked around for you.

Fuck, Janka, my heart was all grimy and hollow and gross, it
even smelled weird, no wonder I don't go there too often. I was
looking around, like, Jana . . . Jana, it's me! You there? I told the
lady therapist I don't know what to say. She's nowhere in my heart,
my friend Jana. But I don't think anyone's in there. I don't think
anyone'd wanna step foot in there. It's not even a heart, Janka, it's
like a damp asshole, pardon my French, how'm I suppose to invite
anyone inside a place like that!

The lady therapist told me that our anus is actually an important
muscle, just like our heart, and that all the parts of our body, mind,
and spirit can help us exercise love.

I always hated exercise. That's some prissy shit, I told her, I'm
already skinny, why I need to run around? She told me that she
thinks that I know what she means and that I am uncomfortable
with it, so I am trying to make it into a joke. She also told me I have
a very good sense of humor, and I don't always need to use it to
conceal myself, but rather to reveal myself. I was like, shit. I mean
she kinda had a point there. It was actually really fucking hard,
with the lady therapist, I mean I was kinda hoping she'd be a bitch
or something, but she was just . . . I mean, no one had ever listened
to me . . . like that . . . like time stood still and everything about me,
even my sniffing and cussing, that it all had meaning and she was
knitting me back together somehow!

Is that how you were taking me in back then, Jana? Fuck, I dunno, I didn't notice much, I guess. I was too busy thinking about how to get back at Mamka or Mr Bolshakov or any of the other assholes who looked at me like I was a piece of shit on the daily!

Jana, it really pisses me off that I can't remember. Like all those years are one clenched fist. I don't know what I had inside of me . . . that was worthwhile . . .

*

When Jana opened her eyes, there was an odd ring of space around her, as if the dancing crowd had backed up, leaving a circled corridor between her body and theirs. Her gaze lowered and she saw that this space was not empty, in fact, but occupied with smaller dancing bodies, children of some sort, six or eight or ten years of age, too old or too young for their proportions. Their hair was uneven and sticky as if they had cut it themselves and scrubbed it with jam. Their clothes were misshapen as well; as they billowed on their skinny bodies, she could make out that they bore logos and patches, but couldn't make out the colors or images, it was just shadows folding and crevicing on their frames. She could smell them though. It wasn't jam at all. It was something honeyed and stringent all at once. Jana tried opening her eyes wide, then squinting, to focus on their movement. Yes, they were moving, moving around her. They were all holding hands and moving around her in a circle, singing. Their mouths moved, but their voices were being chopped up by the electro music. Jana followed the succession of their heads, the lips forming the same phrase, over and over and over again, like a carousel, and then, that's it, that is what they are singing, and Jana touched her own mouth, because it was singing along with them, *Kde domov můj?* Where is my home . . . ?

*

When Jana opened her eyes, she was touching her mouth and Zorka was laughing at her as her body zigzagged to the music, the flashing lights falling onto her tongue and down her throat. When Zorka lowered her head, she kept a soft grin and began pumping her fist into the air to the heavy bass fragments. Jana's hand was also in the air now, her fingertips grazing her scalp in circles to dips in the rhythm.

"I think she's cool, you know," Zorka shouted over the music.

"Who?" Jana shouted back.

"Your chick."

"Aimée?"

"Yeah," Zorka yelled out, "she seems cool."

"She is cool," Jana replied. "Don't need your approval, though."

"Yeah, I know," Zorka jutted her hips to the electronic pulse. "Just wanted to say it, that's all."

"Message received," Jana replied. Then she raised both hands and lowered them like rain to a computerized melody.

"I lost my Zebra!" Claire yelled at Jana's face.

"What?" Jana put out her hands to deflect her and Claire's body pivoted around.

"Oh, here you are!" Claire sprung her arms around Zorka. "I missed you . . ."

Claire bent her knees and tried to hang off her, as Zorka tilted her head to the side toward Jana.

"Listen, Zorka, I'm gonna go," Jana shouted.

"Wait," Zorka yelled, as she undid Claire's arms from her neck. "Hold up," she grabbed Jana. "You . . . uh . . . want me to call an Uber for you?"

"No, it's fine."

"Come on, I got an Uber account and fingers . . ." Zorka grinned.

"Now who's the 21st-century lesbian . . ." Jana replied.

Jana was making her way through the crowd upstairs when her shoulder was pulled back again.

"Jana, Jesus, just wait!" Zorka was out of breath.

She reached out her hand toward Jana, then opened her fingers. "You forgot your phone," she said.

"I did?"

"Yeah," Zorka replied. "And um . . . heads up, I put my number in. It's under *IM SORRY*. Just so you know."

Jana took the phone and put it back into her trouser pocket.

"So," Zorka continued, "if *IM SORRY* calls you one day . . . maybe you could pick up . . . ?"

*

Jana was walking outside, away from the club, through the loitering bodies smoking, waiting for a friend, reformulating their night, holding out their phones, texting exes or hook-ups or following their Uber driver taking the wrong street toward them on the screen. Jana was teetering, footsteps on and off the curb, making her way around the people and puddles in the gutter, her stride uneven, as if stepping over branches.

*

There was the buzzing again, against her hipbone. She reached into her trouser pocket and pulled out her phone, which trembled and flashed in her palm. She re-read the caller's name once, twice, *M-I-L-E-N-A*. Milena was calling again. Jana matched her index fingertip to the green circle and the name disappeared, time, advancing per second, taking its place, and within the ticking, a voice.

She brought the phone up to her ear.

"Hello . . . ?" Jana said hesitantly.

"Hello? Hello? Can you hear me?"

"Yes, I hear you, your French is really good, by the way."

". . . Thanks . . ."

"I just left the club and—I thought you were dead?"

"What?"

"I thought you were dead."

"Who?"

"You."

"Excuse me?"

"DEAD."

"WHO?"

"YOU . . ."

"What do you mean?"

"AREN'T YOU DEAD?"

"Who's dead??"

"YOU! YOU!"

"ME?"

"YES!"

"WHAT?"

"YOU'RE DEAD, MILENA!" Jana was shouting into her phone.

"This is Aimée."

*

"I see you . . ." Aimée said.

"You do?"

"Yes, Jana, that's you, isn't it?"

"Where?"

"Um . . . pacing around the lamp-post across the street . . ."

Jana halted her step and looked up. The lamp-light drenched her eyes, she squinted, and looked back down, then traced her gaze across the street toward the building. There was a window, lit, with one side of the curtain drawn open and a silhouette touching the glass.

Jana lifted her left hand and wiggled her fingers at the window. The hand on the glass wiggled her fingers back.

"Well . . ." Aimée's voice came out of the receiver. "Do you want to come up . . . or keep pacing?"

Amy

Amy steps one sneaker carefully in front of the other at the edge of the wall of the house with the brown roof and gray satellite dish. Low-waisted flared jeans, soil-stains on the knees, dark-green zip-up, navy-blue backpack on her shoulders. One hand tracing the pallid stone, she moves around the house.

A wind picks up the loose blond hairs straying from her thick ponytail, and wisps them across her cheek.

The emptiness is shifting around her. She turns her head back to the lone dirt road, stringing away into the dimness shared by the soil and the trees and the night and the man's departure.

She's seen the man leave, from the bushes, where she was waiting and watching. He was in his gray suit, with shined shoes and a shined head, locking and bolting the door with even-handed accuracy, stopping only to cover his mouth with a sky-blue silk handkerchief when he coughed.

Below, in the dirt, at the tip of her foot, there is a stone. She picks it up, steps back, and tosses it at the window with the three iron bars. It clinks against the glass, then drops onto the ledge of the windowsill. There is no echo. The darkness makes foam of noise. Her arms are crossed over her gut, the backpack straps dangling against her jean pockets.

"Dominika . . ." she whispers with her head tilted up, "it's me!"

From inside the house, a heavy chain is dragging, the links pulling apart then hitting against each other.

"It's me, Dominika!"

She's made her way to the door, wide and wooden, with a dark iron frame. Near her belly button, the keyhole is a black copper, made for a bulbous key. There is a thin light coming from the hole. She watches it. Just then, it disappears, and through the hole, an exhalation.

The keyhole looks like it's breathing.

"*Amy . . .*" the breath filters out of the keyhole. "*O my Amy . . .*"

"Dominika? Dominika!"

"*O my sexy Amy!*"

She crouches down carefully, palms on the door, and approaches her eye to the keyhole. She squints, then opens her eye wide and feels a warm breath on her eyeball, then squints again.

"But I can't see you . . . !" Amy whispers.

The chain lifts and drops and Amy flinches, then catches herself on the door and peers back into the keyhole.

"I see . . . red . . . is it your dress?"

"*I wearing it for you, my love!*"

"I want to see your face."

"*I cannot, my beauty . . . chain not long enough.*"

Amy unzips her backpack and takes out the toolbox and sets it at her feet. She begins to feel around the iron door frame, wedging her fingernails between the metal and cement lining.

"Geez, it's really . . . solid!"

"*Yes, he made very strong!*"

"I need like a blow torch or something!"

"*You bring this with you?*"

"No . . . All I brought was like . . . my dad's toolbox, and most of the tools they took away at security, they were asking me why I needed a wrench and a hammer and different-sized screwdrivers, I got nervous, I didn't know what to say, I told them I wanted to make art. 'What kind of art?' The security guard was asking me. I really had to think on my feet, and to be honest, I don't really know too much about art, so I just said I want to build something . . . like a small house . . . as an art project, but the security guard kept asking me to explain further, so I told him that I was going to build a doghouse around myself using only my father's toolbox as, like, people came and went and there was a sign that said they should, like, bark at me, as they watched, until they got bored and wanted to leave. I dunno, I just kind of ran with the idea . . . Then I stopped talking and the guard was just staring at me. He asked me if I make feminist art. I got nervous again, 'cause I wasn't sure, but I think it was definitely a trick question. And I couldn't remember anything from my European History class, ugh, I really should have listened better, like, was feminist art illegal in Europe or something? Just in case, I told him I didn't know what feminist art was. He raised his eyebrows at me and said, 'All right, well what kind of art do you make, then?'

"All I could think about was you, Dominika, I was afraid he wouldn't let me through, I was trying to be very careful, watching his facial expression, thinking about my words, and I could kind of feel the tears coming up and I was squeezing my chest shut so they wouldn't come up, I was telling him, 'Sir, I just want to make a doghouse actually, for a dog I love very much, sir, and, um, the dog lives here and, um, the reason I am using my father's toolbox is because my mother does not have a toolbox, sir, because in my country, most women don't own toolboxes yet, and, um, of course, after the doghouse is made, I will return the toolbox to my father, sir, and myself back to America before my 90-day tourist visa is up.' I showed him my return ticket, and he handed me back the half-empty toolbox and I walked through the security gate . . ."

"*Oh my darling! My clever girl! What long journey you had. And now you are here, so close to me!*"

"But how am I supposed to get this door open now . . ."

Amy hits the door with her flat hand.

"Fuck!" Amy yells out.

"*Shhh . . . my angel, please . . .*"

"I'm sorry," Amy whispers, "I . . . don't know . . . what to do . . . I feel like such an idiot . . . with this stupid toolbox and . . . I love you, Dominika! Ugh, I wish I could dismantle this door and this house and everything and we could just be together! But they only left me the shitty tools I can't do anything with! I can't even scrape off the wood of this fucking door if I wanted to, how am I supposed to break you out of here—"

"*Kiss me.*"

"What?"

"*Kiss me, my love.*"

"I want to! But . . . shouldn't I try to get this door down first?"

"*One kiss, please!*"

"Um . . . okay! But . . . how??"

"*Put your lips to hole where key goes, my angel.*"

Amy looks at the black copper keyhole.

"My lips?" she says hesitantly.

"*Yes, my Amy, my sexy Amy!*"

"But what if . . . he comes back and . . . and—"

"*Amy, my beautiful girl, I wish I can hold you, you so nervous.*"

"I'm scared, Dominika. I . . . I'm stuck out here, you're in there, and he—he—he's going to come back!"

"*Shhh . . . everything be all right. Kiss me and I show you everything all right.*"

Amy glances around, still nothing but the forest and the lone road. She looks back at the wooden door, focusing toward the keyhole.

"Okay . . ." Amy murmurs.

She begins to lean in, pursing her lips as her face comes closer to the wood and her eyes close. The cold metal ridge touches the skin of her lips.

"Come closer, my love . . ."

She leans in closer, pressing her lips into the copper-framed keyhole, pushing the pulp of them inside the thumb-sized space.

"My angel, come closer . . ."

Amy is pushing her face up against the door, the key-shaped ridge prodding into her teeth.

"Closer, closer . . ."

Her nose is bending into the wood, the grain stamping her forehead.

"Clo—" the voice drops.

*

The night is cut in two with one sharp shriek from inside the house.

*

Amy jumps back away from the door, her hands over her mouth.

"Dominika . . . ??" she is getting up to her feet. "What's happening??"

The shriek comes again from inside the house and Amy winces, stepping away from the door.

The shriek is stretching into a scream and the chain is clanging against itself frantically.

"H—H—Hel—" Amy is stuttering as she continues to stumble away from the door.

Her breath is beating faster than her heart, as the scream is ripping a blood-lined voice from inside the house. Amy turns toward the forest and takes a hurried step to run, but jolts to a halt as her sneaker hits the ground.

On the lone dirt road leading to the forest, the man is walking. The man is walking with even steps along the lone road toward the house. He is looking at her, directly at her, and yet his body flickers as he walks. He is approaching and his body is flickering strangely, as if he is flesh one second, and digital data the next, then flesh again, but his eyes remain solid points of vision, pointed without a doubt at Amy, on the doorstep of the house.

"H—, He—, He—, Hel—" Amy is gagging, her throat clutching itself.

And then,
you went
to Hell . . .

The man lifts his arm and extends it toward Amy, the muscles and bones flashing like running input.

"HELLLLL . . . PPPpppppuuuhhh!!" Amy is wheezing.

Her eyes clamp shut and she squeezes them tighter and tighter, sucking herself into her pupils.

*

Amy is not sure how long she has been waiting, but she remains still within her own darkness as time goes up like an elevator, in a clean, straight line within the immaculate silence inside her.

*

The wall is completely blue, and at the corner of the ceiling, a blue speaker hangs like fruit off the crux.

The girl is unconscious in the blond woman's arms. She is holding the girl up, one hand around her waist, and the other beneath her armpit, the girl's sneakers dragging on the floor.

I was a different woman then
Had an apartment near Madeleine . . .

*

The lights begin to flicker and one of Amy's sneakers tenses, flexing toward the floor, and then the other, both making contact, setting themselves firmly, and pushing upward through her body.

*

Amy is lifting her head and opening her eyes. She stands on her own two feet and Aimée takes her arms off the girl and steps back. Amy is looking around at the listless clientele sitting in pairs at the tables, then at the bar stools, all empty except for the middle one with the little girl in the oversized pink cap, then at the bar-woman, who is lifting a blue bag of lemons from the counter to wipe beneath it, then setting it back down in its spot.

Amy tilts her head back and shards of light from the disco ball rain into her eyes.

*

"All right, all right, come on." The old lady with the velour scrunchie is tapping Amy's shoulder. "I'll take you to the metro. It's prime time for coins."

Amy turns toward the old woman.

"Oh good, you got a toolbox with you," the old woman continues. "My amp is coming undone from my cart, you think you can tighten the wires?"

Amy looks down at her other hand, gripping the black toolbox by the handle.

"I can try . . ." Amy says, "but they took most of the tools away at security . . ."

"Did you tell them you make feminist art?"

Amy is shaking her head, and as she does, tears drop from her eyes.

"Hey, easy, what's the matter? You want to go home? Is that it?"

Amy shakes her head again, pulling her quivering lips into her mouth.

"It's this music, isn't it? It's really fucking too sad in my opinion. They should change it up, though who am I to critique, I've been singing the same drippy *chansons* for God-knows-how-many years . . ."

Amy wipes her cheeks with the side of her hand, and then her nose.

"I don't want to go home," Amy mumbles. "I just . . . don't know where to go . . ."

"Well, for starters—to the metro, with me!" the old lady says, pushing the cart with the amp through the long blue curtains.

*

The blue curtains open and the two technicians roll in the empty bed toward the monitor. Once it's in place, they begin matching the colored wires to their receptors, then hook the main plug into the floor socket.

Together, they pull the plastic casing off the bed frame. Around the deep mattress, the panels are a solid beige with a shapely apparatus attached to the left-hand side.

"Hey, what do you think this is for?" The first technician touches the nozzle of the pump-like device.

The other technician shrugs and crouches to adjust the wheel stops at each foot.

The first slides his fingers around the handle and the pump separates from its holder. His hips begin to sway and his hand brings the pump up to his lips. He crosses his other arm over his chest, squeezing his shoulders, pursing his mouth, and closing his eyes.

"Hey, man, cut it out!" The other technician is standing. "This thing's expensive! Put that down and let's go."

The first technician lowers the pump into its socket, tilting his head with glowing concern, gazing at the large V sewn into the top of the bed with thick blue threading. Once the pump is back in its holder, his hand releases the apparatus and comes back up to his mouth. His lips give one kiss to his fingertips and those fingertips release his kiss to the new, vacant bed.

"*Allez*, Michael, we have to hook up the others!"

Acknowledgements

Зовётся - Жизнь: Irina, Valeriy, and Valentin Moskovich, and the late Lev Kantolinsky and Isabella and Alexandra Burle.

Mes amours, mes ami(e)s: Rick Kinner, Kaisa Kinnunen, Vanja Hedberg, Ida Skovmand, Scott Cooper, Nadja Spiegelman, Amélie Rousseau, Rosa Rankin-Gee, Theodore Haber, Nicholas Miloš Mestas, Linda Lämmle, Sophie Gonthier.

Thank you for your support: Katya Duzenko, Annie Prossnitz, Kate Kornberg and Matthieu Vahanian, Olga Tsiporkina, the Divinsky family, Elena Peskovatska, Lauren Elkin, Derek Ryan, Jayne Batzofin, Silke Schroeder, Dr Claire Finney.

This novel was partly written during the course of the following generous residencies, both by chance in Scotland, where the rain is writer's manna:

To the Bothy Project and Shakespeare & Co. for sending me to Sweeney's Bothy on the Isle of Eigg in May of 2016, thank you Sylvia Whitman, Adam Biles, Bobby Niven, and Lucy and Eddie Scott on the island.

Thank you to Cove Park, Polly Clark and Julian Forrester, for welcoming me as the International Artist-in-Residence in August of 2016.

An excerpt of *Virtuoso* was published in Dyke_on Magazine Issue 0, thank you to Annabel Fernandes and the Dyke_on team, and in Issue 6 of JANE by the Grey Attic Magazine, thank you to Divya Bala and the JANE team.

Unending gratitude to my editor, Nick Sheerin, who gave me compassion and freedom, and to the whole Serpent's Tail team, dear reader, I cannot emphasise enough how much comradery goes into every book, thank you Hannah Westland, Hannah Ross, Pete Dyer, Patrick Taylor, Sarah Chatwin.

And continued gratitude to Eliza Wood-Obenauf and Eric Obenauf of Two Dollar Radio.

To Jane Finigan, my agent, my advocate, my sidekick, thank you.

Lastly, a kindred bow to all those who subvert with a big heart, together, incognito, our cosmic song, our lyrical transgressions.

Two Dollar Radio
Books too loud to Ignore

ALSO AVAILABLE Here are some other titles you might want to dig into.

SOME OF US ARE VERY HUNGRY NOW
BY **ANDRE PERRY**

← "A complete, deep, satisfying read." —Gabino Iglesias, NPR

ANDRE PERRY'S DEBUT COLLECTION of personal essays travels from Washington DC to Iowa City to Hong Kong in search of both individual and national identity while displaying tenderness and a disarming honesty.

SAVAGE GODS BY **PAUL KINGSNORTH**

← "Kingsnorth's is a voice worth listening to."
—*Kirkus Reviews*

"For all the confessional memoirs so popular at the moment, this is the real deal." —*The American Conservative*

SAVAGE GODS ASKS, can words ever paint the truth of the world—or are they part of the great lie which is killing it?

THE BOOK OF X NOVEL BY **SARAH ROSE ETTER**

← "Etter brilliantly, viciously lays bare what it means to be a woman in the world, what it means to hurt, to need, to want, so much it consumes everything." —Roxane Gay

"A powerful novel." —*Minneapolis Star-Tribune*

A SURREAL EXPLORATION OF ONE WOMAN'S LIFE and death against a landscape of meat, office desks, and bad men.

TRIANGULUM NOVEL BY **MASANDE NTSHANGA**

← "Magnificently disorienting and meticulously constructed, *Triangulum* couples an urgent subtext with an unceasing sense of mystery. This is a thought-provoking dream of a novel, situated within thought-provoking contexts both fictional and historical." —Tobias Carroll, Tor.com

AN AMBITIOUS, OFTEN PHILOSOPHICAL AND GENRE-BENDING NOVEL that covers a period of over 40 years in South Africa's recent past and near future.

Thank you for supporting independent culture!
Feel good about yourself.

Books to read!

THE WORD FOR WOMAN IS WILDERNESS
NOVEL BY **ABI ANDREWS**

← "Unlike any published work I have read, in ways that are beguiling, audacious…" —Sarah Moss, *The Guardian*

THIS IS A NEW KIND OF NATURE WRITING — one that crosses fiction with science writing and puts gender politics at the center of the landscape.

AWAY! AWAY! NOVEL BY **JANA BEŇOVÁ**
TRANSLATED BY **JANET LIVINGSTONE**

→ **Winner of the European Union Prize for Literature**

← "Beňová's short, fast novels are a revolution against normality."
—Austrian Broadcasting Corporation, ORF

WITH MAGNETIC, SPARKLING PROSE, Beňová delivers a lively mosaic that ruminates on human relationships, our greatest fears and desires.

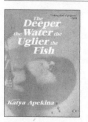

THE DEEPER THE WATER THE UGLIER THE FISH NOVEL BY **KATYA APEKINA**

→ **2018** *Los Angeles Times* **Book Prize Finalist**

← "Brilliantly structured… refreshingly original, and the writing is nothing short of gorgeous. It's a stunningly accomplished book." —Michael Schaub, NPR

POWERFULLY CAPTURES THE QUIET TORMENT of two sisters craving the attention of a parent they can't, and shouldn't, have to themselves.

THE BLURRY YEARS NOVEL BY **ELEANOR KRISEMAN**

← "Kriseman's is a new voice to celebrate."
—*Publishers Weekly*

THE BLURRY YEARS IS A POWERFUL and unorthodox coming-of-age story from an assured new literary voice, featuring a stirringly twisted mother-daughter relationship, set against the sleazy, vividly-drawn backdrop of late-seventies and early-eighties Florida.

THE UNDERNEATH NOVEL BY **MELANIE FINN**

← "*The Underneath* is an excellent thriller." —*Star Tribune*

THE UNDERNEATH IS AN INTELLIGENT and considerate exploration of violence—both personal and social—and whether violence may ever be justified. With the assurance and grace of her acclaimed novel *The Gloaming*, Melanie Finn returns with a precisely layered and tense new literary thriller.

Books to read!

Now available at **TWODOLLARRADIO.com** or your favorite bookseller.

PALACES NOVEL BY SIMON JACOBS

←·· *"Palaces* is robust, both current and clairvoyant… With a pitch-perfect portrayal of the punk scene and idiosyncratic, meaty characters, this is a wonderful novel that takes no prisoners." —*Foreword Reviews*, starred review

WITH INCISIVE PRECISION and a cool detachment, Simon Jacobs has crafted a surreal and spellbinding first novel of horror and intrigue.

THEY CAN'T KILL US UNTIL THEY KILL US ESSAYS BY HANIF ABDURRAQIB

··→ **Best Books 2017:** NPR, *Buzzfeed, Paste Magazine, Esquire, Chicago Tribune, Vol. 1 Brooklyn,* CBC (Canada), *Stereogum, National Post* (Canada), *Entropy, Heavy, Book Riot, Chicago Review of Books* (November), *The Los Angeles Review, Michigan Daily*

←·· "Funny, painful, precise, desperate, and loving throughout. Not a day has sounded the same since I read him." —Greil Marcus, *Village Voice*

WHITE DIALOGUES STORIES BENNETT SIMS

←·· "Anyone who admires such pyrotechnics of language will find 21st-century echoes of Edgar Allan Poe in Sims' portraits of paranoia and delusion." —*New York Times Book Review*

IN THESE ELEVEN STORIES, Sims moves from slow-burn psychological horror to playful comedy, bringing us into the minds of people who are haunted by their environments, obsessions, and doubts.

FOUND AUDIO NOVEL BY N.J. CAMPBELL

←·· "[A] mysterious work of metafiction… dizzying, arresting and defiantly bold." —*Chicago Tribune*

←·· "This strange little book, full of momentum, intrigue, and weighty ideas to mull over, is a bona fide literary page-turner." —*Publishers Weekly*, "Best Summer Books, 2017"

SEEING PEOPLE OFF NOVEL BY JANA BEŇOVÁ
TRANSLATED BY JANET LIVINGSTONE

··→ **Winner of the European Union Prize for Literature**

←·· "A fascinating novel. Fans of inward-looking post-modernists like Clarice Lispector will find much to admire." —NPR

A KALEIDOSCOPIC, POETIC, AND DARKLY FUNNY portrait of a young couple navigating post-socialist Slovakia.

Books to read!

THE DROP EDGE OF YONDER
NOVEL BY **RUDOLPH WURLITZER**

← "One of the most interesting voices in American fiction."
—*Rolling Stone*

AN EPIC ADVENTURE that explores the truth and temptations of the American myth, revealing one of America's most transcendant writers at the top of his form.

THE VINE THAT ATE THE SOUTH
NOVEL BY **J.D. WILKES**

← "Undeniably one of the smartest, most original Southern Gothic novels to come along in years." — Michael Schaub, NPR

WITH THE ENERGY AND UNIQUE VISION that established him as a celebrated musician, Wilkes here is an accomplished storyteller on a Homeric voyage that strikes at the heart of American mythology.

SIRENS MEMOIR BY **JOSHUA MOHR**

→ **A Best of 2017** —*San Francisco Chronicle*

← "Raw-edged and whippet-thin, *Sirens* swings from tales of bawdy addiction to charged moments of a father struggling to stay clean."
—*Los Angeles Times*

WITH VULNERABILITY, GRIT, AND HARD-WON HUMOR, Mohr returns with his first book-length work of non-fiction, a raw and big-hearted chronicle of substance abuse, relapse, and family compassion.

THE GLOAMING NOVEL BY **MELANIE FINN**

→ *New York Times* **Notable Book of 2016**

← "Deeply satisfying." —*New York Times Book Review*

AFTER AN ACCIDENT LEAVES her estranged in a Swiss town, Pilgrim Jones absconds to east Africa, settling in a Tanzanian outpost where she can't shake the unsettling feeling that she's being followed.

THE INCANTATIONS OF DANIEL JOHNSTON
GRAPHIC NOVEL BY **RICARDO CAVOLO**
WRITTEN BY **SCOTT MCCLANAHAN**

← "Wholly unexpected, grotesque, and poignant." —*The FADER*

RENOWNED ARTIST RICARDO CAVOLO and Scott McClanahan combine talents in this dazzling, eye-popping graphic biography of artist and musician Daniel Johnston.

Books to read!

THE REACTIVE NOVEL BY MASANDE NTSHANGA

→ **A Best Book of 2016** —*Men's Journal, Flavorwire, City Press, The Sunday Times, The Star, This is Africa, Africa's a Country, Sunday World*

← "Often teems with a beauty that seems to carry on in front of its glue-huffing wasters despite themselves." —*Slate*

A CLEAR-EYED, COMPASSIONATE ACCOUNT of a young HIV+ man grappling with the sudden death of his brother in South Africa.

SQUARE WAVE NOVEL BY MARK DE SILVA

← "Compelling and horrifying." —*Chicago Tribune*

A GRAND NOVEL OF ideas and compelling crime mystery, about security states past and present, weather modification science, micro-tonal music, and imperial influences.

NOT DARK YET NOVEL BY BERIT ELLINGSEN

← "Fascinating, surreal, gorgeously written."
—*BuzzFeed*

ON THE VERGE OF a self-inflicted apocalypse, a former military sniper is enlisted by a former lover for an eco-terrorist action that threatens the quiet life he built for himself in the mountains.

THE GLACIER NOVEL BY JEFF WOOD

← "Gorgeously and urgently written."
—*Library Journal*, starred review

FOLLOWING A CATERER AT a convention center, a surveyor residing in a storage unit, and the masses lining up for an Event on the horizon, *The Glacier* is a poetic rendering of the pre-apocalypse.

HAINTS STAY NOVEL BY COLIN WINNETTE

← "In his astonishing portrait of American violence, Colin Winnette makes use of the Western genre to stunning effect." —*Los Angeles Times*

HAINTS STAY IS A NEW Acid Western in the tradition of Rudolph Wurlitzer, *Meek's Cutoff*, and Jim Jarmusch's *Dead Man*: meaning it is brutal, surreal, and possesses an unsettling humor.

Books to read!

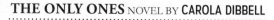

THE ONLY ONES NOVEL BY **CAROLA DIBBELL**

→ **Best Books 2015:** *Washington Post*; *O, The Oprah Magazine*; NPR
← "Breathtaking." —NPR

INEZ WANDERS A POST-PANDEMIC world immune to disease. Her life is altered when a grief-stricken mother that hired her to provide genetic material backs out, leaving Inez with the product: a baby girl.

BINARY STAR NOVEL BY **SARAH GERARD**

→ *Los Angeles Times* **Book Prize Finalist**
→ **Best Books 2015:** *BuzzFeed*, *Vanity Fair*, NPR
← "Rhythmic, hallucinatory, yet vivid as crystal." —NPR

AN ELEGIAC, INTENSE PORTRAIT of two young lovers as they battle their personal afflictions while on a road trip across the U.S.

THE ABSOLUTION OF ROBERTO ACESTES LAING NOVEL BY **NICHOLAS ROMBES**

← "Kafka directed by David Lynch doesn't even come close." —*3:AM Magazine*

A RARE-FILM LIBRARIAN mysteriously burned his entire stockpile of film canisters and disappeared. Years later, a journalist tracks the forgotten man down to a motel on the fringe of the Wisconsin wilds.

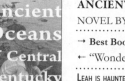

ANCIENT OCEANS OF CENTRAL KENTUCKY NOVEL BY **DAVID CONNERLEY NAHM**

→ **Best Books 2014:** NPR, *Flavorwire*
← "Wonderful. Deeply suspenseful." —NPR

LEAH IS HAUNTED BY the disappearance of her brother Jacob. When a mysterious man shows up, claiming to be Jacob, Leah is wrenched back to childhood.

CRYSTAL EATERS NOVEL BY **SHANE JONES**

← "[Jones is] something of a millennial Richard Brautigan." —*Nylon*

REMY IS A YOUNG GIRL living in a town that believes in crystal count. When her mother becomes sick, she sets out to accomplish what no one else has, and increase her mother's crystal count.